Exclusive

A novel

by
Yasmin Shiraz

Rolling Hills Press

RHP

ISBN 0-9718174-1-3

Library of Congress Control Number: 2004096257

Published by Rolling Hills Press, LLC

For more information:
Rolling Hills Press, LLC
PO Box 220053, Chantilly, VA 20153

email: **RHP@yasminshiraz.net**   **www.yasminshiraz.net**

Exclusive

"How much time do we spend in relationships with people who are nothing like us—people who don't like the things that we like and aren't interested in the stuff we're interested in? Isn't it about time we sought out mates exactly the way that we want them? I want somebody made just for me."
—Tisha Ariel Nikkole, excerpted from her article, "Get the Relationship You Want"

Chapter 1

Washington, D.C.

Magazine journalist Tisha Ariel Nikkole busied around her apartment getting ready to interview Shout, the biggest rapper in the United States.

For ten months the five-seven, twenty-eight-year-old freelance writer had collected various newspaper and magazine clippings that featured Shout and watched his numerous interviews and performances on television. Less than a year ago Tisha was watching Shout on BET and heard him say, "I could definitely fall for a girl who's smart, loves herself, and knows how to take care of me." Staring at the screen, Tisha thought she heard harps playing in her head. *Was that a personal invitation for me?* Tisha thought. *Yes. That was a sign.*

****

Tisha opened the trunk at the foot of her bed and pulled out Shout's biography and articles. She smiled when she looked at the pictures of him. He was finer than Usher with a body like 50 Cent. Butterflies danced in her stomach beneath her silver flower belly ring.

For years, Tisha had all-access passes to the hottest rappers, actors, and singers in the country. She always used them to interview the star, take pictures backstage and then go to the after party. But now she realized that she had to use her access pass as a relationship pass to Shout.

Just then, she heard a knock on the door. She walked over to the door. Her best friend Charmaine Bukola waited on the other side.

At five-five, twenty-eight-year-old Charmaine was a successful government lawyer. Sporting black dreadlocks pulled to a bun at the nape of her neck, the heavy-set Charmaine's sweet scented African musk oil permeated the air. Her dark skin was smooth and she wore her dreads impeccably like she should be on a jar of beeswax. Born to a Nigerian father and African-American mother, her style was unique—a compliment to both Africa and Mississippi. Charmaine often wore a Dashiki dress in the morning and ripped jeans with a tank top in the afternoon. Her strong southern drawl often slipped out of a face that looked like it should have an African tribal accent.

Tisha yanked the door open. "Hey, Charmaine. You could have called me." Leaving the door open and Charmaine standing in the doorway, Tisha walked to her bedroom and stared in the closet.

Charmaine slowly walked up behind her friend and responded, "Called you for what?"

"Because I'm on my way out. I told you yesterday that I was going to the MCI Center for the interview. Had ya gotten here thirty minutes later, I wouldn't have even been here." Tisha walked past Charmaine and stood in the living room.

Charmaine followed her. "Oh yeah, you did tell me about that. That's why I'm here." Charmaine held up a bag in her left hand.

Tisha jumped out of the chair, ran over, and grabbed the bag. She dug inside and saw some blue jeans with silver studs down the sides and a crisp white T-shirt that read HOT CHICK in red sequins. She put the shirt up to her chest then hugged Charmaine tightly.

"Thank you, thank you, thank you. I was getting ready to go to this interview to meet my husband-to-be, and I didn't know what I was going to wear. I was looking through my closet, and I didn't have anything to wear."

Charmaine sat in the recliner and said, "That's what best friends are for." Charmaine reached into her purse and got her car keys.

"I know how much you're looking forward to meeting this rapper, but don't set yourself up for a letdown. You may not like him at all. Or, after you meet him, you may find out that he's not even all of that."

"Please." Tisha put up her hand.

"I believe in fate, and I believe that God has a blueprint for my life. Shout is in my blueprint."

"I must admit, I have never heard you talk about any guy as much as you talk about Shout. And I never heard you ever talk about a guy in the music business like this at all."

"C, I know you're my best friend and everything. I know you don't want to see me hurt but it has to work out between me and Shout. There has to be someone out there for me that has the same passions that I have. Look at all the years that I've loved hip-hop music. Well, he loves hip-hop music. He writes lyrics. I write articles. I always tell the truth in my writing. He speaks the truth on wax and in his interviews. It's a match made in heaven. Don't discourage me, just tell me that you'll be my maid of honor."

Charmaine let out a loud guffaw and dropped her keys. "That's what I like about you, you're eternally optimistic." She picked up her keys from the floor and headed toward the front door.

Tisha and Charmaine walked to the door and hugged. As Tisha closed the door, she looked up to the ceiling. "Thank you, God."

****

Shout sat on his couch and let some unidentified groupie suck his dick. He closed his eyes and kept his hand on the back of the girl's head. He felt weave, tracks and glue but he didn't care. If the groupie wasn't good for anything else, she was good for a nut, maybe two. Images passed through his mind. He saw himself winning a Grammy, an MTV Video Award, and an ASCAP writer of the year award. He looked down at the groupie. *I hope she doesn't choke*, he thought. *But then again, as long as she doesn't bite me, I don't give a fuck.* As Shout was getting closer to coming, his mind went blank. He shot off in the girl's mouth. She swallowed. *That was alright. It wasn't the best, but I ain't backed up either.* Shout thought and smiled.

Shout didn't have much to smile about last week when he stood in front of a judge in Fulton County as a result of a paternity suit. His body was damp all over. A stripper that he had sex with was accusing him of fathering her child. As the judge prepared to read the paternity results, Shout felt faint.

"Miss Julia Gaines, Keyshawn Lane is not the father of your child. The test are 99.9% accurate." The judge stated in his Georgian southern drawl.

"He has to be. He has to be," the stripper yelled.

Shout took a bandana out of his suit pocket and wiped his forehead.

"Jesus walks," Shout mumbled to himself.

As the stripper's lawyers tried to calm her down, she kept yelling.

"He has to be the father. I poked holes in the condom. It has to be his baby."

Shout looked at her. "You bitch," he yelled. And at that moment, Shout realized that it was truly a miracle for that child not to be his.

****

Tisha pulled her new T-shirt over her head and slipped into the skin-tight studded jeans. Tisha's shoulder length reddish brown hair was pulled back into a ponytail. The tight fitting tee revealed her defined abs and toned arms. Tisha's skin was a warm brown tone. From the corner of her bedroom, she grabbed her black leather backpack and checked to see if her handheld tape recorder and notepad were inside. She sat on the edge of her full-sized bed and put on her favorite Nike sweat socks. The thick cushioning in the heel and toe of the sock made her feel as if she was walking on air. Reaching down to put on her Air Force Ones, she paused and decided to kneel and pray.

"God, thank You for this opportunity to meet my husband. Thank You for bringing Charmaine over here today. You let her know what was on my mind. You made it happen, God. In today's world, people might think that me going after a certain person for a mate is crazy. But, You don't think so, do You, God? I want someone with whom I can be compatible. God, Shout's going to be compatible with me. I believe that. Well, anyway, God, protect me although I don't think Shout is a psycho. But, God, as hard as I've worked, I deserve a little loving and a companion also. Eve had Adam. Can I have Shout? Amen."

Tisha grabbed her backpack and headed to the door.

****

The air felt moist and warm as Tisha got on the U Street Cardozo Metro train and settled into one of the bright orange seats with yellowish tan trim. It had to be one of the hottest days of the summer. Near the subway's door were plenty of posters about safe sex, HIV testing, and infections. Tisha sat and mentally reviewed Shout's background.

Shout was the hottest and most profitable rapper signed to World Music Records, having received a half-million-dollar signing bonus after the A&R executive heard his five-song demo tape three years ago. Shout had fan clubs spread throughout the United States and worldwide. In fact, his fan clubs hung out in front of his hotel in every city where he performed. Girls and women from sixteen to sixty threw panties and bras on stage at his concerts. There had been several lawsuits where women alleged that he was the father of their children, although it was later proven that he hadn't slept with those women, one of whom told newspapers and magazines, "It was immaculate conception." Shout held the *Guinness Book of World Records* and *Billboard* magazine's top spot for selling the most albums in one week by a rapper. Two years earlier he had built Shout and Sound, a Philadelphia studio where he could work on his music any time, but the traffic in front was so crazy that he could hardly get into the studio without a police escort.

The train stopped and several young women got on the train talking loudly about Shout.

"Shout is so fine. Oooh, when I get backstage it's over."

"Girl, you gon' have to wait in line after me."

"Oh, that's alright, as long as I get mine."

The girls giggled loudly.

Tisha noticed one woman was wearing a lime-green bikini with a tube top on her bottom disguised as a skirt. Every time the girl moved, her butt cheeks were exposed. Disgusted with the girl's appearance, Tisha rolled her eyes and mumbled under her breath, "Groupies."

Just then, another heavy-set girl who looked to be about eighteen got on the train with two friends. Her bra size exceeded a 38DD, but she was wearing a white tank top with no bra, super-short cut-off jean shorts, and platform heels, and she had a plant sprayer bottle attached to her belt. Tisha regretfully listened as the girl and her friends discussed the concert. Every time the train moved, the girl's breasts moved up and down.

"Girl, we're going to be in the front row tonight. It's going to be so live."

"I know, I know. I'm going to get with Shout tonight. After he sees these big titties, it's over. You know every man wants a girl with big titties."

The girl's small-chested friend replied, "Lawanda, we know you think so." All three of the girls laughed.

The other friend said, "I don't know if you forgot to water the plants or something, but your mom's plant sprayer is on the side of your shorts." The girl laughed.

Lawanda replied, "No shit. If Shout seeing my breasts without a bra ain't enough to get him, I'm going to have my own wet T-shirt contest. I'll be watering my chest like a bed of roses. " All three girls started laughing again. Just then the train doors opened and Tisha stepped off.

*"I won't complain
About my lot in life
Thanks to this rap game
I got a lot in life
It ain't been easy
Hard times
And I've paid the price
But wit' my winnin's
I'ma keep on gamblin' right
Rappin's a lot easier
Than a hustla's life"*
—Shout from his single "Rap Life"

Chapter 2

Boom Tillman sat at the mahogany desk in his Washington, D.C. hotel suite waiting for his star client, Shout, to arrive. Beads of sweat in the center of his back dampened his crisp white Prada cotton shirt. He continually picked barely visible flecks of lint off of his Armani black pants. His outfit, complete with Gucci loafers, were a long way from the hand-me down clothes he wore growing up in Raleigh, North Carolina.

****

Shout had not arrived as planned on the 1:15 P.M. plane that had departed from Philadelphia and was scheduled to arrive at Ronald Reagan National Airport. Boom had planned a huge media reception for Shout and had invited every press contact—from *The Washington Post* to *The City Paper* to Howard University's *Hilltop*. He had even gotten Tisha Ariel Nikkole, one of his college friends, to do a cover story on Shout for *Life Music* magazine.

After receiving a call from the limousine company telling him that Keyshawn "Shout" Lane never showed up at the airport, Boom felt a minor headache coming. "What am

I gonna tell Sydney?" Boom mumbled to himself as he rubbed his hand on the back of his freshly cut neckline.

Artists and missed flights were something that Boom was used to. But at his new job as head of urban publicity for the Sydney Warren Public Relations Group—known industrywide as the SWPR Group, he was told precisely to "Keep those rappers in line." Rappers got a bad rap in the music business—some of the flack deserved, some of it not. Rappers were notorious for showing up to interviews and other engagements late with all kinds of excuses—from sick cousins to baby mama drama.

At twenty-eight years old, Boom was the most aggressive publicist at the SWPR Group—and the only black. He had a reputation for making sure his artists got media coverage in every part of the globe. If there was a magazine in Japan writing about hip-hop, Boom knew who to contact. For Boom, no story was too far-fetched and no contact too far away. His goal was simply to get his artists coverage by any means necessary.

Boom's new boss, Sydney Warren, pursued him for months once she heard about all of his successful media campaigns with rappers Big Todd, CRYME, and Miss Lovely. While working at World Music Records, Boom met a number of these artists who had just signed their deals. He talked to them, shaped their images, taught them how to speak, and what clothes to wear. He single-handedly made them stars before one record was ever sold, before one article was ever written about them.

Boom and Sydney had met during an album release party for Miss Lovely held in a Manhattan waterfront loft. Sydney, one of a select group of white publicists who specialized in African American urban music clients, was a well-known public relations maven in New York City. She had handled clients like Sean "P-Diddy" Combs, Jay-Z, and LL Cool J. Sydney had confided in Boom that she wanted her firm to hire a competent African American so that the firm could relate to its black clients better.

Boom recalled his first meeting with Sydney. A confident blonde, Sydney had walked up to him and created such a stir that the loft seemed to quiet almost instantly. In fact, Boom thought he felt a spring breeze work through the already closed windows.

"Hi, Boom. I'm Sydney Warren."

"It's a pleasure to meet you," he said, shaking Sydney's hand.

She held on to Boom's hand longer than expected and said, "I was wondering if you would consider heading up the urban music relations department at my company. I've heard many wonderful things about you, and I think you would be perfect for me—I mean perfect for the firm." Sydney smiled mischievously.

Although he had never dated white women, Boom was somewhat attracted to Sydney. Her neat two-piece mini-suit, toned, tanned body, fly Manolo Blahnik heels, and shoulder-length highlighted blond hair all turned him on. As he looked at her walk away, he thought, *She looks like she can handle hers in bed.*

****

New York, NY

Sydney powered away on the elliptical machine in her bedroom and looked at the uncut edition of Shout's new music video, "Shout's The Name." The video had pictures of Shout walking through a record label's front office. The scenes reminded Sydney of her start as a publicist five years ago.

While working in the pop music department of World Music Records, black artists and their management would often stop into Sydney's office and complain about their publicity campaigns. The artists would say, "I ain't on the cover of *The Source* and ain't nobody selling more rap records than me." The female R&B artists would complain about Mary J. Blige being featured in every magazine from *Essence* to *Vibe* to *Ebony* while they weren't getting much mention at all. So, Sydney began to investigate and found that many publicists were sending in their artist's music, but they weren't fighting enough to get them on the cover. Subsequently, when the black artists offered to pay Sydney to help with their media coverage, Sydney's idea for The Sydney Warren Public Relations group germinated.

****

Boom walked out on the balcony. It was already two o'clock. Boom decided to try to reach out to Shout again. He knew Shout was in Philadelphia the last time that he checked and that was only two hours from Washington, D.C. The show started at eight and the press reception was scheduled for 6:30. If he could find out where Shout was, there was a chance that the press reception could still happen. Boom looked in his cell phone's address book and dialed Shout's home number. The phone rang five times and on the sixth ring, Boom decided to hang up.

"Hello," a high-pitched woman's voice answered.

Boom placed the phone close to his ear. "Yes. Hello. This is Boom Tillman. I need to speak with Shout."

"Shout, Shout, somebody named Boom is on the phone. Shout, get the phone," Boom heard the woman yell.

****

"Oh shit." Shout looked at his clock on the night stand and saw that it was two o'clock. "I missed my damn plane." He looked at the cinnamon-skinned girl with turquoise eyes who was wearing a midriff tank top with the word *sexy* on the front. Residue from her platinum-colored lipstick formed a crusty ring around her mouth. He sat up on the bed.

"What's your name?" he asked.

"Bonisha." The girl, who wore blond braids and a black choker with a cross dangling from her neck, wiped her eyebrows, making sure not to harm the two-inch red painted nails that extended from each of her fingers.

Shout stood over and looked at the girl.

"What? Never mind. Whatever. You gotta go. Get your stuff."

A bare-chested Shout grabbed the cordless phone and pulled the covers off the girl in one motion. Green-and-gray plaid boxers fell just beneath his hip bone. A tattoo reading GOD HAS CHOSEN ran across his stomach, dipping and grooving with his breathing and the definition of his abdomen.

"Boom, man. I'm sorry. It was a late night. I missed the plane. I know, I know, I gotta get to D.C. What time do you need me there?"

"Four-forty-five."

"Okay, okay. I can get there from Philly in that time. I'll call you when I hit the city."

****

Bonisha began to collect her stuff. Shout went to his bedroom door and yelled, "Greasy, Greasy."

Three seconds later, a burly six-six, light-skinned man wearing a navy-blue skull cap with a blue bandana, white T-shirt, jeans, and Timberlands appeared at Shout's door.

"Yo, Greasy, get her out of here."

Greasy stepped inside the room and walked toward Bonisha. "Alright, sweetie. You heard the man."

The girl backed away from Greasy until she bumped into a wall.

"But, Shout, can I get your number? Here's my number."

The girl tried to throw a piece a paper on the bed as Greasy grabbed her by the arm. Shout barely noticed the paper falling to the floor as he went to the bathroom, shut the door, and sat on the toilet.

****

Sydney worked on her laptop. Her clients, all African-American hip hop and R&B stars paid her firm $40,000 per month plus expenses. She was once called 'The Head Mistress of the Hip Hop Plantation' by a New York newspaper. Sydney found the title complimentary since it was true. She created the images of her black clients and she was 100% Caucasian. Her clients believed that she knew what was best for them and so they followed her every word.

Sydney jotted down some strategies to go over with Boom and then sent him a two-way message: AFTER DC LETS SIT DOWN AND TALK ABOUT OUR CLIENT LIST. I WANT TO OWN NEW YORK CITY. SYD

"In a recent poll, 65% of the women questioned said that they would lie to get a man. They said they would lie about their age, how many times they've had sex, if they had kids, how much money they made, and if they were currently in a relationship. It seems that the respondents were willing to be deceitful if they believed they had met Mr. Right, especially if it was the difference in getting the man or not. Are man-getting lies any different from white lies? And if the lie can get you to a place where you want to be, isn't the lie worth it?"

—Tisha Ariel Nikkole, excerpted from her article "Lies, Lives & Relationships"

Chapter 3

New York, NY

From the bay view of her twenty-fifth-floor Manhattan office, Jordan Ellis saw all the busy New Yorkers going back and forth—men in their trench coats, women with rainbow-colored umbrellas, families with strollers, and older women with plastic scarves flattening their hair, all walking frantically. Jeans, underwear, and record advertisements hung prominently over Broadway, one of Manhattan's busiest streets. Screaming fans holding homemade signs for Eminem stood outside of the MTV office, jumping up and down in excitement. "Kids, the things they'll do for a superstar," Jordan mumbled.

Jordan was a petite, light skinned woman of mixed racial heritage. Her naturally wavy hair was kept in a short, Halle Berry-esque style. She had hazel-eyes that were often hidden under baby blue contact lenses. Her curvy frame barely reached five feet, and most of her 110 pounds were distributed to her shapely thighs and curvy bottom, save her 36B breasts.

She was born thirty years ago in Norfolk, Virginia, to a white mother and an African American father. Her family had traveled all over the world, moving from Army base to Army base. As a small child, Jordan had to move as soon as she made friends at the military bases. When Jordan was twelve years old, a teacher had sent a note home complaining that she did not play well with others and was very anti-social. When a concerned Mr. Ellis asked his daughter what the problem was, she responded, "Every friend that I ever had, you moved me from. If I don't play with anyone, I won't make any friends."

Jordan looked at her achievement plaques on the wall testifying to her success in the music industry. Starting in the business as an assistant/girlfriend of record label owner Sean Simmons six years ago had served Jordan well.

Her mind wandered and Jordan thought about the next radio programmer that she had to pay off. Her job as the radio promotions director for World Music Records had her running money all up and down the east coast and across the continental United States. The Federal Communications Commission had laws that forbid record companies from paying record stations to play their artists' records. But, FCC rules weren't really laws. They were a myth. Any artist on the radio was being heard because some radio executive had greased a station owner's palm. Jordan didn't care about breaking the FCC's laws. She was finally a part of a winning team. World Music Records loved her and paid her 250K a year to work for them. If she had to break some laws in order to remain a starter, she was willing to do it.

Pulling her compact mirror out of her desk drawer. She reapplied her lipgloss and got up from her chair. She brushed off her low-rise Seven jeans and straightened out her Bebe sequined tank top. The promotions assistant, Latavia Jenkins, sat at a crème wooden desk stationed in the reception area in front of Jordan's office.

"Damn it, Latavia, I told you to make the meeting at 6:30," Jordan scolded her assistant.

"Oh, sorry Jordan, it's just that you had a train to catch at six, so I thought that you wouldn't have been here," Latavia responded nervously.

"Well, what time is it now?" Jordan screamed, looking down at her platinum-linked watch. Complete with twelve diamonds, the watch was Jordan's favorite piece of jewelry because it reminded her of the success that she'd had in the music industry. Her watch was given to her by World Music's president, Dan Bellows, after five of her last six artists reached number one on *Billboard* magazine's coveted rap chart.

Gently opening the door of Jordan's office, Latavia leaned in and said, "It's 5:15. Would you like me to cancel your appointment with DJ Stylix?" Jordan looked at the papers on her desk and her cell phone and grabbed her two-way pager. "No, it's fine. I'll meet with him."

Stepping inside the office, Latavia asked, "Well, will you still be catching the six o'clock Metroliner?"

Jordan became irritated at Latavia's redundant question. She got up and walked over to Latavia. "Listen, I know you just started and everything, but in this business we have to remember our priorities. This meeting is a priority, so's the concert in D.C. Try to see if you can pay attention to what I do and learn how I operate. It's a quick pace here. Think before you ask questions." Jordan turned away. "That's all for now. You can leave."

****

Dressed from head to toe in an all-white velour sweatsuit with a silver logo, DJ Stylix strolled into Jordan's office. The Puerto Rican radio programmer was in charge of the hottest rap show at New York City's WQHT radio station, also known as Hot 97. The platinum-link chain and miniature boom-box medallion sparkled brightly. The medallion looked to have at least thirty diamonds.

As he lounged on the comfortable purple leather couch that sat perpendicular to Jordan's desk, Stylix said, "What up, Blue-eyes? What's the latest?"

Unimpressed by his smug comfort in her office, Jordan responded, "Nothing. Why don't you tell me?" She twirled her gold-engraved "Queen Jordan" pen between her French-manicured fingers.

"You know the callers ain't feeling 'Sweat Me.' I can't play the song if the callers aren't requesting it," Stylix said.

"Just last week, you said that you were spinning it in the hip-hop show. What changed?" Jordan asked.

"I was spinning it, but the phones weren't ringing, so I had to pull the record from rotation," Stylix said.

Jordan sighed, reclined in her wide leather chair and propped her feet complete with Gucci flip flops on her desk.

Latavia buzzed Jordan's office.

"I'm in a meeting. What?" Jordan demanded.

"Mr. Bellows called and he wants you to cancel the trip to D.C. and meet with him in his office as soon as possible."

Dancin' naked, showin' skin
Anything to get with him
'Cause the Range
Is on their brains
Seein' jewels they'll never obtain
They'll do ya crew
Sniff the blow
What kind of soul
Does a real trick know?
—Shout from his single "Real Tricks"

Chapter 4

In the backstage area of the MCI Center, Boom supervised the decorating of the press reception for Shout. Five round tables were draped with white cotton cloths. For every expected journalist, each chair had a Shout compact disc, a postcard of Shout, a copy of his biography, and a totebag filled with record label give-aways. Posters of Shout covered every inch of wall space. Smaller flyers had been placed on the ceiling.

Boom had both his two-way pager and his cell phone attached to his belt. Every few minutes he looked at his watch. It was 5:50. Time was ticking, and he hadn't heard from Shout.

Boom paced the floor. A few reporters from the local newspapers had arrived and were enjoying the spread of cheeses, breads, shrimp, chicken, and beef kabobs. A bartender was set up in the corner mixing drinks. The bartender's stand had a poster of Shout taped along the bottom.

Boom walked out of the conference area and headed down the hallway to the men's room. He passed a bunch of sound engineers who were sitting by the speakers, tour managers leaning on walls talking on their cells, young girls in tight jeans and too much makeup, and two guys handing out after-party flyers the size of a CD cover. Boom stepped into the men's room and exhaled. Just as he was about to unzip his pants, he heard a door open and Shout stepped out of a faded brown stall.

"What's up, nigga? I told you I wouldn't let you down," Shout yelled, punching Boom on the shoulder.

Relief swept across Boom's face. "What you doin' coming out of that stall?"

"I got to pee in private 'cause I don't want a picture of my Johnson on VH-1. You smell me?"

Shout and Boom laughed.

"I heard that."

Shout walked over to the sink and washed his hands. Boom resumed his business.

****

Just outside the loading area for the MCI Center, Boom and Shout stood near Shout's brand-new, champagne-colored Cadillac Escalade. The burgundy leather interior had Shout's name embroidered in the headrests. The twenty-two-inch chrome rims stood out in the daylight like four miniature metallic ferris wheels. Shout's manager, Pockets, and his cousin Antonio, sat in the truck rolling blunts. They passed one to Shout who reached in his pocket, grabbed a lighter, and set the joint ablaze.

Boom looked at Shout and then looked at his watch. "It's 6:30 on the dot. I have a roomful of journalists. Let's go in there and talk to them. They'll write some articles and help us sell more records. I'll be straight up with you and you know this already, you'll probably get asked the same question twenty times or more. Some of them may prefer to just look at you, but in the end we gotta give 'em some time in order to get the stories written. I'll be right there with you."

"Journalists are assholes," Shout said as he took a pull from the blunt.

"Some are, not all. But in the end, if they're gonna help keep you paid, you can deal with a couple of assholes. Are you feelin' me?"

Shout took his last pull on the blunt, formed a fist, gave Boom a pound, and said with smoke seeping from his mouth, "Let's roll."

****

The back area of the arena looked dismal. Everything was either a dull gray or black. Stagehands walked by pushing equipment. Young men who looked like they still belonged in high school stood by the artists' dressing rooms. Tisha thought that they might be relatives or male groupies. As she walked down the long hall, she saw a handwritten sign that read, SHOUT PRESS RECEPTION. It was written in the same script as her name on the envelope for her ticket and all access pass. She knew that handwriting because it belonged to her dearest college friend, Boom Tillman.

As Tisha entered the room, she surveyed everyone inside, looking for a recognizable face. As she scanned the room, she looked at the bored expressions of the journalists. Three television crews were there.

Where was Boom? Tisha wondered. She walked over to the food spread and got a small plate and filled it with cheese, crackers, a few grapes, and a strawberry. As she ate her cheese, the door to the media room opened. She looked up and Boom walked in.

"Ladies and gentlemen, I would like you all to welcome the biggest artist of the year, soon to be the biggest rapper that hip-hop has ever seen, Shout," Boom proudly stated.

Everyone in the room began to clap. Boom nodded in approval.

As Shout walked in, Tisha dropped the cheese on her plate. She was mesmerized by his looks. His high cheekbones, narrow nose, and white teeth all had superstar appeal. She stared directly at him, hoping to make eye contact. Shout stood a slim six-two. His brown skin shone as if he had just come from a Caribbean holiday. The white du-rag on his head ended at the top of his back. Most of the du-rag was covered by a baseball cap that had a white embroidered "S" on the top. His red-and-white baseball shirt had *Shout* written across the front in red lettering trimmed with white. His white Nike Air Force Ones looked out of the box fresh.

****

As Boom walked Shout from journalist to journalist, Tisha couldn't keep her eyes off the rapper. Every time Shout turned so that she was not facing him, she moved so that she could see his face. She thought, *This is the man that I'm gonna marry. I'm already in love.*

Tisha was the last journalist to be introduced. Boom looked at her and smiled. "I'm so glad you made it," he said. "This, of course, is Shout."

Shout extended his hand for Tisha to shake. "It's a pleasure to meet you," Shout said in his deep Barry White–like voice. Tisha did not respond. Boom broke the awkward silence.

"Shout, this is the journalist that I was telling you about who went to North Carolina Central with me. She's real cool. She'll be doing the one-on-one interview with you for *Life Music* magazine after the concert."

"Aiight. I'm feelin' that," Shout replied.

Standing so close, Tisha could smell Shout's familiar cologne. *Is it Michael Jordan's cologne? Is it Tommy Hilfiger?* she wondered. "I know that scent," she said, forgetting Boom and Shout were standing in front of her.

"I didn't hear you. What did you say?" Shout asked. "Never mind. It was nothing," Tisha responded.

"I know what you said. You're trying to figure out the cologne. Well, sweetheart, keep guessing."

Shout looked at Tisha. Their eyes locked for a moment.

"Boom, is it time to go? I want to get hyped up for the show tonight."

Boom looked at Tisha. He had never seen her at a loss for words. "Yeah man, but I'll need you to do three short interviews before the show. I have an area set up in your dressing room."

Boom and Shout headed to the door. Tisha just imagined the muscular bottom that was hiding in Shout's baggy jeans.

"At the sold-out concert in the Comcast Center in Philadelphia, platinum-selling R&B superstar Raphael electrified the audience with a 75-minute performance. When he sang his signature hit, 'Hearts of Gold,' the entire stadium swayed from left to right with their lighters, cell phones, and pagers in the air. As I walked to the backstage area to interview Raphael, I noticed the line of groupies trying to enter his dressing room was as long as the line in the ladies' bathroom."

—Tisha Ariel Nikkole, excerpted from her article, "Raphael: The Concert"

Chapter 5

The arena was sold-out. The deejay's cutting and scratching had everybody in MCI Center standing and dancing. Tisha sat in the third row from the stage writing in her tablet. The room was so dark, she could barely see the lines on the paper. Tisha looked around the audience. The concertgoers were of all ages and every color imaginable. There were teenagers, kids being chaperoned by their parents, and thirty-somethings who wished they were still teenagers.

Concertgoers had already begun to jump up and down. The energy in the crowd was infectious. The music from the speakers was so loud that Tisha could not hear herself think. She put down her tablet and started dancing. She imagined Shout dancing with her, pushing his chest against her shoulder blades.

The concert's emcee, a dreadlock-wearing WPGC radio personality stepped on stage and hyped the crowd. "When I say hip, you say hop." The emcee chanted, "Hip" and the audience enthusiastically responded "Hop." With every chant, the crowd became more excited. The back-and-forth continued for at least five minutes.

After the two opening acts left the stage, the center went black. Then, a voice came out of the darkness. "Alright, y'all. Now that you've been warmed up, I got the hottest rapper ever, ready to step on the stage. He's gonna tear this motherfucka down!" the emcee yelled. "So, show some love for Shout, y'all! Show some love."

The crowd went wild and began clapping, flicking their lighters, and hollering.

The house lights came on quickly and then shut off. Silence filled the auditorium. Then a nasally voice yelled to the crowd, "Y'all ain't ready for Shout. I said y'all motherfuckas ain't ready for Shout."

The lights on the stage came on. Shout's five-foot hype man was on stage looking like a human pit bull. He was trying to anger the crowd to get more hyped. The women were going berserk. There were screams from both male and female fans.

"We're ready for Shout!" a female fan exclaimed.

"Bring that motherfucka out," a male concertgoer yelled.

"Listen, D.C., we love y'all, but we only perform for live motherfuckas. So if y'all want my boy Shout to come out here and do his thing, y'all had better make some motherfuckin' noise!" The crowd went wild. Screams exploded throughout the MCI Center. Tisha thought that she had gone slightly deaf. She wiggled her index finger in her ear.

Shout entered from the left side of the stage wearing a white tank top, baggy jeans, and yellow Timberlands. The tattoos on both arms made his biceps seem even bigger than his frame would allow. "What's up, D.C.? Where my peoples at?" Shout yelled, grabbing the crotch of his jeans. "I want to thank y'all for coming out tonight. You didn't have to be here. But you are. That's real for a nigga like me. To show my appreciation, I'm gonna do the first song that y'all loved me for. Y'all remember this one?" He walked over and put his foot on a speaker. The track "Representin' for Me" played and the crowd rapped with Shout word for word.

Tisha found herself dreamily staring at Shout. She envisioned herself being held tightly in his arms. She imagined her hand feeling over Shout's bicep. Her nipples became aroused at the thought.

Two young women tried to walk by Tisha to the front of the stage. "Excuse me. Excuse me," the girls said to Tisha. Realizing that the girls wanted to get by, Tisha stepped back. The two girls passed Tisha and stood in the aisle. One girl, wearing a halter tank top, untied the top of her shirt and shook her bare breasts, yelling, "Shout, Shout, I'm representin' for you. Shout, Shout I'm representin'!"

Her friend, wearing a one-piece tangerine halter dress, turned her back to the stage and lifted her skirt. She bent over and shook her bare bottom, making her butt cheeks wiggle.

It's not gonna be easy getting Shout. Every girl in this concert wants him, Tisha thought. *It looks like I'm going to have to be more aggressive to get him to notice me.*

Tisha looked intensely at Shout and wondered if he saw the women who flashed their body parts at him. There were dozens of them in the crowd. It was almost as if one girl saw another girl do it, and a breast tidal wave began. A lot of girls were wearing pants low enough to show the top of their thongs. Several girls danced provocatively, like they were having sex right in the aisle.

Tisha put her pad in her back pocket and decided to move to the aisle. She pulled her fitted T-shirt down, then realized that it was supposed to expose her pierced navel. She adjusted her shirt to show her belly button. She moved through the crowd and stood at the rail at the front of the stage.

"Women are an important part of my life. My mom is very special to me. She taught me how to treat women right. I'm single right now. But I'm looking for a perfect lady."

The women in the crowd shrieked. Tisha stared at Shout, concentrating on his every word. This was the time in the concert where he was going to ask for a female participant. She prepared to jump when he asked. Her voice was ready to reach unforeseen octaves. Shout continued, "I believe my future lady might be in here tonight. I want to bring her up to the stage."

Right then, Tisha jumped and said, "Keyshawn, Keyshawn, Keyshawn, Keyshawn, Keyshawn."

Shout looked directly at Tisha and recognition dawned. He pointed to her and then pointed to the bodyguard who reached over the rail and picked up Tisha under her arms. He lifted her over the iron railing and pointed to the steps of the stage. Tisha gave her backpack to the bodyguard, adjusted her clothes and walked toward the steps. The other girls who were standing by her said, "Bitch," loud enough for Tisha to hear.

Shout's hype man returned to the stage with a chair, and placed it near Shout. As Tisha walked on the stage, girls continued to wave their arms in the air, still screaming, "Shout, pick me. Shout, pick me. That ho can't do nothing like I can. Shout, pick me. I'm a better ho."

Tisha stuck out her chest and stood tall. She strutted on stage, looking at Shout every step of the way.

Shout yelled into the microphone, "Oh, and she's fine, huh?"

His hype man said, "Hell yeah. If you don't want her, you know I'll freak her."

Shout smiled and said, "Oh, I ain't givin' you nothing yet."

As Tisha got within arm's length of Shout, she put both of her arms in front of her as if to say, "Well, what's next? You got me up here, so now what?" Guys in the crowd began to whistle. Shout eyed Tisha up and down. He walked toward her and grabbed her hand. "So, you're the lucky woman tonight."

Tisha gently nodded. She stood on her tiptoes and whispered in Shout's ear, "No, you're the lucky man."

Shout motioned for Tisha to sit in the chair. She removed her pad from her back pocket and placed it on the side of the chair. The deejay began to play the intro for Shout's hit single, "Perfect Lady." He kneeled in front of Tisha and put one hand on her thigh. As he rhymed, Tisha watched his every move. *Being on stage with Shout is not a coincidence. This is the beginning of our relationship,* she convinced herself.

As he kneeled, he put his leg on one of her thighs and the crowd screamed.

"Don't hurt yourself," Tisha said with a chuckle.

Shout looked up at her and then stood between her legs. Tisha reached to undo her ponytail. She shook her head and her shoulder-length hair fell. The crowd hollered and whistled. Shout smiled at Tisha.

Taking the microphone away from his mouth, he said, "You're a pro, huh?"

He walked to the edge of the stage and ripped off his T-shirt.

Tisha was looking at his back. A trickle of sweat was dancing down the center. He had a picture of a man over his right shoulder blade with the name Vonnell written under it.

He turned to Tisha, then reached back and threw his shirt into the crowd. An overcharged teenager grabbed it with one hand and then put it to her face and inhaled. She then fell out. Two large security men carried her out of the concert.

As the song ended, Shout grabbed Tisha by the hand and said, "Alright, D.C., give it up for my perfect lady." The audience erupted with applause.

Tisha smiled and bowed her head. She squeezed Shout's hand, which caught him off guard. He looked at her and said, "I want everybody in D.C. to know your name. What's your name, sweetheart?"

Licking her lips, Tisha said, "Tisha Ariel Nikkole."

"Thank you, Miss Tisha Ariel Nikkole." The crowd applauded. Shout walked Tisha to the side of the stage and his hype man walked over to her. Shout returned to his performance at the front of the stage.

The hype man gently touched her arm and his hot breath was in her face. The scent of marijuana, stale beer, and sour-cream-and-onion potato chips stung Tisha's nose.

"Hey, baby. Thanks for being a part of the show. You know this shit is stage shit. You don't really have a chance with Shout, but, we're staying at the Four Seasons tonight. Here's the room number." He gave her a wrinkled piece of paper with something handwritten in pencil. "We'd love for you to stop by. And you can bring a couple of friends if they're as fine as you." He reached over and attempted to feel her butt.

Tisha moved so that she was out of his reach.

"Yeah, whatever. I wish you were as fine as Shout."

"What you say? What you say?" The hype man puffed his chest out and tried to walk closer to Tisha.

Tisha kept walking faster and giggled to herself. The pimple-faced, pint-sized, hype man-child was not her type.

She quietly asked herself, "Why is it that the most arrogant, funny-looking people are always a part of an artist's entourage? And, when will they understand that joints, chips, and beer smell like hot garbage?"

She stepped down the backstage steps. "Let me just find Boom and see how long Shout will be on stage. I'm ready to do this interview."

Tisha continued through the backstage area until she reached the media room.

"The hardest part about the music business is separating the snakes from the saints. There is definitely a good-versus-evil element in hip-hop. In order to make it, you need an angel on your shoulder."

—Shout, interviewed for the magazine article, "Shouts and Saints"

Chapter 6

Jordan was on the elevator at World Music Headquarters. She pressed the button for the twenty-eighth floor. She leaned with her back against the elevator's wall, slowly inhaling and exhaling. Jordan jumped when she heard the elevator's bell ring. As she made a sharp left off the elevator, glass doors with the World Music logo awaited her. The receptionist saw Jordan and pushed the remote-controlled unlock mechanism for the door.

"Hey, Jordan."

"Hi, Samantha."

"Love those flip flops."

Jordan looked down at her sandal's white background covered with black double G designs. *These are fly* she thought to herself.

"Thanks. I had to have 'em."

Jordan walked off and took long strides on the plush coffee-colored carpet. Her bang, which touched her eyebrows, moved with every step. She stopped at the glass doors and pushed the buzzer to Dan Bellows' office.

"Jordan, come on in," a voice from the speaker announced. Jordan looked inquisitively at the chrome-colored speaker. That was a voice that she hadn't heard before.

Taking a right and then walking down a long hallway filled with platinum and gold records, Jordan noticed there were still many employees working.

"What's up, Jordan?" Tahib Miner, an attractive executive, said as he walked in the opposite direction. Pointing to his two-way pager, he said, "Hit me on the hip. We should talk."

Jordan nodded and smiled, briefly.

Several offices had opened doors. Executives in their twenties and early thirties were at their desks on the phone, listening to music, or meeting with other executives. Poster-sized pictures of World Music's most famous artists adorned the walls.

Jordan's face tensed and her stride slowed as she approached Dan's office. His assistant, Natalia Manetti, was sitting at her wooden L-shaped desk.

As Jordan approached, Nancy looked up and said, "I hear you've been out and about today. Has it been a rough one?"

Jordan smiled. "Just another day in the record business. Is Dan ready to see me yet?"

"Ready?" Natalia retorted. "He's been waiting for the past hour. Go right in."

Dan Bellows was in his early forties. He wore a baseball cap with WM on it to cover his headful of brown hair that had begun to slightly thin at the top. A handsome white man who stayed tanned, Dan was tremendously fit for his age. He lived in jeans and sneakers. His five-eleven frame showed no evidence of the stomach bulge that usually plagued men his age.

He was practicing his golf swing when Jordan entered his office. "Close the door," he said without looking up at her. He hit the golf ball and it moved too fast on the putting green and came back to him.

"Still working on your swing, huh?" Jordan sat on the tan leather couch. She leaned forward with her hands clasped in the middle of her stomach.

Dan nodded. "How did everything go with that deejay from Butter 93?" Dan asked, continuing to practice. Looking at Dan's pathetic swing, Jordan touched her

Adam's apple and looked at the tips of her nails; some of the French manicure had begun to chip off.

"It went alright."

"Pour me a shot of gin."

Jordan got up and headed toward the liquor cabinet. She poured two glasses. She took one over to Dan, who set the glass at the end of a broad wooden desk with a marble top.

"Is everything handled?"

She picked up the shot glass and threw the gin straight down her throat.

Dan looked over at her and returned to his golf swing.

"He said that he would increase the spins of the record. So, expect to hear more of it. But, I'll tell you this deejay is greedy. He's going to bleed us and bleed us and bleed us. It's just something about him."

"Is that so? The last guy that I ran across like that, I had to hang out of a window." Dan laughed and reclined in his chair.

"I got some ideas of my own on how to handle this clown. It's better that you don't know, " Jordan replied.

Jordan looked at the glass french doors that opened to a tiled veranda in Dan's office, which was at least forty-five floors in the air.

"What do you want me to do next with Butter 93?"

"Arrange for Shout to do some special radio promotions. Do some exclusive shit for that particular deejay. And if all else fails, give him a sex party. Unless he's a homosexual, we'll get some spins for buying him a few hookers. And even if he's gay, we can arrange something for that too."

Leaning forward in his high-back leather chair, he asked anxiously, "How close are you to Shout? Can you get him to understand this part of the music business?"

Exasperated, Jordan protested, "You know how artists are. They think it's all about their music. They don't understand what my job is. Shout's just another knucklehead. I'm not close to him."

Dan raised his hand. "Look, a lot of our financial future rests on our ability to make this a really successful record. This is the last hoop that we have to jump through and that's it. We'll be at the top of our game longer than any other record label in recent memory."

Dan got up from behind his massive marble-topped executive desk and sat down in a black leather chair diagonally across from the couch.

"We need to make this happen. We have to make this happen. Work whatever angle you have to use. This artist needs to be in our back pocket so that we can get this deejay in our back pocket."

"Hasn't Shout already sold like six million albums worldwide? We've already made our money off him. Isn't it time for us to look for World Music's next superstar?"

"Yes and no. We renegotiated Shout's contract so we need his next two albums to be three million–plus sellers for us to make the money off him that we made off the first five million albums we sold. And, don't you worry about that anyway. I want this deejay and Shout in our back pocket. Work on the deejay for now."

"We pay every other deejay. Why do we have to do something different for this asshole? Outside of buying cars, clothes, hookers, what else can we do? Shoot, if I take him out, we still gotta train somebody in his place."

Dan chuckled. "If I didn't look at you and couldn't see that you were a woman, I would believe that you're a man. You think like a man, you act like a man. But, Jordan, you are not a man. Maybe it's time for you to use what runs the world."

Perplexed, Jordan asked, "And what's that?"

"Pussy," Dan Bellows responded.

"You can't curl up to a laptop at night. A business report can't warm your feet on a cold winter's night. Working 12-hour days won't guarantee you a life free from loneliness. If we know this is true, why do we continue to let work get in the way of love?"

—Tisha Ariel Nikkole, excerpted from her magazine article, "Work vs. Love: A Fight We're Not Winning"

Chapter 7

Shout had barbells, weights, and a sit-up board strategically sitting inside his dressing room. The all-gray area had open wooden lockers along the left wall. Three lockers had signs with *Shout Only—Don't Touch* written on them. Inside the three lockers were new sneakers and boots, three pairs of jeans, three velour sweat suits, three tank tops, three pairs of sweat socks, and three baseball caps with "S" on them. Tisha looked around the room.

"He likes working out, huh?" Tisha said to Boom who was leaning near an open closet. Six pairs of new sneakers and Timberlands were lined up at the top of the closet.

"Yeah. He's into his appearance. He takes working out seriously. His commitment to things like that is part of what makes him a huge star."

Tisha got up, walked over to a dressing table, and sat down. Gazing in the mirror, she looked at herself and smoothed her hand over her hair.

"Did you see me onstage?"

Boom stood straight up, "See *you* on stage? When were you on stage?" Tisha spun around in the chair and faced Boom as he walked over to her.

A wide grin crossed Tisha's face as she coyly stated, "I wanted to be a part of the show so when Shout had his audience-member-onstage segment, I volunteered."

Raising his voice, Boom said, "You must be kidding. You're going all out for this story, aren't you? I noticed how you were looking at him earlier. You don't want to go there. Trust me, Tisha. You don't."

Boom's pager went off and he looked at the message: HOW'S THE CONCERT GOING? CALL ME LATER, SYDNEY. Boom closed the top on the pager and put it back on his hip.

"I don't know, Boom. I think I might have felt something when I first looked at him. Love at first sight can happen." Tisha looked at herself in the mirror again and twisted her long ponytail around her finger.

Boom reached into a narrow plastic trashcan full of sodas and bottles of Cristal champagne. He grabbed a soda and quickly began to drink.

"I never thought I'd hear you sound so naïve. As a journalist, you know artists aren't always what they seem. You know what the climate is."

Just then, the screams of the crowd got louder. The mirror shook and the door to the dressing room was kicked open. Shout's two hype men entered, followed by two bodyguards, Shout, and three of his associates.

Shout had a small white towel in his hand and he wiped his forehead and yelled, "Yeah, boy. It's on. It's on." He beat his hands on his chest like a warrior.

Simp, the hype man, headed straight to the trashcan cooler and grabbed two bottles of Cristal. He passed one bottle to Shout and opened the other and began to pass it around the room after he took the first sip. He looked over at Tisha and nodded, "What's up?"

She just rolled her eyes at him. Simp looked over to Shout and then to the other men in the room and said in a huff, "It's a bunch of niggas in here. Where are all the bitches? I gotta get the bitches for our party." He pointed at one of the men and said, "Come on, let's go get the chickens." The man took a long drink on the Cristal, and put it on the table.

Boom clicked into publicist mode and stepped to Shout.

"If you're up to it, the journalist that I introduced you to earlier is here. The interview will be about twenty minutes. It's a cover story and it'll give your fans who weren't at the concert another chance to get close to your music," Boom stated.

"Alright. Give me like five minutes. I'ma get my head right."

"Cool. Me and Tisha are going near the showers. It's quieter back there. We'll be waiting on you."

Simp re-entered the dressing room with four women and directed them to sit on the black couch in front of the barbells. Tisha got up from the dressing chair and noticed that one woman was playing with the weave that hung down to her waist. Another girl was standing in five-inch heels, wearing short-shorts. Her gold belly ring had an "eat me" charm dangling just below her belly.

Standing confidently, Tisha looked at the other women. She picked up her backpack, switched her hips energetically passed them and hissed. The sight of groupies in a rapper's dressing room was always unnerving for her. Boom reached out toward her and she grabbed his hand. Boom yelled to Shout, "In five, ten minutes. It'll be quick, aiight."

"Yeah, man," Shout responded.

Tisha and Boom walked in the back area of the dressing room. It was actually the showers except neither Shout nor any of his entourage used them at concert venues. They always got dressed in the hotel room instead. A couple of chairs were set up in front of wall-length mirrors.

Tisha sat in one of the black vinyl-and-steel chairs and began to pout.

Sitting in a chair opposite from Tisha, Boom asked, "Why do you look like you're trippin' already?"

Tisha did not respond. She looked at the floor and then at her bag.

"Oh, I get it. You're trippin' because you saw some groupies in the dressing room. Come on, Tisha. It really ain't that deep. Rap stars and groupies go together like fat asses and spandex." Boom chuckled but Tisha barely smiled.

"Why is it that groupies have such easy access to stars? But a journalist or a photographer has to get ten levels of clearance to write a story or take a photo. These groupies can get through like one, two, three, Tisha said, exhaling and rolling her eyes.

"Yeah, I feel you. But it's all a part of the game."

****

Boom remembered countless arguments with Tisha when they were in college. For an entire year they debated about the importance of belonging to sororities and fraternities. Tisha always asked if the organizations really served a higher purpose.

"Dag Tisha. Everything doesn't answer a life question. Some things you do because they'll help you in the long run," Boom told her.

"I don't know. Shouldn't we have better reasons for pledging than that?"

Boom couldn't answer all of his friend's philosophical questions. They both pledged anyway. His fraternity gave him the line name Clotheshorse and her sorority gave her the line name Confuscius.

****

Shout entered the back of the dressing room with a white towel draped along his shoulders. His chest was bare and his light blue boxer shorts showed just above the top of his baggy jeans.

"What up? What up? What up?" Shout exclaimed. He walked over to Boom and shook his hand.

"You remember Tisha, don't you?" Boom asked, pointing to Tisha with his left hand. Shout clasped his hands together and nodded with a knowing smirk on his face. "She's here to do the cover story for *Life Music* magazine," Boom continued.

Shout said, "Oh, I remember the pretty lady. She was in the show tonight."

Tisha swiveled her chair toward Shout and seductively looked at him. She slowly rose from the chair, maintaining eye contact. Tisha turned sideways, holding in her stomach even tighter. She was sure that Shout was examining her profile. She bent to reach her backpack. In slow motion, she bent her knees, then extended her arms into the bag, gently moving her hips.

Shout was looking at Tisha but quickly glanced at Boom. "Um, are you sure she's a journalist? She look like she might be something else," Shout said and chuckled. Tisha wondered if he had ever had sex with a journalist before.

"That ain't funny," Tisha said.

Turning to Shout, Boom said, "There's an after party tonight. I'll probably stop through, but I won't have any press set up for you there. So, you'll be on your own tonight."

"I doubt that," Tisha said looking at Shout, rolling her eyes playfully and then looking back at Boom.

"I'm going to go ahead and look for some of the other journalists. I'll be setting up photo opportunities for them to take pictures with you after your interview with Tisha," Boom said.

Boom headed toward the door, then turned back and looked at Tisha and winked.

"Where do you want to do this?" Tisha asked seductively in a tone that was a cross between a whisper and a low groan.

"Well, I have a lot of energy, right, so, sometimes, I just like walking around during the interview. If you can stay with me, we can do it in here. Just walking."

Tisha turned on her handheld recorder. "My first question is why did you want to become a rapper?" Tisha held the recorder just below Shout's chin and looked at his navel and noticed a small band of hair circling it. As he spoke, his stomach contracted and his navel moved. "I've always loved music." Shout looked at the ceiling and continued, "I've always wanted to express myself through music. When my moms didn't want to listen to me, I turned to music, so I express myself through my rhymes." Tisha felt Shout looking at her but did not make eye contact.

"What you looking at?" Shout asked.

"What? Oh. I'm just trying to concentrate on the questions."

"Yeah right. That's new."

Tisha thought that she just lost major cool points by staring at Shout's navel for too long. Maybe he thought Tisha was a groupie just like all the others. Looking up at Shout, she asked, "What are the three greatest things that you've gained from being a successful artist?"

Shout walked into an open shower stall and looked down at the drain. He kneeled down, exposing more of his blue boxer shorts and coughed, clearing his throat. "Money, of course. I can eat now. I gained a certain amount of freedom. I can do things that I couldn't even dream of before." Shout paused. He bit his bottom lip. "Cool, what's the third thing?" He stood and walked to a bench in the nearby area and sat down.

"Is the third thing that you gained love?" Tisha inquired.

Disbelieving, Shout responded, "Love? Love? I don't know what you mean."

"From meeting all these people, surely you must feel that the people love you. Surely you must have met that person who is your true love. Come on, all the places you've been, all the cities that you've traveled. Surely, you've found love," Tisha said, hoping that Shout truly hadn't, but speaking as if he should long for it.

Shout shook his head. "Nah, man. It's not like that. Sure your fans love you, groupies love you. But, what do they love you for? Do they love you for the dough? Do they love you for your music? They can't love you for you, 'cause they don't know you. I've been a lot of places. But, I'm like the man who gained the world and lost his soul."

"Deep. That's deep. What's it gonna take for you to regain your soul?" Tisha asked. While walking toward Shout, she bumped into his arm and they stood face-to-face. Silence. It was awkward. He stepped back. Then Tisha stepped back.

"What kind of interview is this? You're asking things that people don't ask me. Are you a journalist or a head doctor?" Shout tightly grabbed the ends of his towel.

"If I'm making you feel uncomfortable, I'll stop," Tisha said. "But there is so much more to artists than their music. A real story goes beyond the music. It adds an element of the person's true personality. It takes off the mask."

"I ain't wearing no mask. What you see is what you get," Shout said, huffing.

"So what is your public getting?" Tisha asked, unimpressed.

"They're getting an in-your-face rapping phenomenon. I'm here to speak the ills of the ghetto over a phat-ass beat. That's who I am. It's simple. You're trying to make it much more complex than it is," Shout explained.

"Tell me something, off the record, What are your groupies getting?" Tisha looked at Shout slowly from head to toe before walking over to her bag. Shout stared at her the entire way.

Caught off guard, Shout remembered the times he and his best friend, Vonni, would run game on chicks. He felt more confident when he was kickin' it to girls when Vonni was around. Vonell "Vonni" Jones was a well-known, much-respected street hustler who was about to turn a ten-dollar crack hustling gig into a multi-million-dollar empire—until he was involved in a high-speed chase with police officers. When his SUV hit an embankment wall, he died instantly. He left his best friend behind to mourn him.

Sitting on the first pew at the funeral home, listening to Vonell's uncle eulogize him left Shout numb. He stared at the handles of the casket, he stared at the sides of Vonell's face. He expected that Vonni would get up at any moment with his trademark line, "Man, you know I be trippin'." Shout stared at the open casket until the minister closed it. Vonell never got up, and Shout never got over it.

"Let me ask you again. What are your groupies getting?"

Blankly looking at her, Shout responded, "A stiff one."

"I know you think that's amusing but I don't. I wanted you to be different from other artists, but you're not. You're just like the rest of them. It's a shame. You're such a talent. For once, can't someone really take off the mask and show the world who he really is? I guess you're not ready for that. Thanks for the interview."

Tisha walked out of the back dressing room area as Shout looked at her.

"You don't really know me, so, you don't know shit. You don't know if I'm different or not. The most that you know about me is my music. You need to stop trying to be deep and write the damn story."

Tisha saw Simp in the corner feeling on the buttocks of one of the groupies. She noticed someone wearing Timberland boots was in a corner booth with his black jeans around his ankles and a girl in a pink short set was on her knees. A curtain was drawn so Tisha couldn't really see what was going on but it was obvious.

She walked past six groupies sitting on the couch. Two of them were licking their lips. One was kneeling on the couch with her hand on her backside. Two others were sitting on the ends of the couch with their legs open and one was showing one of Shout's entourage member's her nipple ring.

Tisha let out a loud groan. She frantically followed every red-lighted exit sign that she saw. She began to walk fast from one hallway to another stairwell, practically jogging out of the building.

Once she got outside, she flagged down the first yellow cab she could find and jumped in. She leaned her head against the window all the way home.

"I haven't changed. I'm the same nigga I was when I grew up in Philly. I'm a little deeper though. I think about things more. I got a lot more fallen soldiers in my camp and I pour out a whole lot more liquor when I'm celebrating."

—Shout, interviewed for the article, "Shout: On the top of the pile"

Chapter 8

The morning after the show, Boom was resting peacefully in his hotel room. Around three A.M. he heard a loud banging. He was not sure if he heard an alarm, something outside, or the door. He raised his head from the bed and looked around and realized he had left the bathroom light on the previous night. It was still dark outside. He lay his head back on the pillow.

He heard the knocking again. They were quick, rapid thumps. Boom got up and walked to the door. Shout was standing there, breathing heavily, his eyes large.

"Did something happen with your room?"

"Man, I had to come here."

Boom groaned and said, "What is going on?" He stepped aside and Shout walked in.

Shout sat on the couch, bowing his head, and began to speak slowly. "I was in the suite upstairs, chilling, watching ESPN or something. My cousin Broady and Simp were downstairs with the groupies. It started getting loud and rowdy. You know how that is." Shout paused and inhaled deeply, then exhaled.

"So, I hear this one girl saying, 'Smack my ass harder. Smack me.' Them messing around was so loud, I decided to leave the room for a while. I put on my sneaks and sweats and headed to the gym. I ran on the treadmill for like forty-five minutes. And I pumped iron for like another thirty minutes. Well, when I headed back to the room, I stepped off the elevator and looked down the hall and the police had Broady and Simp in handcuffs. I turned around and got back on the elevator."

"They're in handcuffs?" Boom asked.

"Hell yeah. I got off the elevator on the second floor and walked down the stairs to the parking lot. By the time I got to my truck, there was a police car parked behind it, and police were walking around the parking lot. So, I ran all the way up to your floor."

"Damn. That groupie sex is a recipe for disaster. Why do you think the cops arrested Broady and Simp?"

Shout sat back on the bed and said, "I don't know. Man, I don't know. When I saw the police, all I was thinking was, *'Shit, this is the end of my career.'*"

Sitting on the couch, Boom said, "You were right to leave the hotel room. You can't afford the association with this right now."

Boom walked to the closet and got a pillow and blanket and handed the items to Shout. "This is what we're going to do right now. I want you to get some sleep. You didn't have anything to do with this. Around nine, I'll call New York and talk to legal counsel at the label. I'll see what they advise us to do. Don't stress this right now. You're alright by just chillin'. We'll figure it out in the morning."

****

Three light taps sounded at Boom's hotel room door. Shout's loud breathing practically silenced the knocks. Boom, dressed in gray wool slacks and a black knit top, opened the door for Warren Goldsmith, a middle-age white attorney with balding gray hair. He wore a brown-pinstriped suit with a white shirt and brown multicolored tie.

"Thanks for your time," Boom stated as he shook Warren's hand. "I'll brief you quickly and then we'll wake Shout up, and we can go from there."

"Well, if it's all the same to you, let's just go ahead and get him up. I've already called the police department.

It's confirmed. They have issued a warrant for his arrest.
We need to get started so this can be resolved as quickly as
possible."

Boom walked over to Shout and tapped him
repeatedly on the shoulder. "Shout, Shout, get up, get up.
The lawyer's here."

****

Shout stepped out of a limousine, escorted by
Goldsmith, Boom, and Greasy. He nervously rubbed his
hands together. His platinum cross dangled solidly in front
of the black-and-gray athletic jersey's number 33.

Goldsmith looked over at Shout who was solemn-
faced.

Inside the Washington, D.C., police precinct,
Goldsmith stepped to the oversized, wooden information
desk that appeared to be sitting on stilts.

"Good morning. I need to speak with Detective
Ward."

The desk sergeant looked up from the remaining half
of a bran muffin. "What's this regarding?"

"An arrest warrant that was issued last night. He's
expecting us."

The desk sergeant looked over at Shout and eyed
him quickly. He moved his steaming cup of coffee and
picked up an antiquated black telephone and dialed several
numbers. Within minutes, a lanky, tall, African- American
male appeared. The desk sergeant pointed to Goldsmith.

Leaning forward and extending his hand to
Goldsmith, the detective said, "Good morning. I'm Detective
Ward. Thanks for coming in. Follow me."

Shout and Boom were sitting on a wooden bench in
front of the information desk, and Goldsmith motioned for
them to follow.

In the interview room, Shout looked at the bars that
covered the windows.

"You can have a seat," Detective Ward stated and
pulled out a raggedy metal chair for Shout.

"I prefer to stand for now," Shout responded. Boom
and Goldsmith sat down facing each other and Detective
Ward sat at the head of the table.

Looking at Shout's back, the detective asked, "Are you aware of the charges that you're facing?"

Shout did not respond and an awkward stillness filled the room.

Goldsmith began to speak. "Detective Ward, Mr. Lane is fully aware of the two charges of rape and assault, as well as the two charges of false imprisonment. But he can tell you where he was last night and we're absolutely certain that his alibi will be verified."

Shout stepped over to the table and sat opposite Detective Ward. "Last night, I was in my hotel room at The Four Seasons after my concert. The show ended around 11:30. I got some food and went to my room around 12:30."

Detective Ward asked, "Were you alone in your hotel room?"

Shout wiped his hands on the knees of his jeans. "No, I wasn't. My cousin Broady and my boy Simp were there. But my hotel room was more of a suite. There was a front area and a back area. They were connected. I was by myself on one side and my cousin and them were on the other side."

"And them? Who is that?"

"The groupies. The chicks. The females."

"Were you on your side of the suite all night?" Detective Ward asked.

"No, around 1:15, I went to the workout area in the hotel. I had to sign in on some piece of paper. There was a hotel worker in the gym the whole time. I stayed there about an hour and a half. When I left the gym, I went up to my room. But when I got off the elevator and looked down the hall, I saw police arresting my cousin and Simp. So I went up to Boom's room." Shout slouched down in his chair.

"Who is Boom?" Detective Ward asked.

"That's me. I'm his publicist. I work for his record company, World Music Records. I can verify the time that he came to my room. I was asleep and I looked over at the clock when I heard banging on the door. He stayed in my room overnight. We called Mr. Goldsmith first thing in the morning. The hotel can verify that he was in the exercise room because of the sign-in sheet."

Shout looked at the bars on the window. He stood and faced the door. "Detective, I need to take a walk. Can I go?" Shout asked.

"Can you stay for a few more minutes?" Detective Ward asked Goldsmith. "If I can get some of the contact information from you, Mr. Lane can leave now."

"Yes, I'll be here," Goldsmith responded.

****

Back in the limousine, heading to the hotel, Shout's cell phone rang.

"Hello, hello. Who is this?" Shout put his finger in his ear and strained to hear the voice on the phone.

"It's your Aunt Mae. Broady's in jail. He called me collect this morning. Keyshawn, you know better than this. What was he doing with those hussies? Did you know 'em?"

"Aunt Mae Mae. Aunt Mae Mae, calm down. I know Broady's in jail. No, I didn't know those girls."

"Keyshawn, you gotta get him out. I don't have no money. He asked me to put my house up. You promised me you'd take care of him when he started working for you, Keyshawn Lane. Don't make me call your mama."

"I'll get him out. Don't worry. Don't put your house up. I'll take care of it."

Shout removed the cell phone from his ear, slammed the phone shut, and threw it on the floor.

Boom looked across at Shout and asked, "What's wrong? What happened now?" Boom leaned toward him and put Shout's cell phone on the seat.

"Family issues."

"Oh."

"They be trippin'. My cousin already called his mom. Now, she's trippin'. I got to get him outta jail. This shit shouldn't even be happening." Shout laid back in the car and rolled down the window. "I'm hungry. Tell the driver to take us to get some food."

"No problem." Boom got up and tapped on the separating window to get the driver's attention.

****

Boom's phone rang. He clicked the button and put it on speaker.

"Hello."

"What the hell is going on? My pager keeps going off. Reporters from the New York papers are calling me. What is going on with Shout down there?" Sydney asked.

"Nothing." Boom replied.

"Don't bullshit me. Something is going on. Newsbites are being run on the noon broadcasts."

"Sydney, it's a misunderstanding. One of Shout's cousins and a friend had a sexual encounter with some groupies last night in Shout's suite. He wasn't even there. But, because it was technically his room, they charged him. Shout was working out in the hotel, so he has an alibi. The charges will be dropped against him by tomorrow morning—probably around ten. The detective is just checking out everything."

"Well, up here they're acting like he killed somebody."

"Isn't that always how the media acts when it involves rappers? It's always blown out of proportion." Boom looked out the window.

"Please continue to resolve the issue, and two-way me or call me as more information comes in. We'll have to do our own press conference on this matter if the heat is turned up any more. I don't want this incident to reflect badly on the firm and my name specifically."

"The lawyer has assured us that the alibi is going to check out. I know the press is all over you, but I had to handle the legal aspects first. Sydney, I'll be back in the office in like three hours. I'll just have to handle it then."

Boom disconnected the phone and sat in the space next to Shout. "I know you want to handle the situation for your cousin, and I want that as well but we have to get someone else to post his bail and hire his attorney. It would be too much negative media exposure. Some New York papers are already running headlines."

Rolling down the window completely and sticking his head out, Shout exclaimed, "No shit!"

****

Jordan spent her Saturday morning searching for shoes at the Manolo Blahnik boutique on 54th street in Manhattan.

Jordan sat down in the chair alongside her extra-large pocketbook. While bending over, trying on a pair of open toe slides with a platinum chain mesh on the top, Jordan head-butted a young woman trying on the exact same pair.

"Oww," they both said in unison.

"Nice shoes," the young lady who stood about five foot six with light peach skin said to Jordan.

Jordan looked up and smiled. The lady was wearing a leopard print camisole and a pair of low-rise black jeans.

"Look, if we're going to be doing all of this head-butting, we should at least know each other's names," the young lady said with a chuckle while rubbing her head.

Jordan laughed also and with her left hand on her head, said, "I can't remember the last time I laughed. My name is Jordan. It's a pleasure to meet you."

Jordan extended her hand, but the young lady grabbed her arm and gently hugged her.

"My name is Juicy. It's nice bumping in to you," she replied and continued to laugh infectiously, throwing her head back and forth.

Jordan noticed Juicy's pointed chin and small nose. "You're in such a good mood. Does buying heels do this for you?" Jordan inquired, walking over to a display with purple heels on it.

"No. Life does this to me. Making choices for myself, and living does this for me," Juicy said, following Jordan. Juicy's bright brown eyes were clear and warm. She wore a blondish wet and wavy weave that was done so tight, it looked as if the hair was growing from her scalp.

"I would love to know what you do for a living. Are they hiring?" Jordan asked sarcastically, trying on the purple shoe.

Juicy walked over to a nearby rack of shoes and picked up a patent leather shoe. "I can tell from your vibe that you wouldn't believe me if I told you."

Jordan snickered under her breath. "I'd believe you. You have no idea what I do for a living. And, believe me, I have to come across everything."

Stepping closer to Jordan, Juicy said, "What do you do?"

"I work for a record company. I'm an executive. What do you do?"

"I'm a Nubian escort."

Jordan gave Juicy a perplexed look. "Am I supposed to know what that means? I'ma little slow today."

"I go out with men of my choice. If I like them, I have sex with them. And I make a lotta money." Juicy's face was serious. Her eyebrows were raised.

Jordan took off the purple shoe. "Well, I'm glad it works for you, but I can't hustle like that!" Jordan retorted.

"Don't knock it 'til you've tried it."

"I hear you. I hear you."

"Tell me about your job" Juicy asked, standing next to Jordan, adjusting her brastrap and feeling underneath her each of her DD sized breasts.

"Money controls everything. Now my boss wants me to seduce people. He believes that it'll make me more effective in my job. The next thing I know, he'll be asking me to have sex with a radio programmer to get a record played."

"Well, it seems like you're in the same game as I am, just under a different name. Before long, you'll be having sex on the job. But unlike you, I chose who I have sex with."

Jordan gave Juicy an icy stare. Then she shook it off. After she straightened out the bottom of her blue jeans, Jordan headed toward the door.

"I'm ready to bounce. You want to have a drink?" Jordan asked.

"Yeah, I'm game. Let's go," Juicy said.

****

The smell of pasta, cheese and fresh vegetables filled the air at the upscale Bice Restaurant on 54th Street. Cherry woods and Italian art were throughout the dining area. Jordan and Juicy sat at a small table in the back of the restaurant.

"What would you two like to have to drink today?" the waiter asked.

"A Diet Coke," Jordan and Juicy said in unison. They looked at each other and laughed.

"Hmm. I wish my life was as hilarious," said the waiter, chuckling as he looked at them. "I'll be right back with your sodas."

"Now, he was fine," Juicy said.

"Yeah, but he looks like he might be still in high school."

"And what's wrong with that? A little education on the right subject never hurt anybody," Juicy said with a wide grin.

"Girl, you are crazy."

Jordan and Juicy laughed some more.

"Do you ever worry about getting caught?" Jordan boldly asked, staring intensely at Juicy.

"Getting caught ordering lunch?" Juicy laughed. "I hardly think I can be arrested for that."

Jordan smiled and sipped her soda. "You know what I mean."

"I know, Jordan. Lighten up. I used to be afraid. But, I've been in this game for eight years. When I was new to it, I let people take advantage of me. I did whatever I was told. I never thought about protecting myself. I was thrown in jail once." Jordan leaned forward, pushing the soda to the side and putting both of her forearms on the table.

"Really. What happened?"

"I just got in a situation. I was young, naïve, and I got caught out there. Ever since then, I realized that if my ass is on the line, I can't expect anybody else to watch it."

Jordan's eyes glazed over. She began to think about Dan Bellows. While staring blankly, Jordan began to speak, "If someone were to ask what we did for a living, no one would guess that what we do is so similar." Breaking her gaze, Jordan looked back at Juicy. "I mean you no disrespect but you're a prostitute. But, the way that you handle it, it's like you're the pimp and the ho. I never met anybody who said that she could be both. That's some deep shit. I'm in a similar situation in my job. I'm breaking laws—federal laws—and my boss probably wouldn't know me. If I were to get caught out there, my boss would have no love for me. I definitely need to rethink looking out for me."

Juicy reached over and touched Jordan's hand. Her short French manicure looked freshly done. "Sista, if you gon' be out there like that, you got to look out for self."

"She's never met her fiancé, but she believes that she knows him. Relisa and Crazy Ken have been corresponding from a hundred miles away. She lives in Delaware and her fiancé has been in a New Jersey jail for the past five years for drug possession and attempted murder. In two days she's driving to the penitentiary to marry Ken. Relisa says, "I know more about him than what his sentence says or what the media says. I know love." Relisa states this so passionately that I believe her. Sight unseen and beyond scrutiny, perhaps their relationship really has a chance."

  —Tisha Ariel Nikkole, excerpted from her article, "Jailhouse Love: Conquering All"

Chapter 9

The day after the meeting with Detective Ward, Boom was back in New York City taking his usual stroll to the subway. Boom stopped by a newsstand and got a bottle of orange juice and looked down at the newspaper.

The headline read *HOT RAPPER? HOT RAPIST! SHOUT ARRESTED IN D.C.* Boom read the headline, and a look of terror swept across his face. He picked up the paper and spun around on his heels. "Goddammit," he yelled. Crumpling up the paper he screamed toward the sky, "Why does this bullshit keep happening?"

The foreign newsstand owner looked at Boom in disgust.

"You gotta pay for that, Papa. You gotta pay."

Boom looked at the turban-wearing man, reached into his pocket, and put the change on the counter. He walked across the street, sat on a park bench, and quickly read the story.

Rapper Keyshawn Lane, known to his fans as Shout, allegedly raped two women after his concert at the sold-out MCI Center in Washington, D.C. One woman claims to be pregnant with his child.... Apparently the Lane family has a history of sexual assault. Lane's cousin Broady Anderson was arrested four years ago on a statutory rape charge and is currently being held without bail. Anderson is charged with raping the woman as well. According to police reports, it was a gang-rape situation.... Because of Shout's status in the music industry, he was able to turn himself in and be released though Anderson is still being held.

****

"The story is full of lies Sydney," Boom said during a heated argument in the conference room at his job.

"Well, Boom, we still have to do something about it. This will make the firm look bad. You were brought on board to keep this kind of thing in check. And it's way out of check," Sydney yelled. Boom closed his eyes for a moment, wishing that he was in another place. "This is not the time to sleep on the job. I think too much sleeping is what got y'all in this predicament," Sydney retorted.

"Y'all? Who is y'all? Who's y'all?" Boom asked, huffing. Sydney rolled her eyes at Boom and looked at the wall. "That's alright. I know who y'all is. You wanted to say, y'all niggas. First of all, you're overreacting based on a biased story in the newspaper. For the record, that paper is always printing stories that are incorrect. Second, Shout was not in the hotel room or around those hoochies when the *alleged* rape took place. He has an alibi. The detective already checked it out. And the charges are being dropped."

"Well, you didn't tell me all of that. And you don't have to put words in my mouth. You don't know what I'm thinking."

"I did tell you that. I told you that when I was leaving the police station. But it doesn't matter that I told you already. You only want to hear what you want to hear. That's what the real problem is."

"That's not the problem. The problem is that we have a rapper who doesn't know how to handle himself in public. As a result we have a public relations nightmare on our hands. Not to mention the questionable people that this rapper hangs around—family included."

Boom stood. "That's it. I've had it with you. Ever since I've started working here, you've had me on a tightrope. But no more. I'm outta here after this. But, first, I'ma say what I gotta say. You have no real reason to think so negatively of Shout. You think that way because you're biased. Sydney, you really think you're the only white woman running to be around black people and black culture when you don't even like the music? It's so many of y'all, to use your term. You think I don't know you, but I know you. That's how I know what you're thinking. You're just another white woman who is in love with the black man's dick—or at least the myth. You think the industry brothers aren't talking about you and how many of them sexed you? Come on. Get real. If you think for one minute that you're going to keep your company going strong and be biased against your clients and the people who work with you, you're truly mistaken. Good-bye."

Sydney's face became deathly pale. She put her hand on her face, and her bottom lip began to quiver.

Boom turned to leave the conference room and paused when he heard Sydney begin to cry. "You know, I really liked you. But, if you can't respect me, you can't respect my work, how am I supposed to deal with this job? If we could ever deal in truth, it would be a different conversation." With that said, Boom stopped by his desk and grabbed his coat, laptop, and all of his essential belongings and headed for the office's front door.

****

Juicy relaxed on the plush couch in Jordan's office and looked around the office.

"Girl you must work your ass off to get all these plaques on the wall."

"Yeah, like a slave," Jordan dryly replied. The phone in her office rang. She hit the speaker button.

"This is Jordan."

"Whaddup girl? Where you been?"

"I've been around? What's up?"

"The Shout record needs to be movin' more units in Texas. What's up with your street team in the dirty south?"

"It sounds like they lunchin'. Let me check Soundscan and get right back."

"Alright, holla."

Jordan disconnected the phone.

"Rappers from up north betta get some love for the dirty south or their records are gonna be double copper. They'll never go platinum again," Jordan said as she smiled and took a sip of her soda.

"When are we going to lunch?" Juicy asked.

"I can't today. I got some stuff I need to handle with this record. For real, I got like twenty more minutes and then I need to be on the phones."

"I wanted to talk to you about my clients."

"What? That's your business. You don't have to come to me about that."

"Nah, I got a lotta doctors and lawyers, but I know those record people got that chedda. I'm trying to expand my clientele."

"I gotta think about that. We use prostitutes. I mean hookers on the street. Um. What I'm trying to say is I don't know if the music peoples are high-class enough to hire somebody like you. They're kinda scrungy with theirs."

"With all that loot? They using $2 hookers? Please. Jordan, take me to one party with some of them, and I'd have every record exec in my black book."

"Would you now? That's ambitious. If you can accomplish all of that, I'll give you a plaque." Jordan laughed.

"When you taking me to meet somebody?" Juicy stood up and straightened her form-fitting tank dress.

"Um. I'm gonna think about that."

Jordan's phone rang again. As she picked up the phone, Juicy left her office and sashayed down the hall.

****

Boom sat on the Aztec decorated rug, leaning against some matching throw pillows in his eleventh-floor apartment. He was wearing his favorite faded blue jeans and his North Carolina Central University T-shirt.

Boom reached over and took out a bottle of Chardonnay and poured himself a glass. The curtains were drawn and the light was shining in brightly through the cream-colored sheers.

He reached up and grabbed his two remote controls off the couch and turned on his chrome-colored stereo, which was pre-selected to play a mix of Floetry, Maxwell, and Mary J. Blige. As the sounds filled the room, Boom took the bottle and poured himself another glass.

Looking at his clock, Boom realized that it was not even 12:30 P.M. yet, and he was already on his third glass of wine.

With the other remote control, Boom turned on his fifty-six-inch television and began to watch music videos on BET. As he downed the third glass of wine, his cell phone rang. Boom got up slowly and went over to the bar to get the phone. Checking the Caller ID, he realized that it wasn't Sydney and decided to answer. "Yeah," a less-than-energetic Boom said.

"What's up, Boom?" Tisha asked in her usual perky tone.

"Nothing."

"I wanted to call you because I was tripping the other night," Tisha said.

"What do you mean?"

"With Shout. I wanted him to be the one for me. And, I thought he was," Tisha said.

"Yeah, girl. Well, you were trippin'." Boom sat on the barstool, eyeing the bottle of wine.

"What are you doing now? You sound relaxed."

"I'm at home. I had some wine. I just quit my job."

"Already? What happened?"

"Just some publicity, white woman, power-struggle nonsense."

"Oh, I feel that. How's Shout?"

"You have to ask, don't you? You must not be reading the newspapers."

"No. I've been meditating and doing my yoga. What happened?" Tisha asked, her voice escalating.

"He was arrested the day after the concert."

"For what, lewd behavior at the concert?" Tisha giggled.

"No, for rape."

A silence echoed over the telephone.

"You're kidding me. Just goes to show that he wasn't the guy for me. I'm so glad that I didn't take it there. I can't see myself dating a rapist."

"Hold on! Hello! Aren't you going to wait for the judge and jury before you convict him? Hello?"

"Hell no. You know how rappers get down. Apparently he's no different."

"Of all the people who would say that, I can't believe you said it, Tisha. You know hip-hop culture much better than that. It's not what you see on TV. Two days ago, he was your dream date, now he's Jeffrey Dahmer. Girl, I gotta go. Right now he's not even my client, so I can't worry about it, and I definitely ain't up to arguing about it."

Boom hung up the phone, walked over to the couch, stretched out, and fell asleep.

****

A light rapping sounded at Boom's door. He looked at his black digital clock and realized that four hours had passed. He got off the couch and lethargically walked over to the front door and looked through the peephole. It was Sydney. Boom opened the door.

"Hi, Boom. Can I come in?"

Boom didn't respond. He stood to the side and used his left arm to motion for Sydney's entrance.

"What are you doing on this side of town? Conducting more research?"

"Ha ha—very funny."

"Who's laughing?" Boom looked around the room. "I'm not."

Sydney walked tentatively to the couch and sat. She reached to adjust her oriental-designed hair clip, smoothing her hair in place.

Boom leaned on the bar, staring at Sydney. His eyes were bloodshot.

"I see you had a few drinks," Sydney muttered, picking up the empty bottle of wine.

"I wasn't on the job, so I'm allowed," Boom said sarcastically.

"Yeah, that's what I wanted to talk to you about— the job."

"I don't think we have anything to say. It's clear where you stand and what you think of me," Boom said.

"I came here to apologize for overreacting today." Sydney turned to face him. "Could you come over here and sit down? I'm straining my neck to maintain eye contact."

Boom walked into the living room and sat in a chair in the corner diagonally across from Sydney.

"We had a misunderstanding today. It's true I jumped to conclusions and I didn't respect where you were coming from, but it's not like we can't work together. I know that you're the best person for the Shout campaign."

Shaking his head, Boom said, "Every time something doesn't go the way you want, I'm not feeling being in an argument with you. It's a waste of time. If you hired me to do a job, you have to let me do it. And you know papers slant stuff, so why overreact every time you see a story? That's what I can't understand."

Looking at Boom with pleading eyes, Sydney said, "I need you to come back to the company. I promise to work on my overreactions. I realize that we're a team. So when something happens, it's irresponsible of me to get mad at you. I realize that now. I'm sorry."

Boom's cold stare softened.

Sydney walked over to him and extended her hand. "Can we shake on it? Will you come back to work tomorrow?"

Boom just looked at Sydney's frail hand with the frosted pink manicured nails. She had a diamond ring on her index finger and her pinky, as well as a gold bracelet with diamonds in the middle.

Boom stood slowly and shook Sydney's hand. "Yeah, I'll come back to work tomorrow."

"Thank you. Thank you." Sydney hugged Boom tightly around the waist. She barely reached his chest.

She took her leather purse off the couch and walked to the door. As she grabbed the handle, she turned and looked at Boom. "Oh, and another thing, you actually should return to work today. We have a crisis going on with

Shout. People think he's a rapist. You have to do major damage control." Sydney winked at Boom, ran her hand through the back of her hair, and closed the door.

Boom stood staring at the door, still smelling Sydney's expensive perfume that permeated his apartment.

He looked down and noticed a slight erection. "What's that all about?" he said to his blue sweatpants and headed to the shower.

****

In the offices of *Life Music* magazine, Tisha sat in the conference room with the editor-in-chief, Freedom Miller. "I love all of the articles you've been doing on the hip-hop and R&B artists. They've been tight, but have you ever thought about doin' an investigative story on the corruption in the music business?" Freedom asked.

"An investigative piece? I don't know. Interviews and reviews, stuff like that, that's my thing."

"Yeah, but you ask the good questions, and that makes a good investigative reporter."

"Well, what does the story entail exactly?" Tisha asked.

"We've been given some tips regarding executives who've been breaking FCC laws, engaging in harassment, bribery, and things of that nature. I've been collecting the research, but I didn't have a trustworthy reporter to put the responsibility of this story on."

"It's a complete departure from what I've done in the past. Let me think about it, do some preliminary research, and call you later. You know if I do it, I have to feel comfortable with the assignment. Right now I just don't know enough. Give me a couple of weeks to learn about this side of the business, and we'll talk."

"That's all I wanted to hear you say, Tisha. Thanks. And if you need any information, call me."

Tisha got up and left *Life Music*'s office and took the Metroliner back to DC.

You say you hate me
Then you love me
Swear you'd put no one
Above me
Then you put your foot
On my neck
Won't show a brotha respect
The world is how it is
Full of negatives
It's about more than cribs
So what you gonna give?
—Shout, from his song, "Hate Me, Love Me"

Chapter 10

Feeling the cool air conditioner Tisha put on her blue Adidas warm up pants and pulled the eight-by-ten glossy color photo of Shout from her backpack. She rested on her bed and gazed at the photograph. "What have you gotten yourself into now? Do you still feel that you're Mr. Tough Guy? Can I convince you that you don't need groupies, that what you really need is me?"

Tisha pulled the photograph close to her chest, opened her nightstand drawer, and pulled out a crystal picture frame that her mother had given her when Tisha graduated from college. She put the picture of Shout in the frame and tidied up the area on the nightstand. She headed to the kitchen and began to cut up a bell pepper, onions, and red peppers. As she placed them in her dutch oven, there was a knock on the door.

"Come on in, it's open," Tisha yelled.

Charmaine came bouncing through the door dressed in a long African skirt with a black T-shirt and holding some French bread and a box of spaghetti noodles.

"What's up, girl?" Charmaine asked with a giggle.

"You know what's up. It's Spaghetti Thursday, and I'm 'bout to sauté it up. Thanks for the noodles and the bread. You know how it is on a journalist's budget." Tisha smiled as she grabbed the bag from Charmaine and placed it on the counter.

"So, you're going to give up on Shout already, huh?" Charmaine asked.

"Well, I was really thinking about it. But that groupie thing, that's just a phase. It's my job to convince him that he doesn't need the groupies. I think it's my calling to pull him outta the depths of hell and to enlighten him. I have to cleanse his uncleanliness."

"Amen, Sista, amen," Charmaine said, chuckling. "But Reverend, before you beat him about the head with the Bible, don't you have to get him to notice you, or to pay attention to you, or to somehow separate you from the other women and hoochie mamas who are coming his way?"

The butter began popping and the vegetables were browning quickly. Tisha opened up a can of Italian-style tomatoes and dumped them in the skillet.

"Yeah, I have some work ahead of me, but I have to believe that Shout is the man for me. And, if I believe it, I know it'll happen. I just have to keep focused."

As Tisha and Charmaine were cleaning their plates, the telephone rang.

"It's kinda late for a work call, and we know you don't give anybody else your number so who is that?" Charmaine asked sarcastically.

Tisha grabbed the phone. "Hello?"

"Tisha, I'm so glad you answered the phone."

"Oh, Boom, it's you. What's up?"

"I want you to spend some time with Shout to try to clear his name. I need you to go to Philadelphia as soon as possible. I'll meet you there. Can you do that?"

"Yes, when?"

"Tomorrow. I'll have a train ticket for you at the station. You'll go from Union Station to the Thirtieth Street station, and I'll have a car pick you up, okay?"

"Yeah. I'll be there."

"Bring some clothes. It might be more than a day."

"What?"

"Just as a precaution. This media situation is getting out of control right now."

"He just got caught up with his cousins trying to have a ménage à trios. And, you know—guilt by association. Listen, I need you to write an emotional story about Shout, talk about the kind of person he is. I need you to show his humanity. I want people to read your story and know that Shout could not possibly rape any girl. It isn't in him."

"Um, you're asking for a lot. We didn't hit it off that well. So I don't know how much of that bulletproof armor he's going to be willing to take off to let me get to the emotional side. He seems real jagged."

"Let's get real, Tisha. Being jagged is part of the rapper's mantra. You can get past that. Good luck. I'll talk to you later."

"Oh, okay. Bye."

Tisha hung up the phone and yelled, "Yes, yes, yes! He's the one. He's the one!"

****

Juicy and Jordan met for lunch at Justin's Restaurant in Manhattan. In the reception area they waited for their table to be available. Jordan wore a pair of cut up jeans, a fitting beige mid-rift tee and a pair of tan Louis Vuitton sneakers.

"Isn't this P-Diddy's restaurant? I've heard about this restaurant but I've never been here," Juicy admitted adjusting her denim pleated miniskirt. The miniskirt showcased Juicy's model thin legs.

"Yes P. Diddy owns this. I like to come here for the macaroni and cheese. The barbecue chicken ain't bad either."

The maitre'd motioned for the women to follow him. Juicy's jeweled flip flops clapped the whole way to the table. After they ordered their food, Jordan stared at her new acquaintance. Juicy had pulled her blond hair into a high ponytail at the top of her head. The ponytail was big and curly. Jordan noticed that Juicy had light brown freckles on the bridge of her nose. As Juicy fidgeted with the napkin on the table, Jordan admired how Juicy's manicured nails didn't have any chipped polish.

"What makes you so special to your clients Juicy?"

"I'd tell you, but then I'd have to kill you." Juicy smiled and both dimples appeared in each cheek.

The lunch crowd in the restaurant was noisy.

"I'm special to my clients because I know how to use my body to give others pleasure," Juicy confidently stated.

"Anybody can have sex."

"Yeah, anybody can, but everybody doesn't know what turns men on. Everybody doesn't know that a man wants to live out his fantasies when he has sex. I know this. I play my role in his fantasy. And I get paid very well to do it."

"Umm. I'm not convinced," Jordan said while leaning her head to the side.

"Seeing is believing and tasting is proof. I'll invite you over the next time I have a client and you're in town."

"Yeah, you'd probably like that."

"Don't get me wrong. I'm not a freak. But I decided a long time ago why should I give my good pussy away for free when somebody is willing to pay for it."

As Jordan's two-way pager vibrated, Juicy went into the ladies room and washed her hands. As she looked at herself in the mirror she remembered wanting to run away from home when she was eight. She never met her father and was close to her mother until drugs came between them. When crack ravaged through Juicy's working class neighborhood, her mother became addicted. At first nobody really noticed. She would just disappear for an hour or so at a time. She managed to go to work and keep her job as a secretary for the first six months of her crack addiction. Then, the hours became days. At eight Juicy was going two and three days at a time without seeing her mother at all. On one night when Juicy was laying in the bed sleep, her mother came to her door and woke her up.

"Jocelyn, I need to you do me a favor."

A sleepy-headed Juicy, rubbed her eyes, "Ma, what are you talking about?"

"Listen to me Jocelyn. There's a man out there I need you to do a favor for. It's for me. I owe him money. I'm gonna bring him in here."

"Why are you gonna bring him in here?"

"I need you to be nice to him and do whatever he says and then I won't owe him no more money."

"Okay ma."

Jocelyn stood against the wall and a tall slender man walked in her bedroom. His yellow track pants almost blinded her sleepy eyes. He walked over to her and touched her thighs.

"You are prettier than your mama."

Jocelyn didn't say anything. The man kneeled down on his knees and rubbed his hands between both of Jocelyn's thighs.

"I don't like you touching me."

"We're just playing a game. Didn't your mom tell you to do whatever I say?"

"Yes."

"Well, we're gonna play doctor. Did you know I'm a real doctor?"

"No," Jocelyn said feeling a knot develop in her throat.

"Go lay on your bed and take your panties down," the man said, undoing his pants.

Jocelyn lay there. She didn't remove her panties.

"You're not supposed to let strangers see your panties."

"I'm no stranger. I'm the doctor."

The man climbed on the bed, pressed his naked flesh upon Jocelyn and ripped off her underpants. He penetrated her vagina as she screamed and yelled. Her mother was outside of the door with a crackpipe to her lips pretending that she didn't hear her daughter scream.

****

On the train to Philadelphia's Thirtieth Street station, Tisha sang "You Don't Know My Name" to herself while listening to her favorite R&B singer, Alicia Keys. The song had become Tisha's motto when she first began to think about being in a relationship with Shout.

The last serious relationship Tisha had was with Darien Bowman about a year before. Darien was a five-nine, well-built man with brown skin, hazel eyes, and a brightening-white smile. Tisha had met him at the metro when she sat next to him and they struck up a conversation.

Darien was a computer programmer who had recently relocated to the D.C. area. They were both the same age and gainfully employed so Tisha gave him her phone number. Their first date, a week later, was wonderful. Darien met her at an upscale restaurant off M Street, and they had walked in Georgetown for hours afterward talking. Under the light of the moon, Darien looked like a man who could be a runway model. Tisha was attracted to his physical beauty, especially his biceps, triceps, and abs. She had made mistakes in the past when talking to men just for their bodies, but she felt sure that it would be different with Darien because they could actually have a conversation. After three months, their relationship soured. Darien wasn't as hardworking as she thought, and he began to try to sponge off her for what little disposable income she had. She broke off the relationship, except for occasional booty calls. But now, she was ready for a real relationship.

The train stopped at Thirtieth Street station and Tisha grabbed her bag and stepped onto the platform. She walked up the two flights of stairs and took the escalator to ground level where Boom had a black Mercedes sedan waiting for her.

"Tisha Ariel Nikkole," the driver holding a sign with her name said in a thick Philadelphia accent when she walked up to him.

"Yeah, that's me," Tisha said, bouncing and smiling.

"Good." The driver opened the back door on the driver's side. "I'll take your bag."

Tisha pulled her denim duffle bag closed. "No, that's okay. I got it." She sat and ran her hand over the luxurious black leather seat. She smiled to herself as she looked through the dark tinted windows.

The cell phone in the car rang. Tisha overheard the driver state that they were going to the Gladwyne area. She watched the driver hang up the phone.

"Excuse me, driver," Tisha said.

"Yeah. Whatcha need?"

"Could you stop by a good hoagie place on our way to Gladwyne?"

"Uh, yeah. That should be no problem."

Tisha dug in her bag for her cell phone. "I can't find my cell phone. I could have sworn I had it with me."

The driver handed her the car's phone. "Miss, you can use this one."

"Cool." Tisha grabbed the phone and dialed Boom's number. "What's going on, Boom? It's Tisha. I thought you were coming with me to do the interview with Shout."

"I know but he really wants to speak to you on his own. He's going through a lot, and he said he would feel better if I wasn't looking over his shoulder on this one. He doesn't want me there," Boom responded.

"Oh," Tisha said, exhaling. "I wish you would have told me that. How are his spirits in light of the coverage of the rape allegation?" Tisha inquired.

"He wants to feel that he can trust someone to tell his story. He believes it's you." Boom paused, Tisha smiled from ear to ear.

"Are you still there?" Boom asked.

Tisha's voice was slightly higher when she responded, "Yes, I'm here."

"Well, I believe you can write the story that he's looking for. But we have to see what happens when you get there. You'll be fine. If anything goes wrong, hit me on the cell phone."

****

Tisha heard the driver pick up his cell phone and dial. He said, "Mr. Lane, we're outside of the gate." Then there was a pause, and he said, "Okay. Thank you." The driver hung up the phone and the gate opened. The car slowly drove down a hill and parked. He turned around and said to Tisha, "Miss Nikkole, Miss Nikkole, we're here." Tisha was lying with her eyes slightly open. The driver got out of the car, opened the door opposite Tisha, and touched her on the shoulder. She opened her eyes completely.

"Hey, what's up?" She looked out the door. "We're here already?"

The driver nodded as Tisha got her bag and stepped out of the car. She stretched both of her arms, let out a yawn, and looked around the driveway. "This place seems empty. Where is everybody?"

The driver closed her door and got into the car. "Mr. Lane said that you could walk right in. Here's your sub." The driver gave the sub to Tisha. She reached into her pocket and grabbed a ten-dollar bill.

"Thanks. I didn't realize I was so tired."

"No problem. I hope you like it."

"I will. Take care."

Tisha walked past the pool house and the Jacuzzi and opened a side door that was left slightly ajar. She looked at the kitchen and noticed bags of nachos and potato chips and bowls of dip on the counter.

"Hello, hello." Tisha dropped her bag on the floor in the living room and took her sub and put it in the empty refrigerator. The first floor was decorated in honey-colored hardwood and purple leather furniture. African statues, pictures, and miniatures were placed throughout the home. She peeked into the studio, a room carpeted in a plush navy blue and decorated with five framed gold and platinum records with Shout's name and his album or single's name on them. There was a wall-sized, framed poster of Shout. Across from the recording equipment was a sound room with a microphone that had a triangular name tag with "Shout" on it.

Tisha walked next door to the den and heard what sounded like a printer making noise. She walked over and saw a fax machine receiving a paper with the headline that read: RAPPER OR RAPIST! SHOUT CAUGHT IN HOTEL! Tisha grabbed the fax and put her hand over her mouth.

Pacing, Tisha said, "I can't believe this. This can't be happening. It has to be a lie. He wouldn't do this! Or would he?" Tisha stood against the wall with the fax in hand. She noticed a shelf with Shout's MTV Video Award, a Grammy, a Source Award, a BET Award, and various plaques given to him by The City of Philadelphia, The Boys Club of America, West Philadelphia High School, and *Fade 'Em* magazine. She put the fax on a black lacquer desk and slowly walked upstairs.

"Hello, hello." She heard the radio playing and water running in the back of the house. The French doors to the bedroom were open and Tisha walked in.

Shout's platinum and diamond necklaces, bracelets, and rings were on one nightstand. About thirty pieces of paper with numbers were on the other. Magnum condom wrappers were in a pile in the center of the bed. Jeans, T-shirts, and sneakers surrounded the bed. Instinctively, Tisha began kicking the dirty clothes in a corner near the closet and picking up the shoes and putting them in another corner.

Shout stepped out of the shower with a red towel wrapped around his waist. Tisha noticed a dragon tattoo on his calf.

"You're making yourself at home, ain't you? Damn, you betta be thankful you're cool with my man 'cause I don't appreciate you movin' my shit around the room."

"Oh, my fault. Um, I was uh, just um. . . " Tisha responded.

"Yeah, whatever." Shout walked over to the closet and pulled out a pair of jeans. Water was dripping off his sun-blessed shoulders.

Tisha was staring at Shout with her mouth wide open.

Looking over his shoulder, he said, "Do you mind?" and motioned to the door. "I ain't that kind of guy."

Tisha turned around and closed the double doors. "He ain't even all of that," she mumbled to herself and bounced downstairs. She went back into the living room and sat down. She patted her thighs and thought about her white and yellow Serena Williams inspired tennis dress that she was wearing. *Why did I wear this dress? I probably should have worn jeans. But it's too hot outside.*

Tisha's cell phone rang in the tune of Beyoncé's "Dangerously In Love." She reached down to get it, and the Caller ID displayed BOOM'S CELL.

"What's up, man? I'm here," she said.

"How's Shout doing? Is he still in a bad mood?"

"Is that a mood? I thought that was his personality."

"No, stop trippin'. He got the story about him being called new rapper/new rapist, and he's pissed about it."

"Yeah, I saw it."

"Have you thought about any story angles that might make this rapist story go away?"

"I've been thinking. Shout really needs to show people who he is on the inside. Sometimes the music portrays such a rough-and-tough image. So when something happens, everyone believes the image. Everyone believes that a rapper is more likely to be a villain. It sorta goes with the territory."

"Yeah, tell me about it. But good guy rappers don't sell music, unless you're Will Smith."

"There's a lot more to Will Smith than being a good guy. That's what I have to pull out of Shout. All of that intangible stuff that'll make people love him and feel for him."

"You sound like you got some ideas."

"Yeah, a little somethin', somethin'. I won't let you down. But, I don't have it totally figured out yet. Part of it will be up to Shout. I need him to really cooperate with me. Did you tell him that?"

"Yeah, I did. He knows the deal."

"Well, let me get crackin'. I'll call you if he gives me any trouble."

"Alright. Be good. And thanks for coming out on such short notice."

"No prob'. It's all good. See you later."

"Peace."

Tisha hung up the phone and got the sub out of the refrigerator. She sat at the bar with her yellow notepad and began to write a list of questions: *What do your fans need to know about you? How do you really feel about women? How do you feel about violence? Have you ever hit a woman before? Do you know what community service is? Do you have any sisters? How often do you mingle with groupies? How often do you have sex with groupies? Have you and a friend ever had group sex? Who are the people you hang around? Is it possible the people that you hang around don't respect women? Do you respect women? How do you know that you respect women? Give me an idea of the three most positive relationships that you've had with women in your life. What would you do if you found out that one of your friends was hitting his girlfriend?*

****

Jordan arrived at the upscale apartment building and asked the doorman for the penthouse suite.

"Who are you here for?" he asked.

"Juicy." Jordan stated while looking at her reflection in the glass along the wall. Her black Moschino sleeveless turtleneck and fitted white pants hugged her body, accentuating every curve.

"Oh, she didn't tell me she was having company. I have to call upstairs first." The doorman motioned for Jordan to stand by a small desk. He dialed Juicy's apartment and returned to Jordan who was combing her bangs with her fingers.

Maybe it's time I do something else with my hair, Jordan thought. She had been told many times that she looked like Halle Berry.

"I'll escort you to the penthouse," the doorman stated.

Jordan and the doorman stepped inside of a red and gold decorated elevator. The brass was shiny and smudgeless. The crystal ball that dangled about their heads looked to be made of a million Swarovski crystals.

"Prostitution has come up over the past decade." Jordan mumbled to herself as she ran the front of her black slides over the mahogany elevator trim. She stepped off the elevator onto cream marble floors with a hint of black specks throughout. She rang the doorbell and Juicy came to the door with a silver silk robe trimmed in bluish-gray fox fur.

"Hey girl," Juicy said as she hugged Jordan.

"You livin' large ain't you? Just tell me how you got into this building." Jordan walked through the foyer, living room and kitchen. She saw the massive granite countertops, built-in fireplaces, and marble flooring.

"You like it?" Juicy asked pulling her hand through her hair.

"Who wouldn't like it? This is like a palace at the top of Manhattan."

"One of my clients left it for me in his will."

Jordan stepped back and practically stepped out of her black leather slides.

"I need to change my line of business. I can't hardly see any rapper, singer, record label owner or anybody leaving me shit in their will."

Juicy laughed.

"You mean to tell me you got this joint for rolling in the hay? Juicy, I'm seriously thinking about a career change. Your business is unbelievable to me."

"I was hoping that you would say that," Juicy said and adjusted the tie on her robe. "You want something to eat or drink?"

"No, I'm alright."

"Could you really think about changing your line of work?"

A phone with an unusual ring went off in Juicy's apartment. It rang for about five times and then stopped.

"If the right thing came along and for the right amount of money, I could probably do anything. But, I must admit, I love the pace of the music industry. It's quick."

The phone rang again and Juicy got up and answered. Jordan's eyes followed her and noticed that she wasn't wearing any other clothes under her robe.

"Herb, I'm in a meeting right now. I can't meet with you. I'll call you in a couple of hours. Uh-huh. I promise, I'll call you. Bye."

Juicy walked back and sat on the white couch and took one of her zebra striped pillows, positioning it behind her lower back.

"Girl, having addicted clients is a trip."

"You don't have stalkers do you?" Jordan asked.

"No, it's not like that, I just have men who don't want to wait and want to spend too much time with me."

"In your line of work, that must be a great problem to have."

"Sometimes..." Juicy's phone rang again.

"I'm sorry about all of the distractions, it's just that I handle all of my business myself."

The phone stopped ringing and Jordan went to the bar and poured a glass of Courvosier. As she took her first sip, Juicy's phone rang again.

Jordan headed over to the phone.

"Let me get your phone for you. This is ridiculous."

"Hello... No this isn't Juicy. Who's this... Herb, we're trying to conduct a meeting. Unless you're prepared to pay triple of what you pay normally, you betta stop calling today. If this phone rings one more time while I'm sitting here, Juicy's gonna cut you off. All the way off. Do you understand?"

There was a pause.

"What? You'll have $4,500 dollars wired to her within the hour?" Jordan looked at the phone and Juicy with a blank stare. And then she hung up.

"It can't possibly be that easy?"

"What can I say? My clients have money. He's a plastic surgeon. Although I was born looking this good, I have to admit Herb gave me these," Juicy said pointing at her breasts.

"Why did you want me to come over here today?"

"I want you to manage my clients."

"What do you mean? Are you asking me to be your pimp?"

"Pimp is a man's term. Ladies are much more sophisticated."

"Are you asking me to be your madame?"

Juicy smiled. "You could look at it like that." Juicy took off her robe and walked over to the glass door opening to her balcony.

"Since I met you I can tell that you handle your business. And I can't lie. It's hard having to manage 25 people like Herb. It gets crazy sometimes. When I met you, something clicked in my mind."

Jordan walked over to the glass door and stood next to Juicy. Juicy was at least four inches taller than Jordan.

"I've gotta think about that one. I like my job, but I'm not one to knock a good hustle."

Juicy turned to Jordan and embraced her. The front of her robe loosened. Juicy slowly readjusted her belt.

"Would you at least think about it?"

Jordan nodded and headed for the door.

"Most women believe that there are good
men out there. They just don't know where they
live."

—Tisha Ariel Nikkole, excerpted from her
article, "Finding a Good Man"

Chapter 11

Sitting anxiously at the edge of the couch, Tisha wondered, *What is he going to say about this article? Obviously he's going to be pissed—but what if he really did it?*

Shout trotted downstairs wearing a blue du-rag, gray T-shirt, blue jeans, white sweat socks, and blue athletic sandals. He sat in a recliner next to Tisha and began to quiz her. "You consider yourself a journalist, right?" Shout said, pointing at Tisha. He looked away and waited for her to respond.

"Yeah, I'm a writer, a journalist. Yeah." Tisha nodded and looked at Shout, slightly confused.

"Well, instead of you interviewing me, I'm gon' kick a few questions to you." There was an awkward pause in the conversation. "Why is it that most journalists want to portray rappers and black men generally as monsters? Do you have an answer for that?" Shout asked.

Tisha's eyes became the size of small plums. She felt a drop of sweat forming at the nape of her neck. *I can't believe he asked me that. I gotta breathe deeply on that one.*

Shout sat forward in the chair. "Well, why is that, miss journalist lady?"

"Um, I don't think most journalists do that. But for those who do, I don't know if being a black man has anything to do with rappers being portrayed as monsters. I believe—"

Shout cut her off. He stood, walked over to her, and yelled, "Bullshit! Almost any black man who is famous has some kind of black cloud or dark circle around his name. And for the niggas who don't have one, these leech-ass journalists create it."

Tisha stood and walked over near the sliding glass door and noticed a picture of a Zulu warrior on a wall. The warrior appeared to be as angry as Shout. Tisha looked out at the pool. The water was the deepest aqua blue. She turned and walked closer to Shout. "Leeches? Did you just call journalists leeches?" Her voice rose. "I'm a writer, too. I don't know how you could call me a leech. You don't even know me! Yeah, I got your leech." She rolled her eyes at him so hard it took several moments for them to return to their sockets.

Shout burst out laughing and took a chew stick out of his back pocket and rested it on the inside of his jaw. "You are a leech—journalists are, period. If it wasn't for stars, for the people who are creative, y'all wouldn't know how to eat. The only story you can come up wit' is the stuff about us. What y'all don't know, you make up." Shout took the chewing stick out of his mouth and continued to laugh.

Watching Shout walk over to the refrigerator, Tisha envisioned ways that the du-rag could mysteriously fly off Shout's head and wrap around his throat. She believed that a reddish tint had covered the entire room. "Am I in hell?" she said as she walked over to the couch and sat down.

Shout poured some cola into a glass and dropped five ice cubes inside. He stood at the counter and menacingly looked over at Tisha.

Tisha felt a bit of tension around her shoulders. *I can't believe this. Why did I have to pursue the one rapper who understands the media? What can I say to him to make him believe that I'm different. I am different, aren't I?*

"Cat got ya tongue, huh? Yeah, it be like that. Every rapper ain't no idiot." Grabbing the remote control off the television, Shout threw all of his weight in the recliner.

Tisha reached into her denim bag and got her recorder. She then sat back on the couch. "Did you see the New York paper? Boom wanted to make sure you saw it."

Shout shook his head, blew air through his lips, and adjusted his du-rag. He lazily turned in Tisha's direction with a serious smirk on his face.

"Wrong. Wrong. Wrong. I told Boom about the article. I saw it first. He didn't have to tell me. I told him to fax it here so that you could see and realize what we're dealing with. But damn, you're making me see that you don't have to be a genius to be a magazine writer, huh?" Shout continued to shake his head and chuckled.

"You don't have to worry about being compared to other rappers. You're more obnoxious and self-absorbed than any of the rest. And, you obviously think you're smart, but being an asshole to a journalist who is supposed to be helping your image is not smart at all."

Tisha went into the bathroom and slammed the door. She turned on the faucet and splashed some water on her face.

Shout walked over to the bathroom door and yelled, "Bump the media. They didn't make me. That's where y'all get it twisted. And I didn't allow you to come up here to interview me because I want you to write good things about me—"

Tisha put her entire weight behind the doorknob and swung the door open, hitting Shout in the face with the door. He fell back into the wall and put his hand up to his face. "Damn, girl. That shit hurt. I'm gettin' a nose bleed."

Tisha walked past him and gave him a steely glance. She went to the kitchen, put some ice in a hand towel, grabbed Shout's left hand, and lead him to the couch where she sat down. "You got to lean your head back. It'll prevent the nose bleed from being really bad. Let's go." He put the back of his head on Tisha's lap. She removed his right hand and gently put the ice on the reddened area. Looking down at him, he looked so helpless. And, he didn't look like the mean, evil rapper he was five minutes earlier.

Straining to move his face, Shout said, "You know you did that shit on purpose."

Tisha pushed the ice a little harder in to Shout's face. "Oww!" He tried to get up.

"Lay down. I said lay down." Tisha pushed Shout's forehead back. "I didn't do nothing on purpose." Tisha quickly smiled. "I didn't know that I couldn't go to the bathroom in here without being hollered at."

"I was just trying to tell you somethin'. You ain't have to start trippin'."

"What were you trying to tell me? What was so important that you had to chase me to the bathroom?"

Shout moved the muscles in his face. "Now my face feels numb."

"But you'll be alright. What were you trying to tell me?"

"I don't want you to write good things about me."

"What? What are you talking about?"

"I want you to write the facts, the truth. Some artists may want people to make things up about them. I don't want that. Just keep my articles real. I want at least one article in my career that's the truth." He lifted his head and looked Tisha directly in the eyes. "Can you do that?"

Tisha leaned down slightly and Shout rested his head on her lap and put his other hand on his face.

"If you're willing to show me what the truth is, I'll write it. But in order to be real, you have to be yourself. I don't want to create a fantasy."

Shout smiled. "Ahh, that's funny. But my face is hurtin' so I can't laugh really. But a writer who doesn't want to make sumptin' up. That's funny."

Shout closed his eyes, and Tisha looked at the music video on the wide, flat screen television.

****

Sydney asked Boom to have breakfast with her at the Four Seasons in the city. She adjusted her asymmetrical gray shawl and matching tank top. Her faded blue jeans had a golf-ball sized hole at the knee. At ten, Boom walked in the restaurant and Sydney followed shortly after. Her Dr. Scholl's sandals clicked as they walked to the table. They sat at a table covered with a white cloth with a candle in the center. Boom sipped some ice water and asked, "Is this meeting about Shout's rape charge?"

"No. In fact, I don't really want to talk about work," Sydney replied. Sydney reached out and stroked Boom's hand. "I wanted to meet with you because over the past couple of weeks, I've found myself more and more attracted to you."

Boom looked at Sydney in surprise.

"I wanted to let you know because I won't deny how I feel." Sydney looked deeply into Boom's eyes.

"Sydney, I'm truly flattered. But we have too much to lose if we allow our personal feelings to taint our business relationship."

"So, you're just gonna tell me no and that's it? Don't you understand that when you have feelings for someone, it might be once in a lifetime?"

"I understand that," Boom replied, "but, if it's meant to be, it'll be. There's no need to rush anything."

"How can I continue to work with you platonically when I know I want more? Are you in a relationship?" Sydney asked.

"No," Boom said.

"I didn't think so." Sydney picked up her glass of water and sipped.

"Let's make a deal. Let's get through the next couple of months with Shout's campaign and see if our feelings still exist. We can't afford to put our clients or the company at risk."

"That's why I like you, Boom. You're the focused, reasonable one between the two of us. Where would I be without you?"

"You'd be in the same place. You just wouldn't be having as much fun," Boom said with a laugh. "Let's order. I'm starved."

"Me too. Thanks, Boom, for not making me feel crazy."

"The feeling's mutual, but anything worth having is worth waiting for and worth working for."

Sydney leaned over and kissed Boom on the lips.

Things have changed
The pain remains
More than my boy
You was a brotha to me
Schemin' and wildin'
You had my back for me
Teaching me the streets
You took no shorts from me
Although you're gone
You'll always be a part of me
—Shout, from his song, "Vonni"

Chapter 12

Brooklyn, NY

Jordan tightened the belt of her black silk robe and picked up the newspaper on the doorstep of her brownstone. The newspaper headline read, RADIO VP ARRESTED IN PAYOLA SCAM.

"Oh man, they took Norm's S-600 to the impound. Things are definitely getting hectic," Jordan said as she read the paper.

Jordan's house looked barely lived in save a photo of Jordan and her father. The last photograph that they had taken together was three years ago. Jordan had just purchased a camera that could be set to take pictures. She decided to try it out on her Dad.

Jordan had put the camera up on the counter and leaned on her Dad's shoulder. Within fifteen seconds, the camera went off. Two hours later while sitting in his favorite recliner, Jordan's father had a stroke and had been in a coma ever since.

Jordan walked over to her black kitchen counter and poured some orange juice just as her cell phone began to ring. "Yes," Jordan said as she leaned against the kitchen counter.

The voice on the other end of the phone asked, "What counteraction do you have planned for the FCC?"

"Dan, you're kidding me right? I don't make the laws so I can't do anything."

Dan laughed. "Oh, Jordan, you take this stuff too seriously. We don't have any problems with the FCC despite what you hear or read. And, anyway, I called to talk to you about your new job."

"Oh? I didn't realize I was getting a new job."

"I want you to be intimately involved with the day-to-day affairs for Shout."

"I thought that was something that was down the road. I didn't realize it would happen this soon."

"Well, I didn't either but apparently—I mean allegedly—he raped a couple of girls in a hotel room the other night and now the record company is facing a myriad of legal fees."

"Man, I didn't even hear about it." She sipped her orange juice.

"It's been on every video channel and every urban radio station. You must have been hiding under a log for the last seventy-two hours."

"Yeah, to say the least. How am I supposed to do my new job?"

"Well that's the fun part. I just want this rapper under our thumbnail. I don't care how you do it. Make him trust you. Make him want to do whatever you say. Hell, if it's to the record company's benefit, make him love you. But in the end, he's our cash cow, and we need to know what he's doing, how he's doing it, and who he's doing it with. *Capice?*"

Jordan took the phone from her ear and ran her fingers through her bangs. *If I'm not running money to deejays, I'm supposed to operate some kind of spy/manipulation scheme. When is this job gonna be about music and just selling records?*

"Hello, hello. You still there?" Dan yelled.

Silence echoed over the line. Jordan heard the ticks from the clock on the kitchen wall. "Yeah, I'm here. What is

World Music doing to help Norm? The article said he was being held without bail?"

"Nothing. He's on his own. World Music can't get into that mess."

"I don't believe this." Jordan dropped her glass on the floor. She stared as the juice spread all over.

"Jordan, you need to worry about yourself. Start coordinating with Shout's manager Monday." Dan hung up. The dial tone sounded like the pounding of a drum amplified by 100,000 decibels.

****

Like on many nights, thoughts of Vonni entered Shout's mind. Vonni had given Shout his stage name after they met when Keyshawn and his mom first moved into the neighborhood. Shout and Vonni were both twelve. "Go on, make some friends. We gon' be here for a while," Keyshawn's mom had said from the front door of their row house.

"Who you kidding, Ma? You always say that."

"Don't back talk, boy. You betta take your butt outside 'fo I go upside your head."

Keyshawn had hopped down the steps with some drumsticks in his back pocket. Walking down the street, he approached two boys who looked to be his age who were shooting marbles by the fence of a vacant lot. He glanced over at the boys and kept walking.

"Ey yo. Let me holla at ya."

Keyshawn heard someone talking, but he was inclined to keep walking.

"Ey yo, drumsticks. Let me holla at ya."

Keyshawn turned around and walked toward the young man with the dice.

"You're the new kid, huh?"

Keyshawn simply nodded.

"Well, I'm Jayvon. I look out for the newbies on the block."

Keyshawn nodded again.

"What, you can't talk?"

Keyshawn nodded.

"You know how to shoot dice?

"Yeah, I guess." Keyshawn was naturally loud. Even when he whispered it sounded like a lion's growl.

"Oh, that's why you don't talk, you got a loud voice, huh. Did people used to make fun of you or something?"

"Yeah, something like that."

"Well, we don't play that on this block. Got any money to shoot dice?"

"Nah."

"Well, you just like everybody else then."

Keyshawn nodded.

"My mom always told me that the one thing that people make fun of you for when you're little, will be the one thing they'll respect you for when you get older."

"I never heard of that."

"Yeah, man. I got a new nickname for you. I'm gonna call you Shout."

From that short meeting, Vonnell and Keyshawn became inseparable friends.

****

Outside Shout's house, Tisha walked along the pool and pulled out her cell phone to call Charmaine.

"Hello, Charmaine."

"How are you? How are things going?"

"Um, it's not going well," Tisha responded. "I thought I would be able to get through to him in a real significant way. I thought I'd be able to come up here, do a one-on-one interview and he'd open up."

"Don't beat yourself up yet, give yourself more time. You just got there, right?" Charmaine said.

"But, Charm, this could have been the story of my career. This could be the story that finally gives me my due respect, and all of those editors from *Aura* to *O Magazine* would come knocking. This is like the big fish and it's falling through the net," Tisha moaned.

"See the big picture. Stay focused. Don't let him build a wall and keep you out of it, no matter what he says. Remember, you're there to help him with his publicity issues, and he's there to help you further your career. This is about your career, don't forget it."

Tisha sat in one of the pool chairs and held her head down.

"I know you're right. That's why you're my best friend. Thanks for the pep talk."

"You got it."

"I'll talk to you later."

"Bye." Tisha hung up and walked toward Shout's back door.

****

Boom rang the buzzer outside of Sydney's Tribeca loft apartment. Wearing blue jeans, a Vassar Alumni t-shirt, and barefoot, she opened the door.

"Hey, good morning." Sydney smiled.

Boom stepped inside of the elevator. "Yeah, hey. When did we start having meetings at 11:00AM on Saturdays?" he asked.

They stepped off the elevator and into Sydney's apartment. She walked to the walnut-colored dining room table and sat in a matching chair. "Have a seat, Boom. There are a lot of things that are going on with the company, and I think it's time we had a strategy/partnership meeting."

"Partnership meeting?" Boom looked around the room. "I don't see any partners in here. I didn't think you believed in partnerships."

Sydney walked into the kitchen and returned with a cup of coffee. "Would you like a cup?" she asked.

"No, I'm feeling some Red Bull right now. But it can wait. What partnership are you talking about?" Boom sat across from Sydney.

Sydney sipped from her mug. "I realize everything that you've been doing with the company. You're responsible for our biggest client, Shout, of course. And you haven't missed a step." Sydney stirred the spoon in her cup. "I really think the firm could be a lot bigger, and I want us to take on more clients and that means I have to share more of the responsibility. In short, I think I want you to be a partner in SWPR."

"Um. I gotta give you credit, Sid. You know how to shock somebody. This was the last conversation that I thought we'd be having this morning," Boom responded.

"Well, what do you think? Don't you think we could be partners?" Sydney smiled devilishly.

Boom chuckled. "We work well together, but I'd have to understand the direction that you want to take the company, how it'll affect my finances, and all of that. I can't just jump into a partnership with my eyes closed."

"I'm having my lawyers draw up some papers. I just wanted to make sure that you'd at least entertain the idea." Sydney reached across the table and put her hand over Boom's.

Boom feeling aroused, rose from the chair and headed toward the kitchen. As he turned around from the refrigerator, Sydney was standing close to him. Boom stepped back.

"I'm serious about this. We belong together. We're a match, you can't deny that."

Boom opened the energy drink, "I'll look at the paperwork from your attorneys, and I'll think about it. It could probably work, but like I said . . ."

"I know you don't want to jump into bed with your eyes closed," Sydney responded.

Boom walked to the living room, and grabbed his jacket off of the couch. "Is there anything else that we should discuss today?"

"I just offered you the biggest deal in your life, and you're all ready to leave. What's up with you?" Sydney pouted.

"You've given me a lot to think about and I normally do my workouts around this time. I really could use a workout to organize my thoughts."

"Okay Boom. I hear you. I guess that's fair."

Boom walked to the door, and Sydney followed. As Boom opened the door, Sydney squeezed his waist with both hands. Startled, Boom turned around.

"Take this opportunity seriously. It's a big deal, and I wouldn't have offered it to you if I didn't think so highly of you," Sydney said and hugged Boom.

"Alright, Sydney. I'll talk to you on Monday, unless there's an emergency with Shout or something. Peace."

Sydney shut the door and mumbled, "If that doesn't get his attention, nothing will."

****

Outside of Mimi's strip club in northern New Jersey, Jordan sat in her silver Jaguar waiting for Juicy to arrive. She laid her head back on the buttery black leather interior. As she closed her eyes, pictures of her mother entered her mind. She remembered a photo of her and her mother playing with the water hose in front of their house. That was the only real memory Jordan had of her mother. When Jordan was six her mother was hit by a car in a grocery store parking lot. Jordan was in 1st grade. When it happened her father was in San Francisco on military business. The neighbors and the military support group kept Jordan overnight until her father came back home. But Jordan didn't understand how she was supposed to be a "regular girl" and not have a mother.

"Dad, every regular girl has a mother. There's something wrong with me. God doesn't like me."

"You're wrong about that. God loves you."

"Well, if he loves me so much why don't I have a mother?"

Jordan strained her forehead hoping that she would gain some real memories of her mother. She wanted to know what she smelled like, what her hair felt like, or if she was ticklish. Jordan wanted to know things about her mother that her father could never quite tell her. Jordan squinted her eyes tight and then there was a light sound on her window.

"Jordan, wake up."

Jordan opened her eyes and saw Juicy's DD's leaning into her window, revealing two pierced nipples. The black tube top needed some help to keep its contents in place.

"I wasn't sleep," Jordan replied as she grabbed her bag and exited the car. The wind lifted the fabric of Jordan's spaghetti strapped black babydoll dress.

"Why did you want to meet at a strip club?" Jordan asked.

"I'm trying to keep it interesting."

That's for sure, Jordan thought as she looked at Juicy's zebra print mini skirt and black slides with a 4 inch heel.

Jordan and Juicy entered Mimi's Stripclub, an exotic dance club for women. They bypassed the hefty bald bouncers that stood in the lobby. Mimi Paldone walked over to Juicy.

"How you been? It's been a while. Do you want a table, booth or what?"

"Mimi, it's good to see you. Give us a booth."

Mimi hugged Juicy and pointed them to a booth in the right front area of the club.

Jordan looked around the room. Most of the customers at the bar were women. Most of the customers that sat at tables in front of the stage were women.

"Juicy, you are one freaky bitch. You brought me to a lesbian strip club. I didn't know you got down like that."

"I like the atmosphere. I've always gotten excited by being at strip clubs."

The waitress stopped by and brought Juicy a drink.

"She'll have a Hypnotiq as well," Juicy stated to the waitress.

"Jordan you need to relax. I wanted to meet here because I just wanted to show you the game and how my pussy reigns supreme." Juicy laughed. "Guy, girl, homo or straight. It's all good to me."

"You brought me here so that I could watch you trick?" Jordan shook her head.

"I want you to know how serious I am. Men are kinda simple. If you went in business with me, I want you to know that clientele won't be a problem."

"But, why a girl strip club?"

"Most women are far more complicated then men. By the nights end, I will have 10 women in this bar dying to have sex with me. If that doesn't show you that I'm serious, nothing will."

Jordan looked around the room. The butch lesbians looked as masculine as the wrestlers on TV. Some of them looked to have beards. And the lipstick lesbians wearing their Versace dresses and Jimmy Choo heels looked too snobby and selective to be pulled by a pointy-chinned Manhattan call girl with a boob job.

"If you can pull 5 butch and 5 lipsticks, I'll know you're for real." *An impossible feat*, Jordan thought.

"This will be like taking candy from a baby," Juicy replied and pinched both of her nipples.

"Guys walk around in the music videos in sweatshirts, baggy jeans, and Timberland boots. The background could be a scene in Alaska, but every girl in the video is wearing a bikini top, butt-cheek shorts, or skirts so high you can see her panties. Women, sex, and their bodies are being exposed and exploited in every hip-hop video."

—Tisha Ariel Nikkole interviewed on a television news program

Chapter 13

Shout and Tisha were headed to the Women's Nonviolence Crisis Center in West Philadelphia.

"You know what? I'm going to give you something to think about for a minute. I was hard on you earlier today. I'll own that. But my problem with journalists and people in general is that no one believes that rappers have feelings unless you're at the funeral of one of your friends."

"I hear you."

"Well then, listen. Most people think that all rappers do is make records, get money, and have sex. But the real deal is we have families we take care of, we have friends we look out for. There's a lot of emotion going into what we do. Do you remember when the Notorious B.I.G. was gunned down in L.A.?"

"A little bit."

"Well, I'll refresh your memory. There were people, magazines who hyped up hate putting one coast against the other. Then when people started dying they were shocked. But not only that, pictures were taken at the funeral. The media had us on videotape. They acted like we were not supposed to miss Biggie, like we couldn't cry, like we didn't have feelings." Shout looked over at Tisha who was wearing a blank expression.

"That's a lot of what hip-hop artists go through. We write music from our experiences and then nobody wants us to grow from those same experiences."

Shout turned away from Tisha, who did not respond.

"What's this place that you're taking me to?"

Shout looked at her, but did not answer.

This girl refuses to understand where I'm coming from, he thought.

"You'll see, you'll see." Shout reached over and turned up the music.

Tisha pulled one leg under her bottom and looked over at Shout. "Why should anybody believe that you're not a rapist? What is this place that you're taking me to?"

Shout gave Tisha an icy glare. His eyes pierced through her flesh. He saw Tisha's lips moving, but he didn't hear her words.

He looked forward and nodded to Kanye West's song "Get Em High." As Talib Kweli recited his verse, Shout thought *Tisha hasn't met a real nigga yet.*

Tisha reached over and turned the volume down on the stereo.

"I know you saw the *Rush Hour* movies. Watch your hands on my system—aiight?" He reached to turn the music back up but Tisha grabbed his hand.

Their eyes connected. For a moment, no music was heard in the truck. Shout noticed the light flecks in Tisha's eyes, and Tisha saw the half-inch scar on Shout's cheek.

"How did you get that scar on your cheek?" Tisha asked.

Shout ran a finger over it. "Oh, it happened a long time ago. You know I grew up in West Philly, right?" Shout looked at Tisha.

"Yeah, and as I recall it wasn't the best neighborhood."

"Nah, it wasn't the 'burbs, but back then it didn't matter. I was always havin' fun, me and my boy, Vonnell. One Christmas, the Stretch Armstrong action figures came out. It was all we wanted. Everybody in the 'hood was talking about Stretch. Everybody was braggin' about how they were gon' have Stretch, what they was gon' do with it and how they were gon' have wrestling matches and all that. Well, me and Vonni, would get in trouble in school a lot. We would stay out after our moms told us to come in. But, we didn't want to be the only cats in our 'hood who didn't have Stretch. So we came up with a plan. For the whole month of November we did everything that our moms asked us to do. We cleaned our rooms, we did homework, and didn't get in any trouble at school for the entire month."

"Y'all musta been real pressed to do all that for an action figure," Tisha said, chuckling.

"Yeah, you could say that."

"Well, what happened? Don't leave me hanging."

"Christmas morning, we was mad excited. He ran down to look under his Christmas tree, I ran to look under mine. I practically tore the living room up looking for it but, it wasn't there. There was no Stretch Armstrong under the tree. Before I could start screaming, the phone rang. Vonni was on the phone asking me about Stretch, then he told me that he didn't have one under the Christmas tree either. We was so mad that day."

Tisha looked over at Shout and pointed at his face. "That still doesn't explain how you got the scar."

"Oh, you're right. Me and Vonni was mad 'til about noon or so, and then I went over his house. And, instead of playing with Stretch, the action figure, we pretended to be Stretch ourselves. We wrestled for that entire day until we believed that we were Stretch Armstrong. Man, we had so much fun. But, in one of those quick wrestling moves—I think I was trying to put Vonnie in a half Nelson or something—we went flying to the floor. I rolled over on a sharp rock. The rock cut my face, and it bled like crazy. But, I didn't care, I was having fun."

A loud honking came from behind them. Shout looked in the rearview mirror then ahead at the light and floored the accelerator.

"Before you turn the music up again, I want to know why any of your fans should believe that you haven't raped anyone."

Shout rolled his eyes at Tisha.

Tisha inhaled slowly. "Hold up. Before you go off, I know the charges are being dropped. I know you weren't there, but this article is about painting the clearest picture of you."

Shout cut off the radio. He drove straight then turned sharply into a vacant parking lot in front of a big beige house with white shutters.

Shout cut off the car engine and opened his door. He looked over at Tisha, "Come on."

Shout's stride was wide and self-assured. Tisha walked several steps behind him and looked at his tall, lean physique. "He's cocky as hell," she mumbled to herself.

He lifted the cover off a white mailbox on the front of the house and pushed a button.

"Who is it?" a voice asked through the speaker.

Shout looked up at a camera and said, "The Man of Steel," then looked back at Tisha.

The door clicked, Shout pushed it open, reached for Tisha's hand, and pulled her through the door.

"Wait here. I'll be back." Shout moved right and darted down a long, dimly lit hallway.

Tisha stood in the foyer, rummaging through her tote bag until she found her cell phone to check the call history.

Shout returned with a brown-skinned woman with large cornrows gathered in a neat bun at the nape of her neck. She smiled at Tisha and hugged her.

"Hello, Tisha. Call me Ms. Mary," the woman said with a northern accent. "Shawn just told me that you wanna learn more about our facility."

Tisha looked at Shout, puzzled. She noticed that Shout's cheekbones and those of the woman were identical.

Shout looked at Tisha with a sly grin, as if saying, "Just nod and go along."

"This is a place that serves as a refuge for women who are victims of violence. We make sure that our girls are safe while they here. They change some of they old habits so they'll be safer on the outside," the woman said.

Ms. Mary, Tisha, and Shout began walking upstairs. Ms. Mary walked with an unmistakable limp in her right leg.

"Do you usually allow men in this safe haven for women?" Tisha inquired.

"What men?" Ms. Mary said as she looked around the hallway and in the bedroom. The house looked to have about six bedrooms with four bunk beds in each room.

Tisha looked at Shout and then looked back at Ms. Mary.

"Oh, him. Keyshawn's been around these kinds of places since he was ten. I learned about this place because I had to come here a coupla times on my own."

"Oh, I didn't know."

"Of course you didn't, honey. Most people say we look just alike. I thought you could tell I was his mama. Anyway, it's impossible to know what people have been through until they tell you. Shawn has always been a child with a helpin' spirit. So as he got older, he continued to help out at this shelter though we no longer live here."

****

Jordan was in a back room where she could see the entire club. She saw Juicy sitting next to women and sticking her tongue in their ears. Juicy would gently grab a person's hand and bring it to her inner thigh. She would then take their finger and raise it to their mouths. Within minutes Juicy and her selected partner would go to the ladies restroom. In a span of two hours, Juicy had already netted 7 women in the room.

****

The ride back to Shout's house was quiet and dark. Tisha could barely see her hand in front of her. Shout used high beams to improve his night vision.

Shout drove looking straight ahead during the ride. He did not turn on the radio and had not looked at or spoken to Tisha since he'd been in the car. Tisha looked at her watch. When another five minutes passed, she looked at her watch and then at Shout. Time continued to pass and she just stared at Shout. He did not return her glance. He continued to look straight ahead.

Tisha's neck was getting red. "Alright, Shawn. Why can't you say anything? We should be talking on the way back if you're not listening to music. Daggone!"

He smiled. "Tsk, tsk. Just because you met my mom, you think you can call me Shawn?" He shook his head. "We ain't like that. I'm Shout to you still." He looked over at Tisha and smirked. "Ain't a damn thing changed. What's the problem? You can't stand the silence?"

"What are you talking about? Why do you have an attitude with me?"

Taking one hand off the steering wheel, he said, "I know what your problem is. You're afraid of the quiet because you think that you're sitting next to a rapist. You had already judged me from the minute you saw the headline so it ain't even about who I really am. You believed the hype, and you probably still believe it."

Crossing her arms in front of her chest, Tisha said, "That's real bullshit. I didn't know anything about you but your music. I came up here to learn more about you, and all you can come to me with is all of the wrong things that the world thinks about you. Well, guess what? Your attitude ain't helping change nobody's mind."

Shout looked out of the windshield, unaffected by Tisha's tirade. Tisha took off her jean jacket. Already breathing heavily, she wiped the edges of her face and felt the warmth of her skin beneath her fingertips.

Exhaling, and smoothing her jeans with both hands, she said, "For some reason, I think you forgot the purpose of me coming up here. I'm here to learn about you. Period. You. That's the only reason that I'm here. By refusing to help me, you're hurting yourself and you're hurting your fans."

"My fans?" The thought of hurting his fans touched Shout in a way that even he could not explain.

Tisha adjusted her seat's recliner mechanism and relaxed. She inhaled and exhaled deeply and closed her eyes.

Shout looked over at Tisha. The grimace on his face disappeared. He picked up his cell phone and turned it off. When they pulled up in the driveway twenty minutes later Shout leaned over toward Tisha. "Come on, get up. We're here."

Tisha slowly lifted her head and rolled her sleepy eyes at Shout. She opened the door, grabbed her bag, and gently stepped out of the truck. Shout walked over to the passenger side of the vehicle. "You okay?" he asked. She just looked at him and nodded. He walked toward the side door, and she slowly followed.

Sitting on the closest couch, Tisha rubbed her temples and forehead. Shout ran upstairs and energetically returned, jumping down the last three stairs. He had left his boots upstairs. He went over to the refrigerator and got a bottle of soda, grabbed a bucket and filled it with ice. He moved to the pantry, got a bag of chips and two glasses before standing in front of Tisha. "Alright, sleepyhead, let's go. You ain't done yet. You still working. Come on."

Tisha angrily looked at him. She got up and followed Shout down a narrow hallway. He turned on a dim light and the stairs lit up.

Tisha's eyes widened as she began to descend the stairs. At the bottom she noticed reclining chairs and a movie screen at the opposite end of the room.

Shout put the bucket of ice on the bar counter and situated the glasses in cup holders on the sides of the recliners. Tisha stood at the stair landing with her lips slightly parted. Her eyes followed Shout from the bar to the recliners to the stainless-steel casing that held what looked like a hundred movies.

Just before sitting down, Shout told Tisha, "Go ahead, girl. You can sit down." Tisha walked in front of Shout's chair. She looked at him and noticed that he was looking at her backside. She smiled to herself. "Can we make up and start over? Or better yet, can we just start over?"

Putting his chair in full-recline mode, Shout said, "Aiight, whatever."

Tisha kicked off her shoes, then hastily reclined her chair. "See, you always wanna be sarcastic. You can't be sarcastic. Give my story a chance. Give your fans a chance."

"Okay, okay. I hear you. I hear you."

Tisha leaned over and extended her hand. "Hi. My name is Tisha Ariel Nikkole." She looked into his awesome light brown eyes. "I'm here to write the best, most honest story about you that has ever been written. No lies, no bullshit. Just you."

Both of their palms moistened. While firmly holding on to Tisha's hand, Shout said, "I feel that. It's cool to meet you. Shout is what I rhyme by, but all my peeps call me Shawn. I'm this everyday nigga who grew up and saw things and wanted to live my life a different way. Know what I'm sayin'? I ain't in this shit to be famous or to be a role model, for real. I just want to make music, good music. And when my fans stop wanting to hear my music, I'ma step off. I'ma pass the mike to the next man. No problems. You smell me?" Shout smiled at Tisha and she smiled right back. He reached for the remote control and the movie *Scarface* was projected onto the screen.

"Tisha, this is the movie of all movies. You can't be gangsta if you haven't seen it. You've seen it, right?"

"Seen it? You must be lunching. I have a *Scarface* poster hanging in my bedroom closet. It's like that."

"Oh, you gangsta like that? Okay. Okay. I'm feeling that right there."

As the credits for the movie rolled up the screen, Tisha noticed that Shout was asleep. She grabbed a jacket from a nearby closet and placed it across his chest. She leaned down and said good night, and kissed him on the neck.

****

"That was ten chicks in two and a half hours," Jordan said as she opened the door to her car.

"It was really twelve, you missed the two that I caught up with in the hallway," Juicy replied as she sat in the car. Juicy had visited this club many times to pick up chicks.

"Do you ever worry about HIV?" Jordan asked as she drove over to Juicy's truck.

"I make sure I'm protected, especially in dealing with men. You never know how many of them are on the down low."

"What about women?"

"I don't have women clientele." Juicy asked while pulling up her tube top.

"If you want to do some business in the music industry, hey, you might have to get with some females."

"Uh huh. When I look at the music industry, I see guys and that's where I'm focused."

Juicy remembered her last serious relationship was with a lesbian named Marissa. She was a European model - tall with brown wavy hair. They lived together for a year and a half. Marissa couldn't stand the fact that Juicy slept with men for a living. It was all a joke at first, but as the relationship got more serious Marissa wasn't laughing.

"I can't mess with you anymore if you keep sleeping with men. It's like you're cheating on me."

"Rissa, it's not like that. It's my job. I don't tell you who to model for. You can't tell me who to fuck."

"Yes I can. Either you quit or I'm leaving you."

Juicy showed her the door and threw her stuff toward the elevator.

"How many times have you been arrested?" Jordan asked.

"Once. I'm a professional. We don't get arrested."

"You ain't worried about breaking the law."

"They arrested and sent Heidi Fleiss to jail. That's only one madam out of a industry of a lot of them. The chances of me getting arrested are slim."

Jordan turned the music up and thought about what Juicy had said. *Record industry executives face more legal problems than prostitutes? Is it really possible?*

"Staying in the game is harder than getting in. When you're looking for your first break, nobody is feelin' you. But, when you get that break everybody is feelin' you. With that break comes money you gotta pay back, deals that look good but ain't good, and people who are trying to destroy you."

—Shout, interviewed in the magazine article, "Rules of the Game"

Chapter 14

Tisha laid on the purple couch in Shout's living room. She was covered in a cream-and-blue patchwork blanket that she had found in a hallway closet. It was nine o'clock and Shout looked at her resting peacefully. He ran upstairs, hopped into the shower and put on his navy-blue sweat shorts and a gold T-shirt. He went into the kitchen and took some orange juice out of the refrigerator. A few minutes later Tisha sat up on the couch.

"It's about time you're up. We got stuff to do," Shout told her.

"What? What do we have to do? It's early."

"I'm going for a jog, and you're coming with me. I ain't leaving you in my crib by yourself. You might get into something."

"Negro, please. You ain't got nothin' I want."

"Uh-huh. Go ahead and take a shower. Boom should have told you to bring a bunch of different outfits. So put on something you can sweat in."

Tisha got up slowly and hung her head.

"Can I have some orange juice?"

Shout smirked. "Not now. You gotta brush your teeth first. You got the dragon." He laughed and sat in a recliner.

Tisha picked up her bag off the floor and walked upstairs to shower in the guest bathroom. She brushed her hair and put it in ponytail at the nape of her neck.

She bounced downstairs twenty minutes later in her blue distressed jeans, a T-shirt, and her white sneakers. "I'm ready. Where's my orange juice?"

"My maid is off today. You better go for self," Shout said as he hit buttons on the remote control.

Tisha busied herself in the kitchen and made some toast and eggs. She sat at the bar and quickly ate her food. Shout cut the television off and said, "Let's go. By the way, your jeans will be wet when we're done."

Tisha shrugged. "This is all I have to wear."

Tisha followed Shout out of the door and down the driveway. They made a left and jogged along the quiet streets that were as wide as a country road. Shout jogged along and Tisha kept up. Shout moved faster and Tisha stayed with him.

"We'll stop over by the lake," he said while wiping the sweat onto the bottom of his t-shirt.

"Yeah, no problem," Tisha panted, practically out of breath.

When they reached the lake, a family of ducks was swimming on the edge. They sat on a black wrought-iron bench.

"How long have you lived out here?" Tisha asked.

"Like two years."

"Isn't this kind of far from the city?"

"It seems farther than it really is. But what's your point?"

"It just seems like this would be too quiet for you out here."

"That's why I moved here. I wanted to have a place that I could go where I would be away from the city, away from the noise, and sometimes away from the people."

"You have fans who love you. Who do you have to get away from?"

"There you go again with that love shit."

"I'm not trying to act like everything is all love, but a lot of people would kill to lead the life you lead."

"It's a lot of pressure. And nothing is what it seems. There have been times when I wanted to quit this business, but I know that I would let my family, my friends, and myself down."

"What do you mean? Pressure to sell records?"

"That's part of it. The record business is fucked up sometimes. I mean they lure artists in here with the money, fast cars, jewelry, and then the artist has to sell so many records to *not* owe the record companies any money. And then when we sell a platinum record, we look at the money and wonder why there isn't more. We could leave the record companies, but then, what would we have?"

"That's wild. It seems like you're saying that the more success that you have selling records, the less money you have because of what you have to pay the record companies."

"Yeah, that's right. And, the minute that the record executives know that you're hip to their game, they try to take you out."

"Take you out? What you mean?"

"Take you out. You watched *Scarface* last night. Figure it out."

Shout got up from the bench and started to head back to the house. Tisha followed.

"But, this isn't the case with your contract with World Music because you just renegotiated your deal. Right?"

"Maybe, maybe not." Shout looked at Tisha with a sarcastic smirk.

"It's public record that your deal was redone."

"I'm done talking about that."

"Okay." Tisha began to pick up the pace. "Last one to the house has to fix a real breakfast." Tisha took off, running as fast as she could. Shout just looked at her legs moving up the street. He waited until Tisha was about two blocks ahead of him and then he ran behind her and pinched her on the back.

"I want my eggs medium, and don't burn my toast." Shout flew down the street and when he reached the house, he left the door ajar.

****

Ten minutes later, Tisha entered. Shout was upstairs in the shower. Her jeans and T-shirt were soaked, *I don't have but one other pair of jeans here. What am I gonna wear today?* Tisha thought.

She kicked her sneakers off in the living room and walked upstairs. She heard Shout singing in the shower. He sounded like Ginuwine off-key. "I guess he picked the right profession—rapping not singing." Tisha laughed. She entered Shout's bedroom and sat on the edge of the bed. When she heard the water shut off, she yelled to him. "I'm in the room."

"What for?"

"I was just thinking."

"Thinking? Thinking what?"

"I ruined my jeans outside running with you. Let me borrow some shorts. They don't have to be new."

Shout opened the bathroom door with a green towel draped around his waist. Tisha tried not to look at him, but instead looked toward his closet.

"I know they don't have to be new. I don't know you like that."

"You are a trip."

"Yeah. You just lucky you're cool wit' my boy Boom. 'Cause I ain't never let no journalist in my spot like this. And, now you want to wear my clothes. Umm."

Tisha smiled.

"Well, if you can't help a sister out, I'ma be stinkin' for the rest of the weekend. It's your call."

"Whatever, man."

Shout went over to the dresser and took out some gray shorts and gave them to Tisha.

"Thanks. What am I supposed to do for a top?"

Shout looked at her and centered his eyes on her chest. Tisha walked toward him and warned, "Don't go there."

Shout turned around and grabbed a burgundy T-shirt and threw it on the bed.

"Damn. You needy," he retorted.

Tisha left the bedroom and went into the guest bathroom and ran her water.

****

"Where do our adventures take us today?"

Tisha asked Shout, who was driving toward the city in his gray Aston Martin Vanquish.

"You're supposed to be writing a story on me. Correct?"

"Yes."

"I want you to know more about me."

"Right now, I know that you have more than one car."

"Is that supposed to be funny?"

Shout took one hand off the steering wheel and placed it on the car's gear shift. Tisha noticed that his platinum diamond bracelet was at least six inches thick. Tisha reached out and gently touched the bracelet.

"That is so pretty," Tisha said.

"Thanks—a little something from Jacob my jeweler."

Shout exited the highway and they rode through the busy streets of Center City, Philadelphia. Before long, they were stopped in front of some row houses in West Philadelphia.

"Where are we?"

"This is where I grew up."

Shout and Tisha got out of the car and headed toward a row home. Shout pulled out his keys and entered the house that had keyboards, drumsets, and synthesizers lying on the floor. The couch was black leather.

"Do you own this house now?"

"Yeah."

Shout walked down to the basement, grabbed Tisha's hand, and held it as they walked down the steps.

The basement had different pictures of Shout with Vonnell, his mom, his cousins, and other family members.

"This is where I write rhymes," Shout stated as he pointed over to a desk in the corner.

Tisha walked over to the plain wooden desk.

"This is real basic. It's not upgraded like your new house."

"Yeah, well, when you write rhymes you better write from your soul, or it's gonna sound wack anyway."

"Why do you have all of these pictures around?" Tisha asked.

"Most of the time when I come here, I'm by myself and it's late. The pictures of my family remind me of where I came from. Your family is your source of strength. A lot of people don't know that," Shout said as he walked back toward the steps.

Shout turned on the alarm and exited the house with Tisha. When they reached the porch steps they noticed about twenty kids standing by his car.

"Shout, Shout, Shout," they all screamed.

As he walked down the steps, they came up to him and shook his hand.

"What y'all doing out here?" Shout asked the group of boys.

"We saw you was in the 'hood, so we came over."

One of the boys grabbed him around the waist.

"Come on now. We can't get emotional," Shout chided and then punched the boy playfully in the arm.

"Is she your girlfriend?"

"There y'all go. Nah, she's a writer. She's writing a story about my life."

"Can we be in it?" a boy asked.

Shout looked at Tisha who was smiling.

"Alright. I got some more stuff to do today. But I want y'all to stay out of trouble and stay away from them drugs and gang banging."

Shout reached into his pocket and pulled out a wad of cash, giving a twenty-dollar bill to each kid.

"Be safe, shorties." As Shout hit the car's remote control, Tisha opened her car door, and he jumped in his side. As the car pulled off, older men and women stepped out on their porches and waved at Shout. He beeped his horn a couple of times. A few minutes later, Shout asked, "Do you have a boyfriend?"

"No," Tisha replied as she suppressed a smile and looked out the window.

"Grammy award winning rapper Nice X recently filed bankruptcy. Although he sold more than 10 million albums in his career, he says, 'accountants, management, and record labels robbed me blind. You new-school rappers betta watch your back.'"

—Tisha Ariel Nikkole, excerpted from her magazine article, "Ain't Nothin' Nice About Being Broke"

Chapter 15

Tisha sat in her apartment at her black-and-gray laminated desk with one foot in her chair. She reached for her handheld recorder and began to speak into it. "It's the toughest article that I have ever had to write. Keyshawn Lane, aka Shout, is like the toughest person that you ever want to meet. He protects himself. He's a pitbull, a rottweiler, and a Glock all rolled into one. He doesn't want anybody invading his space—not friends, not enemies, not family, and especially not a journalist."

Tisha stood and went over to the window. Three teenagers were walking down the street, singing the lyrics to Shout's song, "Real Niggas." She walked over to her laptop and began to type.

Keyshawn Lane is a rapper accused of being a rapist. But he could never be a rapist because he believes women should be respected. He volunteers at a shelter for battered women that he and his mother fled to when he was ten. He talks to the women there about finding the right kind of man to be with. He tells them, "Don't be with a man who'll hit you. A man who will hit you is a punk." The women can't believe this platinum-selling rapper is telling them that they should find better men. The women at the shelter who meet Shout love him, not only because he talks to them, but because he plays with their kids. When he's at the shelter, he isn't Shout, he's Shawn, Miss Mary's son. So this guy who reveres women and loves his mother is accused of rape. Could he do it? Absolutely not.

In Gladwyne, an exclusive suburb of Philadelphia, Shout lives in a quiet, spacious, upscale community. His house is large and secluded. Unlike many artists who can only survive on the energy of city living, Shout prefers to live elsewhere. Throughout his house, he has artifacts that bring warmth, love, and strength to the environment. He calls this place "A sanctuary. It's where I go to get myself together, to think about the things that are most important in my life." In a time when he's often pulled in many directions from touring, fans, and record company responsibilities, he has a sanctuary that continues to make him whole.

This rapper who talks about brotherhood and friendship still mourns the loss of his best friend who died tragically five years ago. The tattoo on his back is just a reminder of Vonnell Jones, but Vonni's spirit clearly lives inside of Shout. In the mornings after Shout wakes up, he goes jogging by the lake in his neighborhood, sits by the ducks, and takes in the atmosphere. He thinks deeply. He talks about things. "Artists need to be more knowledgeable about their deals. We're volunteering ourselves to be slaves." Even though his contract was recently renegotiated, he cares about the uninformed artists who will never become rich, even after they sell a million records.

Shout's commitment to the people around him not only includes the people who buy his records, but the youngins who live in the area where he grew up. He routinely visits his West Philadelphia neighborhood and talks to the aspiring ballers and rapper wanna-bes. In a hectic schedule, he makes time for everyday people. Despite his public persona, he cares about men, women, and children. He has a big heart and enough love for all of them.

But now, Shout, the rapper that we hear on the radio and see on MTV, is accused of raping some women in a hotel room. Should we believe him or believe them? We don't know much about the women, but there are some things that we know about Shout. Why would someone who volunteers at a women's shelter participate in an act that commits violence against women? He wouldn't. Why would someone who *spends time trying to evaluate the importance of life with every step, involve himself in a thoughtless, senseless act that would diminish his very quality of life? He wouldn't. Shout's behavior, in front of the camera as well as behind, does not support the actions of a rapist or a violent offender. Before we judge him, we need to check the facts and read the résumé.*

Tisha hit her email button and sent the story draft to her editor at *Life Music* magazine.

Tisha picked up her handheld recorder. "I know he's innocent and the fact that I'm attracted to him and that we both love *Scarface* has nothing to do with it."

****

In a first-class trip to Miami, Shout and Boom sat next to each other. "Shout, there'll be photographers there at the same time we're doing the video. They'll be taking stills for a couple of magazines that I'm approaching for cover stories. Okay?" Boom said.

"Yeah, no problem," Shout responded.

"I know you go off sometimes when you don't know who's taking your picture."

"Come on, man. That happened one time and now you won't let me forget it." Shout laughed. "Tell me about Tisha."

"We went to college together."

"Word? Was she wild in college? You know how some girls get down," Shout said.

"No way. Tisha was really a hard worker. She worked at our college newspaper and had a part-time job with a local African American–owned newspaper. She just always loved to write. That's her thing."

"Does she have any kids?"

"You must be joking. No. Why are you asking all these questions about her?" Boom asked.

"I thought she was real cool. That's all."

"Oh, okay. I understand," Boom said, nodding.

"Does she have a boyfriend?"

"Shout, I don't know her business like that. I couldn't really tell you."

Shout reclined his chair and pulled his Burberry rainhat over his eyes.

"I'm outta here," Shout said, pulling the shade over the window and closing his eyes.

****

Miami, FL

Sydney was sitting at an umbrella-shaded table sipping a strawberry daiquiri when Boom walked onto the patio.

"This is a surprise. What are you doing here?" he asked.

"I just wanted to check in on you, see if you needed any help," Sydney replied.

"Oh boy. What's up with you today? I know you can't stand video shoots. So, what's really going on?" Boom said.

"Well, I just wanted to get away for a few days, so I thought I'd come here. You know I love Miami."

"Yeah, you and every entertainment industry person. But I know one thing, it's hot as hell in Miami." Boom took his polo shirt off and revealed his white-netted tank top. He signaled for the bartender to come over.

"When is Shout getting here?" Sydney asked.

"He'll be here in two hours. You know the drill. The director, cameramen, and models should start showing up in the next forty-five minutes. It should be a great shoot."

"I love this location. This house is beautiful and the pool is nice. I was thinking about taking a swim before the crowd got here," she said as she stood up unbuttoning her tank dress, revealing a yellow thong bikini.

Trying not to stare, Boom took his drink from the bartender and said, "Well, you have about forty-five minutes. Go for it."

Sydney walked to the edge of the pool and dived in. "Why don't you join me? The water feels great," she said as she backstroked the length of the pool.

Boom's cell phone rang and he turned his back from the pool.

"It's starting already. I have to go to the gate and clear everything with the guard. I'll be back," he said after he finished the call.

****

Tisha walked through Miami's International Airport, rolling her one piece of luggage behind her. Through the glass, she saw the bright Florida sun. "I just love Miami," she said. When she arrived at the airport's exit, she saw a Latino limousine chauffeur who held a sign with her name on it. She waved and pointed to herself.

She stepped into the limousine, and they rode through downtown Miami until they reached a yellow stucco mansion sitting back from the street with a black iron gate at the entrance. Tisha got out of the car and pushed the buzzer.

"Can I help you?" a male voice said on the opposite end of the call box.

"Tisha Ariel Nikkole for Boom."

"Just a minute."

A few moments passed.

"Go straight back to the pool area. The opening will be on your right."

The gate clicked, then opened. Tisha rolled her bag and walked straight back.

Ten to fifteen women wore an assortment of bathing suits—from thongs to string bikinis to one-piece cabaret-like outfits. There were cameras and their operators all around the area. Tisha surveyed the area, looking for familiar faces. Boom was near the bar, talking on his cell phone. She walked over to him and tapped him on the shoulder.

"What's up, girl?" Boom said and signaled with his finger that he'd be with Tisha in a moment.

"Can I have a Pepsi?" Tisha said to the bartender.

Tisha sat in the chair next to Boom and drank her soda.

Boom hung up his phone and turned to Tisha and gave her a big hug.

"I'm glad you made it. I take it you didn't have any problems with the car, right?"

"Not at all. Everything is fine," Tisha said.

"Did you see Shout yet?"

"No, I just got here."

"I'm glad you had time to stop by our shoot. Why are you in town again?" Boom asked.

"I gotta do an interview with P-Diddy. He's in town too. But the interview isn't until later today."

"Girl, I know you're loving that. Diddy knows how to treat journalists."

"Yeah, I know. Remember I went to his place in the Hamptons for *Mad Rhythms* magazine? That's the first place I ever got reflexology. I love Diddy."

Boom looked at his watch.

"It's time to get the star. I think everybody else is ready. Are you gonna chill right here?"

"Yeah. I'll be in the background today."

"Alright. I'll be back."

After a few minutes, Boom entered the pool area with Shout and his entourage. Tisha had moved to a shaded lounge chair and put her red & white visor over her head. The director had one of the technicians turn Shout's music on and the women started to dance. Shout went over to the director. It seemed like they were talking about which direction Shout should be facing. The music was started over again and Shout faced the camera and walked. He mouthed the lyrics to "Ghetto Politicks" and his hype men nodded and mouthed the lyrics as well.

"Cut," the director yelled. Shout headed over in Tisha's direction. As he got closer to her chair, he slowed down, then he bent and lifted the brim on her visor. Tisha looked up.

"Tisha?" Shout asked her.

"Hey, Shout. How you doing?" Tisha got up off the lounge chair and hugged him.

"I didn't know I was hanging out with you tonight."

Tisha smiled. "Nah, I don't think so. I'm in town for somebody else tonight. You know you're not the only superstar in my life."

"Oh, it's like that?" Shout stood back. He checked out her red velour Adidas short set. *She got a lil' flava,* he thought to himself.

Tisha giggled. "I work with celebrities all the time. You weren't my first. I gotta work."

"Alright then. I'll speak to you later." Shout walked over to the bar and then opened up a can of Red Bull. Tisha sat back down in her chair. The videotaping started again and this time Shout was wearing a different outfit. Tisha just looked at him. *He's still cocky as ever,* she thought. Tisha relaxed in the lounge chair and when she looked at her watch again it was five o'clock.

Tisha walked over to Boom. "Hey, thanks for inviting me out here. The food was great. And you know, Shout is becoming my favorite rapper." She smiled.

"No problem. Call me when you get done with Diddy."

"Tell Shout that I'll catch him in the next city."

"Okay."

Tisha walked to the driveway and got in the waiting limousine.

****

Jordan leaned her short dark blue denim mini skirt against the spotless white convertible Bentley that sat in the driveway. Her red fitted tee matched the red in her Gucci sneakers. She looked at the backside of the mansion. Shout's rented Miami mansion was as beautiful as any palace ever pictured in the movies. Juicy felt the leather interior in the driver's carseat.

"This makes my Escalade's interior feel like plastic," Juicy said while she inhaled a chest full of the new car smell.

"Yeah. Only the best for Shout," Jordan said mockingly. The two women walked past a yellow Lamborgini with both doors up in the air. The yellow and black interior was embroidered with yellow bumblebees in the headrest.

"I need to stop what I'm doing and become a rapper," Juicy said with a chuckle. Her form-fitting fuschia tank-dress hugged her every curve. Juicy's fuschia snakeskin heels had a jeweled snakehead at the toe.

As Jordan and Juicy entered the mansion, they saw girls in bikinis, thongs and short shorts scattered all over like sprinkles fighting for position on a cupcake. A large bathroom on the first floor was equipped with 24 karat gold fixtures complete with a gold tub. Two girls kissed each other in the shower. The water drenched their shoulder length weaves and braless tank-tops. As their hands moved over each other's bodies, one of Shout's bodyguards held up a video camera. Another guy drank from a bottle of Heineken and repeatedly slapped the buttocks of each girl.

Jordan walked past the bathroom and sucked her teeth.

"Are they gettin' paid for that?" Juicy asked.

"Not likely."

Jordan and Juicy continued and walked up a winding crystal staircase. They entered the master suite. Shout sat bare-chested on the bed playing a video game. The bedroom was full of Shout's cronies lined a long the black and white striped walls. Jordan stood in the doorway and contemplated introducing Shout to Juicy. After a few seconds Shout looked in Jordan's direction and nodded his head. The cronies looked at Juicy like she was a steak from Ruth's Chris Steakhouse. Shout's cell phone rang. He went into the bathroom and spoke discreetly.

"It's time to return to the set. Let's go," Shout commanded to the entire room. He walked past Jordan with not so much as eye contact. Jordan felt his steely veneer. And she admitted to herself that he was sexy and had a star quality that spoke volumes without him saying a word. But there was an elusiveness to Shout. He moved quickly like a panther in the night and yet his strength made him seem like he could have been the king of an African jungle in a previous life. He always had a busy look on his face. There was something that went on behind his eyes. Something had his attention.

I gotta find out what Shout is really thinking about, Jordan thought to herself.

Jordan and Juicy went downstairs and sat on the plush couches in the family room. The ceiling–high windows allowed them to view the pool in the back of the house.

Music blared loudly and a line of women playfully ran around the pool topless.

"How much these girls getting' paid to strip, skinny dip and be in the video?" Juicy inquired.

"Nothin.' It's desperation. You don't know? There are girls who would pay to be in a video and suck off a superstar," Jordan replied as she took her cell phone out of her brown plastic Louis Vuitton bag.

"Video hos – that's what we call 'em. They'll do anything to get in the video. They don't care about gettin' money. They tryna be famous."

"I need to talk to some of dem. I could put 'em on my team." Juicy ran her fingers through her hair.

"You probably could," Jordan said while standing up. She stared at Shout who was rapping and standing in front of the pool.

"Those girls look good – too good to be ho'in' for free," Juicy said as she took a glass of Cristal champagne from the waitresses' tray.

****

A week later, Boom and Sydney were in the office, reading the headline of Tisha's article, "The Softer Side of Shout." Sydney and Boom both read the article and Sydney's eyes lit up with every sentence. "This is really a great piece. Your friend outdid herself. Shout should have her on the jury," Sydney said.

Boom picked up the paper from Sydney's desk. "This is a good story. The charges were dropped, but this is the kind of story that will help people forget about the accusation."

"I don't know about that. Rape is a hard thing to forget."

"Oh, here we go." Boom put the paper on the couch and sat down.

"No, no, no. I just like to deal with reality. There are some things people never let you forget. Let's send the writer something special for the piece. Let's start circulating that article."

Boom grabbed the paper and a pen off Sydney's desk. "I'm on it."

"By the way, is that a new cologne? What's the occasion? You seem different today. What's different?"

"I don't know what that is."

Boom left Sydney and went to his office mumbling, "Jungle fever" under his breath.

****

Tisha looked at the entertainment page with her story and the photo of Shout, bare-chested in baggy jeans. She smiled to herself. She opened her closet and taped the story opposite the photo of Tony Montana aka Scarface. She flung the doors to the closet wide. "Picture, picture on the wall, will Shout be able to see the truth in that story? It couldn't have been any truer if he wrote it himself." She fell back on her bed and noticed the posters of Jay-Z, Nas, and Nelly on her wall. She frowned and took down all three posters and put them in the corner as her pager went off. She flipped the cover. WILL YOU INTERVIEW DENIM FOR THE COVER OF AURA? WE WANT YOU TO DO IT. "Can life get any better?" Tisha asked herself as her phone rang.

"Hello."

"What's up, girl?" I didn't know that you were a celebrity," Charmaine said.

"What are you talking about?"

"There's a picture of you and Shout in the newest issue of *Life Music* magazine," Charmaine explained.

"Really? I haven't seen it," Tisha responded.

"Well, you need to get it."

"How do I look?" Tisha asked.

"You look good. It must have been taken at the photo shoot in Miami. The pool looks just like you described. And by the way, you look like you might be his girlfriend."

"Oh, not yet. I'm still working on that one."

Tisha hung up the phone and rushed out to get a copy of the magazine.

"I'm single but looking. Real women only.
Gold diggin' chickens aren't allowed to apply."
—Shout, quoted in the magazine interview,
"Shout: Up Close & Personal"

Chapter 16

New York, NY

Boom was walking down 57th street with Sydney when his cell phone rang as they stopped in front of Mr. Chow's restaurant.

"Hello."

"Boom, give me Tisha Nikkole's direct line. I want to thank her."

"Shout?"

"Yeah, man. What's up?"

"You got the article then?"

"Yeah."

"Well, I'll call her for you."

"No, Boom. You ain't gotta do that, man. Let me do my thing. Just give me the number."

"Cool. It's coming through right now on your two-way."

"Bet. I'll talk to you later. One."

Boom handed his cell phone to Sydney, removed his pager from its holster, and sent Shout the number.

****

Tisha was in her apartment listening to Lloyd Bank's "On Fire" as she danced in front of a mirror. She was doing all of the moves from Aaliyah's old videos. As another song came on the radio, the telephone rang. She looked at her clock. It was 3:30. *This must be Charmaine,* Tisha thought. She lounged on the bed and answered the phone, "What's up, Chey? I'm just gettin' my dance on. I love that Lloyd Banks song."

The male voice on the other end of the phone said, "Oh, is that right? Is he your favorite rapper?"

Tisha knew she had heard the voice before but she couldn't place it.

She sat up on the bed. "Who is this?"

"You should know who it is. And you ain't supposed to like no rapper more than me. That ain't cool."

"Shout? Is this Shout?" Tisha got up and jumped up and down, using her hand to cover the mouthpiece.

"Yeah, it's me. Thanks for representing with the article. I was feeling that."

Tisha twisted her earlobe and bit her bottom lip. "Your approval means a lot. Whenever you need somebody to write a real story for you, get Boom to call me."

"What if I want to call you?"

Tisha grinned. "You got the number, you can call me. It's all good." Tisha walked over to her closet and looked at the article of Shout, putting her index finger on his chest.

"Is it all good? Alright then. We're cool now, so I don't want you to call me Shout, call me Shawn. I like to keep Shout onstage. You know that now, right?"

"Yeah, I know."

"I'm coming to D.C. in a coupla hours to do a promo run. Can you come out?"

"Let me see. There may be someone else I gotta write a story on. Hold on one minute." Tisha looked in her appointment book. "Oh, I ain't doing nothin' tonight."

"I'm doing some small venues for the VIPs who supported my albums. I'll be at Dream nightclub. Just look for the tour bus and ask for Jim Greasy."

"Who did you say to ask for?"

"Greasy. Tell him who you are and he'll find me. Try to get there around seven."

"I will." Tisha poked her tongue into her cheek. "Should I bring my tape recorder?" she asked, putting one leg behind the other.

"Nah, man. You ain't working tonight."

"Alright. I'll be there."

"Tisha."

"Yeah?"

"I'll see you later. One."

Tisha hung up and screamed. She did three cartwheels in the hallway of her apartment and ran back into her bedroom and jumped on the bed before picking up the phone to call Charmaine.

"Charmaine, he called me. He called me!" Tisha kicked her feet in the air.

"Who?"

"Girl, don't even try it. You know who. Shout, girl, Shout." Tisha turned over on her stomach.

"He called you? Really? What did he say?"

"He said that he loves me and he wants to marry me." Tisha burst out laughing.

"I know you're lying now."

"Yes. He read the article that I wrote about him, and he thanked me for being honest."

"Now this is a first. A rapper thanked someone for writing a good article? Wow. Strange things do happen."

"He also invited me to hang out with him tonight."

"Where at? I hope not at his hotel. It is not time for a booty call."

"He's doing some promotional stuff at Dream. I'll be there to talk to him and what-not."

"Oh, that's good. Please be careful. I know you're happy, but you still have to be extremely careful."

"Girl, I've been dreaming about this forever. I can't wait for tonight. It'll be better than Cinderella going to the ball."

"Yeah and you don't even turn back into the unloved stepsister. You're too beautiful for that."

A click sounded on Tisha's line.

"Girl, that's the phone. It might be Prince Charming again. I gotta go. Talk to you later."

"Bye."

Tisha clicked over to the other line.

"Hello."

"Hey, Tisha? How you doin'?"

"I'm fine. Who's this?"

"It's Darien. You know my voice. Stop trippin'. I had to check in wit' you. I want to stop by to see you tonight."

Darien was Tisha's old boyfriend who had disappointed her with his lack of zest for life, thereby ruining their relationship.

"Noooo. That ain't gon' work. How you figure you're gon' be able to call me every two weeks and think you can come over here when you want to?"

"You wasn't saying that last time when I was tapping that ass."

"Well that was then, this is now. Let's just terminate our communications. And let's make a pact: I won't call you and you won't call me either. Bye!" Tisha hung up the phone and headed for the shower.

****

Wearing a blue denim Roc-A-Wear skirt, Timberlands, and a white tank top, Tisha approached Shout's tour bus. The sides were covered with pictures of Shout and artwork from his album covers. Tisha pushed the door open and noticed the hardwood flooring on the bus. There was no driver, so she slowly walked up the steps and found a dark-skinned, heavy-set man snoring with his arms folded across his chest. He had on a red shirt that had *Shout* written in white letters.

"Excuse me," Tisha said, in a barely audible voice. The man continued to snore loudly.

"Excuse me, sir. Excuse me," Tisha said very loudly.

The man looked left and right and made a snorting sound. "Yes?"

"I'm looking for Shout."

"Who isn't, miss?" The man wiped the moisture from the right side of his mouth.

"Oh, I'm looking for Greasy. My name is Tisha Ariel Nikkole."

The man unfolded his arms and pushed himself up out of the chair. "Now we're talking. I got you. I'm Jim Greasy. Hold on one second."

Greasy went to the back of the bus and then returned. "Let's go, miss. He's doing sound check right now."

Tisha and Greasy entered the backstage of the club. Shout was onstage rehearsing. He looked over at Tisha and winked. She smiled at him. Shout yelled to a person handling the sound equipment, "Are we done?" Shout paced across the stage. "That was my last song." He pulled up his sagging jeans.

The handler responded, "Yeah, 'til showtime."

Shout walked over to Tisha and hit her shoulder, "What's up, girl? Who told you you could come backstage? I want to see your pass."

"Very funny. I didn't know you had a sense of humor too. Whew! You're the real package, huh?"

"That's what they tell me." Shout grabbed Tisha's arm and put it in the air. He looked over at Greasy who was standing nearby, "Yo, Greasy, what you think of her? She seem alright?"

Greasy looked over at Tisha, eyeing her from head to toe, and rubbing the stubble on his chin. "Yeah, she straight, I guess."

Tisha stopped walking and looked at Greasy then back at Shout then back at Greasy. Looking at Greasy, Shout said, "She got a tight little body, huh? She must work out."

Tisha's face had turned a light crimson, and she grabbed Shout's wrist. "Will you stop it? I ain't here for that."

"So what you here for?" Shout touched Tisha's shoulder and stopped walking, preventing her from going any farther.

"Greasy, we'll be right here. I'll be on the bus in a minute," Shout said as he signaled Greasy to head back to the tour bus.

"Aiight, holla." Greasy exited the stage and went out the back door.

Shout went and sat on a back stairwell, motioning for Tisha to come sit with him.

Tisha walked over and stood in front of Shout. "So Shawn, why am I here? For you to try to embarrass me?"

"Nah, girl. I just wanted to thank you for writing the truth and to kick it wit' you for a minute."

Tisha walked away from Shout and felt him looking at her. She turned around. "You could have thanked me over the phone."

"Come here, Tisha," Shout said. He stood and she walked toward him. He grabbed her hands and pulled her closer. She could smell the peppermint on his breath. "Close your eyes," Shout said.

"No." Tisha stepped back. "I'm not doing that. You could have some crazy person stashed back here."

"Now, you goin' back to your ol' ways. You know I don't get down like that. Just close your eyes for a minute."

He leaned down, holding both of her forearms, and kissed her on the lips.

Tisha opened her eyes. "What was that for?"

"That was payback for the other night."

Tisha put her hand over her mouth.

"How you gon' try to kiss me when I'm sleepin'? Yeah, you didn't think I knew. Yeah, un-huh. Come on. Let's go to the bus."

Shout and Tisha walked through the narrow aisle, heading toward the back of the bus. They passed four boothlike areas before they reached an open back door where a couch and a bunk bed were situated. A petite woman wearing a tan ruffled top and white pants was on the couch. The lady looked at Tisha and rolled her eyes before saying, "Shout, groupies are not supposed to be on your tour bus."

Tisha pulled her arm away from Shout, stepped in the lady's direction, looking down at her and said, "Excuse me. You need to watch your mouth. I ain't no groupie."

Shout held on to Tisha's hand and raised his hand to the lady. "Jordan, this is my friend Tisha. This is the person who wrote that dope story about me."

"Oh, my fault. I didn't know. It's a pleasure to meet you." Jordan extended her hand to Tisha.

Tisha hesitantly shook Jordan's hand and said, "Yeah, likewise," before looking at Shout.

The back of the bus was small. There was barely enough room to turn around between the bunkbed and the couch. Tisha shot a disapproving glance at Shout.

"Jordan, I need to kick it with Tisha in private. I need some space."

"Okay, no problem." Jordan grabbed her Gucci hobo bag and headed out the door. As she closed it, she looked back at Tisha with a jealous stare.

Shout and Tisha sat on the dingy green-and-blue plaid couch.

"Do you know how to play PlayStation 2?"

"No."

"Well, I'll show you how to get down with my NBA Ballers game. It's crazy."

Tisha lay on the couch and rested her head on her hand. "I don't know if I want to play video games."

"You kidding me? You watch *Scarface*. Video games is in ya blood. Stop playin'."

Shout and Tisha played videogames until Greasy told him it was time to go on stage. He performed for forty-five minutes and Tisha waited at the side of the stage in awe. After his performance, Shout had sweat dripping from his head. He clutched a white towel in his left hand. "I want to take this time to thank all of you out there who have supported my music. I want to thank my peeps in radio; I want to thank the magazine peoples; and I want to introduce y'all to a friend of mine, some of y'all may already know her, but she wrote an article about me that actually told the truth—Tisha Ariel Nikkole. Tisha, come up onstage with me real quick."

Tisha walked out on stage and pinched his waist while nervously smiling. She stood out there for a few moments, and then hid again backstage.

After the concert, Shout walked through the crowd meeting everyone. Tisha stood for a while watching Shout, then decided to leave.

"Ninety-five percent of the artists in hip-hop music are people of color. In fact, African-Americans are the largest group contributing to the library of hip-hop music. Yet the top power structure at the businesses who profit from these artists are an all white, primarily all men's club. How does that calculate?"

—Tisha Ariel Nikkole, excerpted from her article, "The Hip-Hop Power Structure"

Chapter 17

Chicago, Il

Jordan and Shout were at George's Music Room, one of the best music stores in Chicago. Shout was dressed in a dark blue denim outfit with blue Timberland boots and a cream T-shirt. Jordan was wearing a Moschino sleeveless turtleneck with white pants and black slides.

Shout's posters adorned the walls and the table where he was to sign autographs. As he looked through the R&B section of compact discs, Jordan came up behind him and touched him on the waist.

"How's the sexiest rapper in the United States doing?" Shout barely lifted his head out of the CD rack. Jordan continued, "This is the most popular record store in Chicago. You'll probably get an insane crowd here." Shout continued looking through the CDs. "After we do a couple more signings at some other stores, I wanted to take you out to dinner to discuss your career."

"I'll be busy after this. I'll have to take a raincheck on that one," he responded.

****

Charmaine and Tisha were walking through Iverson Mall in Capitol Heights, MD. "I want to stop by the music store," Charmaine said.

"Me, too. Let's go."

They enter the well-lit record store and posters of Shout were at the entrance windows and along the walls. Tisha went over to one of the posters and looked at it. "You can't front. He's fine as hell."

Charmaine looked up at the poster. "He looks good. And, he's ripped. His li'l abs got it going on. I'll give him that."

"Yeah, but ain't nothin' on him little." Tisha laughed.

"Don't go there, Tisha. Don't go there." Both girls giggled.

Charmaine picked out some R&B CDs and went to the cash register. "Do you have any extras of that Shout poster?"

"No, but so many people have been asking for it," the cashier said.

"Really?"

Tisha walked up to the register, and Charmaine lowered her voice, "He's practically her boyfriend." Charmaine pointed at Tisha.

"Yeah, right. He's her boyfriend and everybody else's." The cashier gave Charmaine her bag and smirked.

****

Shout pulled out his cell phone while sitting at the autograph table and dialed Tisha. The phone rang in Tisha's apartment, then the answering machine came on.

"Wish I could talk, but I can't," the answering machine sounded and then the beep was heard.

"Where you at? I'm in Chi-town gettin' ready to sign some posters and CDs. I'll get at you later."

Jordan tapped Shout on the shoulder. "The fans are here. It's time to work. Make your phone calls later."

Shout looked at her and huffed, "Whatever, man."

A bunch of kids rushed the table asking for Shout's autograph.

"You're the best rapper ever," one male fan said.

"Thanks, li'l man," Shout replied.

A girl who looked to be fifteen gave Shout her poster and just stood there crying. She looked at it while he was signing the poster.

"What you crying for? It's all love in here."

The girl looked at her two friends and said, "He talked to me. He talked to me."

A girl dressed in a sequined bra top and low-rise jeans, with her thong showing, handed Shout a folded poster. He opened it up and it was a picture of the girl sitting bare-breasted with her legs wide open. Looking at the picture, Shout sat back in the chair.

"Whoa, I don't think I can sign this. This needs your autograph."

"Okay, fine." The young lady bent over to Shout's side of the table and wrote down her phone number and gave the folded poster back to him. He slid it under his stack of posters.

****

The next morning Shout visited WGCI, a popular urban radio station in Chicago. He was scheduled for an interview with the morning crew. The radio station had the typical well-worn cloth couch, stacks of records on every corner, and promotional material oozing out of every drawer. The walls were spruced up by the platinum plaques by the artists like—50 Cent, Aaliyah, Lil Kim, TLC, Nelly, Jay-Z, and Outkast.

Shout sat across from the two deejays, eating a blueberry muffin and drinking a large cola. He adjusted his earphones and leaned closer to his mike.

"We're here with unquestionably the hottest rapper in the country, Shout. If you have any questions, call in now. So, Shout, how does it feel to have your third album go platinum in less than two weeks?" the deejay, Tim Blaze, asked.

"It's good, man. It's good. To have fans support the music and connect with me, that's love right there. Much love and respect to all the fans out there."

"Shout, did you ever think you'd be as big of a star as you are today?" the deejay, Candy Cane, asked.

"Not really. You work hard, but then things just happen. Nahmeen?"

"Let's do some call-ins from your fans now," deejay Stan the Man said.

"Oh, definitely, go ahead."

"Do you have a girlfriend or any baby mamas?" the first caller asked.

Shout chuckled in his mike. "Nah. I don't have a girlfriend or a baby mama but I am accepting applications. But, you gotta be smart. No dummies."

"You hear that, young ladies. If you want a rapper like Shout, you betta stay in school," Candy Cane said.

"Shout, how do you come up with the concepts for your music, 'cause you're a real deep brotha," the second caller said.

Shout moved closer to his mike. "Man, I'm just inspired by life. Whatever I'm going through, I rap about it."

"Are you feuding with Nas?" another called asked.

"No, man. I love Nas. If it wasn't for Nas's *Illmatic* album, the rap game wouldn't be what it is today. Hip hop music owes a lot to Nasir."

****

During the limousine ride back to the hotel, Greasy rode shotgun with the limo driver and Jordan lifted the front of her blouse and began looking seductively at Shout. She put her hand on his thigh and he removed it. "Shout, you said that you didn't have a girlfriend, so why can't I get a piece?"

Shout moved to the other seat in the limo. "You're not my type, Jordan. Let's just leave it at that."

Jordan sat straight up and pulled her shirt back down. "What, are you a homo?"

Shout smiled slyly. "Not at all. I'm not the gay rapper. I don't believe in mixing business with pleasure. You're a part of the record company. They pay me and they pay you, but we ain't on the same side. So, we're on the same team, but we're not. I can't mess with you."

Jordan licked her lips. "Well, maybe I can change that."

"Maybe," Shout said nonchalantly.

The limousine stopped. Shout and Greasy got out and went into his hotel. Once inside, he picked up the phone and called Tisha.

"Hello," Tisha said.

"Where you been at?"

"Shawn?"

"Yeah, where you been?"

"I was at the mall looking at your posters in the music store, wondering where my poster was."

"It's like that? Good. Why didn't you call me back or hit me on my two-way?"

"Shout, you didn't give me a number."

"What did I tell you about that? You don't want me to treat you like I'm Shout, so leave Shout out of our conversations."

"Alright. Dag. Why are you snappin' today?"

"Man, it's one of dem days. You wonder what you doin', who you doin' it wit' and who you doin' it for. You just wonder. Smell me?"

"Yeah, it's tough. Being a superstar isn't as easy as it looks."

"Write down my numbers," he said and rattled them off.

"How was your signing in Chicago?" she asked after she wrote down the numbers.

"It ain't like home. In the next couple of weeks, I want you to think about flying to a city with me."

"I don't know."

"Just think about it, Tisha. I'll talk to you later."

****

Shout took a cold shower. "It's been a long time since I had a girlfriend, " he muttered.

Shout's old girlfriend, Sade McMillan, had worn Timberlands and skirts just like Tisha. He had brought Sade some pink Timberlands for her birthday during their junior year in high school despite his uncle warning him,

"Don't ever buy a woman shoes—she'll walk away from you." Keyshawn didn't believe his uncle, but years later, he didn't have Sade.

Sade was a cheerleader. When he dropped out in their senior year, her parents told her that she couldn't date him anymore but Sade didn't listen. She secretly met Keyshawn at the mall, at the skating rink, wherever she could go under the guise of hanging out with her girlfriends. When Sade turned eighteen, she was tired of lying to her parents about having a boyfriend, and she told them about Keyshawn. Her parents wanted to lock her in her room until she left for college at the end of the summer.

When she left for Spelman, Keyshawn wanted to go to Atlanta with her, but instead focused on his music. As his popularity increased with performances at local clubs and radio play, he became a star in their hometown. When Sade came home for Christmas break, people would stop them, and girls would give him their phone numbers while she stood there. When he got his record deal, Sade didn't feel that she could compete with all of the women who wanted a piece of him. Sade broke off the relationship and broke his heart. That was the first and last girlfriend that Keyshawn loved. He vowed if he ever dated seriously again, it would be with a girl who was a part of the music industry—one who understood it.

****

Jordan sat on the bed in her hotel room and thought about her perplexing relationship with Juicy. She was intrigued by Juicy's boldness and ability to get things done. Juicy was as determined as Jordan when it came to getting what she wanted. When Jordan was first hired as an intern for World Music Records, she'd often sabotage other interns' work so she'd have her moment to shine in the spotlight. She deleted marketing reports, erroneously changed meeting times and outright lied on people. She did anything to get ahead and to be on top.

Jordan went down to the bar and ordered a shot of gin. In a few minutes, a hotel staffer brought her some papers. At her request, Boom had faxed a list of all of the journalists who received a Shout platinum plaque. Jordan believed that this list would have the name of the journalist that Shout was talking to on the tour bus.

"Tinea, Takiesha, Tisha," Jordan mumbled to herself.

"Tisha, that's it."

Jordan circled Tisha's name with a big circle and drew a devil's face with a pitchfork beside it.

I got clout like Jay-Z
People saying, 'Um, maybe'
If you doubt it,
You crazy
Clock the label I'm rockin'
Check the rhymes I be droppin'
Peep the chicks I be clockin'
To you that be shockin'
Like Will Smith I got paper
Like Biz Mark you got vapors
And nothin' can save ya.
—Shout, from his song, "Talk About It"

Chapter 18

New York, NY

Tisha was at Music World Records getting ready to interview the biggest selling R&B superstar, Alonzo. With his dark chocolate skin, close-shaven look and sexy smile, Alonzo had millions of female fans. He had toured the United States for the past five years to sold-out shows and standing-room-only venues. He had four ballads in the top ten over the past four years and had performed on every show from *Jay Leno* to *Oprah* to *Saturday Night Live.*

The conference room was plastered with Alonzo's posters. Tisha looked over the catered meat, bread, and veggies, but changed her mind and reached into an ice bucket and grabbed a bottle of water.

She collapsed in a comfortable chair and stretched her legs. *Anywhere but here. Any day but today.*

Boom popped his head in the room. "Tisha Ariel Nikkole. What's up girl? You getting ready for Alonzo?"

Tisha laughed. "Ready?... Yeah, I'm alright. Ready to escape." Boom entered the conference room and closed the door.

"Why, what happened? Did Alonzo's people do something to you?"

"No."

"Well, what is it?"

"I used to have a certain energy when doing these interviews. I used to be excited. Now, I just wish I was somewhere else."

"Umm, that doesn't sound like you at all. When did you start feeling like that?"

"I don't know. I just know after I did some stuff with Shout, a lot of my outlook changed."

"Girl, don't tell me this is about Shout. Did he call you? He asked me for your number."

"Yeah, he called me. We've been talkin'."

"It can't be getting serious..." Boom looked over to Tisha for confirmation and she turned away.

"I can't tell you what's happening. I know how I feel and I know how our conversations are and what our time is like. I don't know anything beyond that."

"You have to know that having a serious relationship with a rapper is completely impossible. It's like flying to the moon in an airplane—it ain't gonna happen."

"Boom, I hear you. I know you're telling me this for my own good but being a rapper is his job—it's only a small part of who he is. I'm looking at the other part."

****

Tisha was resting in the Sheraton hotel in downtown Manhattan when her room's telephone rang.

"Hello?"

"Come downstairs. I'm in a black Range Rover."

"Shawn, I'm not dressed."

"Oooh. Well, maybe I should come up."

"Whoa, don't even try it."

"What you gon' do? I'm getting ready to leave."

"I'll be down in a few minutes."

Tisha took a quick shower and put her babyblue Enyce terrycloth sweatpants and a basic white mid-rift T-shirt. She slipped into some white sneaks.

She grabbed her denim bag and dashed out of the door.

As Tisha approached the black truck, it pulled away. She walked toward it and it slowed as she was about to grab the handle and then it pulled away again. She crossed her arms over her chest and turned back toward the hotel door.

Shout rolled down the back window. "Hey, beautiful, can I get your number?"

Two elderly pedestrians heard the voice from the truck and looked at each other, then smiled at Tisha.

"Hey, beautiful, can I take you out to dinner?" Shout opened the truck's door and leaned forward, extending his hand to Tisha.

With her hands crossed, and her lips upturned, Tisha said, "You playing games today I see. I'm too tired for this. I'm going back upstairs."

"Come on, Tisha, I was just playing. You betta come on."

Tisha rolled her eyes and began to walk toward the truck. When she stepped inside, Shout grabbed her around the waist and Tisha fell over in the seat.

"Yeah, I thought so. You wasn't about to go upstairs."

"Get off me. Get off me." Tisha tried to wriggle away from Shout's grasp, but her efforts were fruitless. He snuggled close to her and kissed her on the neck. She looked up and kissed him on the lips.

****

Justin's Manhattan restaurant was busy. Every table was full and the waiting couch had about six people on it. As Shout and Tisha got out of the chauffeured truck, people outside of the restaurant pointed at them and whispered. Shout's bodyguard opened the door for them and stepped inside. He raised his hand to get the attention of the maître d'. The man walked over immediately.

"Good evening. Follow me."

The bodyguard walked slowly behind Shout, who was holding Tisha's hand. They walked to the back of the restaurant to a roped-off section. The maître d' unhooked a red rope and allowed the threesome to enter.

Shout and Tisha walked over to a brown leather cushioned booth. The bodyguard sat at a separate table in front of the booth. Shout ordered barbecued ribs, macaroni and cheese, collard greens, and corn bread. Tisha ordered fried chicken, black-eyed peas, and macaroni and cheese.

"Shawn, how did you know where I was today? I didn't tell you that I was going to be in New York."

"Girl, I'm like the FBI—I can find you wherever you are."

"Oh, that's real cute. Maybe I should have asked you, why were you looking for me."

"Who said that I was looking for you?" Shout said as his cell phone rang. He looked over at the Caller ID.

"Hello. What's up, Ma?"

Shout spoke in a hushed tone, and after a few minutes, he hung up.

Shout looked at Tisha. His face had become tight. He got up and walked to the wall. His bodyguard got up and walked near him. Shout looked at him and put up his hand.

Shout sat back in the booth a few minutes later. "My moms and the shelter got a problem. I gotta make some calls."

Shout pulled out his two-way and sent a message for Jordan to call him. His cell phone rang moments later. "Yeah, what's up? I need a favor," he said.

Tisha overheard Shout ask Jordan to send security to the shelter to protect his mom and the women there. He told Jordan that he couldn't do it himself because he was flying to Los Angeles that evening. He really sounded like he wanted the security to be there for his mom.

"Thanks. I owe you big for this. For real. Hit me on my two-way when it's done," Shout said then he hung up his phone.

"I hate to do this to you, but I got a two-way when you were on the phone. I gotta go. I have to cover another artist right now," Tisha explained.

"What do you mean?" Shout asked, raising his voice.

"*Life Music* magazine asked that I be at Chill B's album release party. They want me to do a feature."

"Chill B? Please."

"Shawn, a car is waiting for me outside. Do you want me to hit you on the two-way after the party?"

"Nah, that's alright. I gotta go to the airport anyway," Shout said.

Getting up from the table, Tisha leaned over and kissed Shout on the cheek. "Have a safe trip."

Tisha exited the restaurant and hopped into a chauffeured midnight blue Mercedes Benz.

****

Jordan had heard a woman's voice in the background on her call from Shout. As Jordan reflected, she remembered that she had broken up more relationships than she could remember. It all started in eighth grade when one of Jordan's classmates liked a popular basketball player. Jordan saw how happy Angie was and immediately started rumors about Kenny. Jordan told people that Kenny kissed her in back of the bus and that he wrote her love letters. None of it was true. But Jordan wanted Kenny as a boyfriend and getting Angie out of the way was simply necessary. When Angie stopped speaking to Kenny, Jordan befriended him. Before anyone realized what really happened, Jordan was kissing Kenny regularly in the back of the bus, the gym and a less traveled hallway. Jordan's infatuation with Kenny lasted all of two weeks. She broke up with him on a Wednesday morning and by Wednesday afternoon she was already focused on somebody else's boyfriend.

After Jordan hung up from arranging security for Shout's mother, she looked over at Tahib who laid naked on her bed. Tahib Miner was the 32-year-old chief legal counsel for World Music Records. The dreadlocked, light-skinned Tahib was a Harvard graduate and matriculated from Yale's law school. He had been Jordan's sexual partner for the past ten months. Jordan and Tahib worked in the same building and engaged in lunchtime sexcapades when Jordan was in town. Because Tahib was married, Jordan viewed the relationship as purely a sexual release. They often had intimate visits in Tahib's office, Jordan's apartment and New York's Essex House hotel.

"Get over here girl," Tahib motioned to Jordan and stroked the shaft of his manhood.

Jordan smiled seductively at him and walked to the bathroom. She returned in a burgundy rhinestone encrusted thong and bra-top. As she climbed into the bed, Tahib bit her gently on the neck.

"I love the way you smell," Tahib said with his deep voice. He inhaled Jordan's Versace fragrance.

"How do I taste?" Jordan asked.

Tahib kissed Jordan from her neck to her nipples and made wet circles around her navel. As he parted her thighs with his tongue, Jordan released a sigh and closed her eyes tightly. She saw visions of Shout in her mind. Shout stood over her with an erection. She turned over on her stomach, positioned on all fours and Tahib pounded his penis into her moist flesh. Jordan panted and pushed back toward Tahib. Tahib laid on his back and Jordan climbed on top. She moved her body rhythmically from side to side. As her juices flowed she thought Shout was inside of her. As she climaxed she said, "Shout you got the best dick." She opened her eyes and saw Tahib lying beneath her cupping her buttocks with both hands. Jordan looked toward his navel and knew that she had just lost interest in another lover.

****

Boom arrived at Sydney's house around 10P.M. He rang the doorbell and Sydney appeared instantly in a pale yellow cotton sleeveless pajama dress.

"I guess it's time we made it official," Boom said while holding up a champagne bottle.

"I thought you'd never sign the papers." Sydney smiled.

Boom walked toward the living room.

"No, Boom. Let's sit on the couch. The Yankees are on tonight. We can celebrate and watch the game."

They both sat down.

"Now that you're a partner, you have to think about who you'll be hiring to help you take care of some of the other clients who we'll be bringing on in the next month or so."

"Already?"

"Definitely. When I first talked to you about becoming a partner, I knew SWPR would be adding a couple of top clients to its list. I should know if we'll have Denim next week."

"That's great. I know we could do a lot more with her than what's been happening."

Sydney leaned toward Boom and put her hand on his leg. "Have you thought about us having a personal relationship?"

Boom bent his head and kissed Sydney softly on the neck. "Sydney, I care about you. The more that we work together, the more I like you, but I don't want to jeopardize what we have."

Sydney grabbed her glass of wine. "Why don't you just tell me that you have a girlfriend, or at least that you're seeing somebody else."

"It's not like that, Sydney. A lot of shit goes wrong when you mix business with pleasure. And, you're right. I have a girl. It's not anything serious, it's more of a physical relationship."

"Oh, you're into booty calls. I thought you were deeper than that." Sydney walked over to the fireplace and looked at a picture on the mantel.

"I'm not a booty call man. I just haven't met anybody that I wanted to have a serious relationship with lately."

"Excuse me? You haven't met anybody or you haven't pursued the person who is standing right in front of you?"

Boom got up from the couch and turned Sydney around by her shoulders and kissed her in the mouth. She pushed him forward to the couch, and they both fell backward. As Boom caressed her thighs and hips, he felt Sydney's bare bottom. Sydney unbuckled his pants and felt his hard erection. She kissed him on his neck, chest and abdomen. She reached inside his athletic cut underwear and cradled his penis in her hand. She kissed the head and her tongue circled the shaft with a slurping motion. Boom let out sounds of pleasure.

When Sydney came up for air, Boom reached into his pocket and retrieved his condom. Once in place, Sydney straddled him and rocked her hips back and forth. Boom enjoyed Sydney on top of him and couldn't believe how long he denied the attraction.

"Rumors persist that there is no such thing as a one-woman man, so I interviewed thirty of New York's hottest bachelors about staying faithful to one woman at a time. Forty-five percent of the respondents stated that they could be faithful to one woman, 'especially if she's giving me everything I need.'"

—Tisha Ariel Nikkole, excerpted from her magazine article "One Woman Men"

Chapter 19

Washington, D.C.

Tisha jogged around the neighborhood listening to her radio headset. She thought about her parents' marriage. Tisha's parents set her image for the perfect union. They were preparing to celebrate their 30th wedding anniversary. Her parents supported each other's careers and rallied around one another's challenges. When Tisha's father was unjustly fired from his sales position at an insurance company, Tisha's mother suggested taking the firm to court. The family didn't have monies set aside for legal fees, but Tisha's mom authorized Tisha's college savings to be used.

"I don't want to use Tisha's college fund to fight my battles," Harold Wilson said as he walked over to the kitchen sink.

"It's not right."

"Listen, Harold, we're going to fight for your job. If we have to borrow the money from Tisha's college fund – it's okay. When we win this lawsuit we'll have more money for college plus money to send her to school in a new car. We don't have a choice."

Harold sat on the couch. Feelings of frustration and the thought that he had disappointed his family surrounded him. He was on his way to becoming a broken man. But Claudia Wilson wouldn't have that for her family. She went upstairs opened the small locked box that contained Tisha's college fund account number. The next day she transferred the bulk of Tisha's college fun to the law firm of Bergman, Schneider and Jones. Before dinner was served the following evening, Claudia had written out the most crucial points of her husband's case for their attorneys. After a nine month struggle, the Wilsons were invigorated when they won their case plus attorney's fees.

Tisha's blue shirt and shorts were getting damp with sweat. "This is the newest underground cut from Shout, called, 'Nicole.' All you young girls out there listen and weep. This rapper is in love," said the deejay through Tisha's earphones.

Tisha stopped and almost fell down. Listening to the lyrics, she opened her arms wide and jumped up and down.

****

Boom and Sydney were in the office when the phone rang at 11:00 A.M.

"This is SWPR—Boom Tillman."

"The new song from Shout is off the meter, man. The phone calls to play it have been crazy," Reggie Black, the program director for WQHT in New York said. "The song 'Nicole' is blowing up."

"I thought that song went to the underground stations only. I didn't realize it was getting major station radio play."

"It's a hot record. I want Shout to stop by the station. The listeners were asking for him. This single alone guarantees his next album is going quadruple platinum. Easy."

"Word? That strong?"

"Mark my words. Four million easy."

Boom hung up and looked at his office phone. Three lights were blinking.

"Hello. This is Boom Tillman."

"How are you, Boom?"

"Fine. Who's this?"

"Jana Smith at *XXL*. We want to do a cover story on Shout. When can we do the photo shoot?"

"I'm getting his schedule together today, but I'm in the process of scheduling press for a party in L.A. for him. I'll call you in two days." Boom disconnected line one and depressed line two. "This is Boom Tillman."

"Hey, Boom. It's Chonita Long at *Essence*."

"Girl, how you doing? That cover y'all did on Alicia Keys was off the chain. You know I can't wait for the men's issue. I got the perfect person for you."

"That's funny. That's why I called you. We want Shout to be a part of a three-person photo shoot for the men's issue."

"That will be tight. Give me some target dates for the photo shoot, and he'll be there."

"Good. I'll have some dates next week. I'll hit you back then."

"Peace."

Boom hung up the phone and yelled, "Sydney, I just got Shout an *XXL* cover, an *Essence* cover, and an radio interview and I haven't even been at work for two full hours yet. I must be the shit."

Sydney walked into his office and sat on the corner of his desk. "Yeah, you the shit alright. That's good. Shout is the hottest artist we got right now, and he just keeps getting hotter."

****

Shout's cell phone rang seven times before Tisha hung up and went over to her laptop workstation. She began to type, "Romance and Rappers: Can It Really Happen?"

She looked over at her telephone and back at the computer screen, then reached for the phone. She dialed Shout's number again. It rang four times. On the fifth ring, an unfamiliar female voice answered on the other end.

"Hello."

Tisha hesitated. "Um, may I speak to Shawn?"

"Who?"

"May I speak to Shout?"

Shout was supposed to be promoting his record in Los Angeles.

"He's sleep and so am I." The girl hung up the phone.

Tisha dropped the phone and ran into the bathroom. She held her head down to her knees and groaned. "My stomach, my stomach hurts." Sweat formed on her forehead and she sat on the porcelain seat for fifteen minutes.

****

Walking into the kitchen, Tisha opened the refrigerator and got some water before going into her bedroom, lying on the bed, and staring at the wall. She picked up the phone and called Charmaine.

"Charmaine Johnson, can I help you?"

"Chey, it's me."

"What's wrong with you? You sound terrible."

"Tell me about it. I just called Shout's phone and some chick answered."

"Oh my God. For real?"

"Yeah, he didn't get on the phone. The girl said he was asleep."

"See, these rappers, you can't take them seriously. You should forget about him. He's probably sexin' hoes in every state."

"I know. I just thought I felt something real between us. I ain't a groupie."

"Well maybe that's all he really wants."

"I'm getting ready to shower then take a nap."

"Are you gonna be alright?"

"Yeah. I'ma call Boom. I need to talk to him."

After hanging up, Tisha rolled over and looked toward the window, curling herself into a fetal position and drifting off.

Her brief sleep was interrupted by a knock on the door. Groggy, Tisha looked at the clock and walked toward her front door. She looked through the peephole and saw a deliveryman on the other side. Tisha opened up the door, rubbing her eyes. "Yes."

"I have a package for Tisha Ariel Nikkole. Sign here."

The man pointed to an X on the sheet and gave Tisha a pen. She quickly scribbled her name and took the small, flat package.

She sat at the kitchen table and ripped the top off the envelope. She peeked inside and saw a platinum-colored all-access pass, a hotel key, and a round-trip ticket to Los Angeles. She looked at the departure date and noticed it was that day. She needed to be packed and at the airport in four hours. Tisha felt around the envelope and found a lone piece of paper. She pulled it out and it read:

Tisha,

Shout wants you to come to L.A. I'll be there today setting up a magazine party.

Please come.

Boom

Tisha laid the envelope and its contents on the table, went to the shower and turned on the water.

****

Los Angeles, CA

Shout was in the living room of his hotel suite, lying on the pecan-brown couch watching music videos in a pair of black sweatpants. There was a tapping on the door.

"Greasy, Greasy, Greasy. Ey yo!"

Shout heard Jim Greasy through the door. Bare-chested, Shout walked to the door and let him in.

Greasy playfully punched Shout in his arm. "Whatcha doin', man?"

"Just chillin'. You know the mathematics."

Greasy sat in a big chair by the television and Shout went into the suite's master bedroom.

Two beautiful groupies who went by the initials "E & W" were lying on the bed naked. E was an extremely heavy-chested light-skinned woman with blond hair. W was a dark-skinned woman with itty-bitty breasts but with an ass the size of two basketballs. She wore her hair bone-straight with a Yak weave to her waist. E & W only engaged in partnership sex. Last night while they stripped for him, Shout asked what the E&W stood for.

"Every Woman," E replied.

Then W chimed in, "Look at us, we represent the what every man wants – beautiful faces, big titties, and bigger booties.

"We're every woman that a man could want," they giggled in unison.

Shout recalled their conversation, "Yall still here?" Shout asked.

E was sitting up on the bed with one of her legs bent and W was lying with her head resting on E's upper thigh. "We ain't tryna leave," W responded.

"Oh, is that right? Put your clothes on." Shout suggested.

W leaned forward to E's right breast and bit the nipple. She kissed her navel, her left breast and then she nuzzled her face in E's pubic hairs.

E looked at Shout and stuck out her tongue. She moved her hand up to her left breast and said, "You know you want some."

Shout reached inside his sweatpants and stroked himself. He watched W fully insert her tongue in E's vagina. Each time W moved her tongue in and out, she moved her ass and spread her legs.

Shout's erection formed a bulge in the front of his sweatpants. He walked over to the nightstand and opened a condom packet. Shout lowered his pants and from the back, plunged his pole in W's hotbox while she was still performing oral sex on E.

E started yelling, "Yeah motherfucker yeah."

Shout thrusted his penis with such force, W had to lift her head up. As Shout came he let out a low groan and fell forward on the bed. As he caught his breath, he called out to Greasy.

"Ey-yo, Greasy. It's clean-up time. You don't gotta go home, but you gotta get the hell outta here," Shout said.

Greasy came in the room and said, "Alright, young ladies, time to go."

"E smiled, squeezed her breasts and said, "Well, it was good for us. I hope it was good for you."

Shout went into the bathroom and began brushing his teeth. W approached Shout in the bathroom with her camera. "Before we leave can you get your boy to take a picture of the three of us?"

Shout looked at her, grabbed the camera, took the film out of it, and gave her a fifty-dollar bill.

The E looked at Shout. "I put our number in your cell phone. We're E&W."

Shout stepped back. "You touched my cell phone?"

"Yeah and answered it. Some girl called this morning and asked for Shawn. Who's Shawn?"

Shout motioned to Greasy to get E &W out of the room and mumbled under his breath, "Damn." He got his cell phone off the nightstand and recognized Tisha's number. "Damn."

"I never said all women are bitches or hoes. They are judged by how they carry themselves and how they act. I can't front on that."

—Shout quoted in the magazine article, *"Livin' Large"*

Chapter 20

Los Angeles, CA

At the edge of the pool, Jordan sat and sipped a strawberry daiquiri while Juicy laid on a floating chaise lounger. Jordan recalled an earlier conversation with Dan where he continued to insist that she get closer to Shout.

"Shout won't get personal wit' me," Jordan explained. "He ain't feelin' me like that."

"You must be doing something wrong then," Dan screamed.

Jordan was perplexed at how Shout wouldn't discuss his personal thoughts, what he wanted to do or even make small talk. If Jordan wasn't specifically talking about Shout's record or a related promotion, he didn't have any conversation for her. For the first time in her life, Jordan was facing a man who wasn't interested, impressed or threatened by her. For all of her cunning, Jordan didn't know what to do next.

Jordan jumped in the water and swam over to Juicy's float. She pulled it closer.

"I can't get next to Shout," Jordan said.

"Whaddaya mean?"

"I'm supposed to be getting closer to him, but he's resisting me."

"He's probably gay, " Juicy said with a smile.

"He ain't gay. But he is difficult." Jordan laid on her back and began to gently kick her feet.

Juicy sat up on her float. Her bikini bathing suit had a head of a cheetah covering each breast. "All guys are the same. Remember that. They're all looking for something. You gotta find out what it is."

Jordan swam away. All she thought about was the tingle she felt in her chest when Shout was around. Jordan wanted Shout for reasons that had nothing to do with Dan or World Music Records.

                              ****

Tisha got off the plane in Los Angeles and was greeted by the cool night air. Her denim outfit kept out the crisp ocean breeze. Walking through the airport, she scanned the crowd for familiar faces. She saw no one as she made her way down to the exit. A male chauffeur was standing with a big white card with her name on it.

She spotted the chauffeur and said, "Hi. I'm Tisha Ariel Nikkole."

"Great, I'll take your bag. Do you have any other luggage?"

"No, that's it."

"Okay, well, follow me."

"Do you know where we're going first?" Tisha asked the driver.

"Straight to the Beverly Hills hotel."

"Oh."

Inside the car, she felt her cell phone vibrating in her jacket pocket and answered it.

"Yes."

"What's up, Tisha? I'm glad you got on the plane. You're in L.A., aren't you?"

"Yeah, you're lucky my schedule wasn't booked."

Boom chuckled. "Whatever. This is about Shout, not me. Shout wants you to be everywhere that there's a press opportunity."

"Hmm. If he wants me to be his personal journalist, he's going to have to pay me. Fancy trips don't pay the rent."

"You goin' off today, ain't you?"

"I just got some stuff on my mind."

"You and your boy. Both of y'all musta had a bad day. The party starts in three hours. Go to your room and rest for a while. Another car will be there to take you to The Playboy Mansion."

"Cool. See you tonight."

Tisha rolled down the tinted window, leaned toward it and inhaled deeply. She stopped short of filling her lungs and said, "Oh yeah, this is L.A. Ain't no such thing as fresh air."

She closed the window and rested against the seat.

****

A ten-foot-tall water fountain planted in a marble base sparkled brightly in the Los Angeles night. Palm trees fifty feet tall lined the street surrounding the hotel. Bright windows glowed with light from the designer boutiques inside. As the chauffeur pulled up in front of the hotel, the bellhop stepped toward the car. The limousine driver removed the partition and spoke to Tisha. "I'll wait here until you return."

The bellhop reached for the door handle, and the driver unlocked all the car doors while simultaneously popping the trunk.

Tisha stepped out of the limousine.

"Good evening, ma'am," the bellhop said and smiled at Tisha.

"Hey." Tisha smiled right back.

"I'll take the bag to your room for you."

"Great. Thanks."

Tisha headed straight to the check-in desk, then felt her back pocket. She pulled out the plastic magnetic room key with #1112 written in black marker. She turned around and signaled the bellhop who followed her onto the elevator.

Reaching the elevator, Tisha took two wrinkled dollars from her front pocket and gave them to the bellhop.

"Thanks, ma'am. Let me open the door for you."

Tisha gave him the key. The room was decorated in cherry furniture with cream-and-gold accents. The bedspread was patterned with cream and gold stripes with golden fringe. As Tisha stepped in the room, she saw a black dress and matching shoes. She looked around the room, stepped forward, and picked up the dress. *Oh my God, this is a Gucci dress—a real Gucci dress.* Tisha reached over and picked up the shoes and noticed little G's across the band. *And matching Gucci shoes. Whose gift is this? I didn't think Boom loved me that much.* Tisha looked at the bellhop with both eyebrows arched in surprise.

"Good night, ma'am." The bellhop left her room and placed her bag in the corner next to a gold towel rack.

Am I supposed to wear this to the party? Tisha wondered while holding up the dress in front of the mirror.

Tisha pulled out her cell phone from her jacket pocket and dialed Charmaine.

"Hello."

"Hey, Charmaine. Sorry to wake you."

"What's going on?"

"Nothing really, but I'm puzzled by something."

"As late as it is, you must be. What is it?"

"I just got to L.A. Shout asked Boom to send me out here for his album release party."

"What's strange about that?"

"Well, I get to my hotel room and there's a Gucci dress and some matching Gucci heels for me. Girl, there's no note or anything. I don't know who this gift could be from. And, I know it doesn't come with the hotel room."

"Are you for real? That's easy. The gift is from Shout. Who else would buy you a Gucci dress and shoes?"

"Really? You think Shout bought me this stuff?"

"Yeah. Didn't you tell me that you called him earlier this morning and some chickenhead answered the phone?"

"Yeah."

"Well, that dress and shoes are his 'forgive me, baby' outfit." Charmaine chuckled.

"Girl, you know this ain't funny. He must think expensive gifts are the way to my heart."

"Well, what about the chickenhead? We can't forget about her."

"Yeah, you're right? Do you think he wants me to wear the outfit to the party tonight?"

"Why else would he have bought it?"

"Girl, I don't know what to think. I'm going to take a shower. If anything else happens, I'll call you."

"Tomorrow. You know I got to get up early."

"Alright, girl. Thanks."

"Have a nice time, and don't even think about giving him no booty just because he bought that dress."

"I know, I know."

"I mean it. Don't become no hoochie over a li'l bit of Gucci."

"Bye, Chey!"

Tisha hung up with a smile. She walked to the bathroom and turned on the shower. As she pulled back the shower curtain, she noticed a black Gucci tote bag staring at her in the mirror. She walked over to the bag and looked inside and found a Gucci wallet and change purse and a cream piece of paper with neat black writing.

To Tisha,

Thanks for keepin' me believin' that everyone ain't deceivin'.

Keyshawn

As the bathroom filled with steam, Tisha thought, *What about you? When are you gonna stop deceiving?*

****

Boom sat at the executive desk in Sydney's hotel room while she put on the last touches of makeup to go to Shout's party. There was a knock at the door.

"Boom, would you get the door for me?"

Boom got up and opened the door. An attractive olive toned man with dark hair said, "I was looking for Sydney Warren. Is this the right room?"

"Yeah, what's up, man? What's your name?" Boom shook his hand.

"Mike Lopez."

"Come on in," Boom said as he walked into the back and got Sydney. His peach shirt set of the coffee brown hues in Boom's face.

Sydney and Boom both entered the front room.

"Hey, Mike," Sydney said as she walked over to Mike and hugged him. "I didn't know you were stopping by."

Boom sat back at the desk and eyed Sydney and Mike's conversation.

"You know I always see you when you're in town. I just wish you were in L.A. more," Mike replied.

Sydney grabbed Mike's wrist and walked him into the foyer and spoke in a hushed tone. Boom couldn't hear what was being said. A few moments later, the door closed, and Sydney walked over to Boom and kissed him on the forehead.

"Who was that?" Boom asked.

"An old friend of mine."

"How old?"

"He's about thirty," Sydney said, giggling.

"Oh, is that supposed to be funny?"

"He's just a friend. Why are you getting angry?"

"I just want to know how you get down, that's all. People can get tricky," Boom stated and walked in the living room.

"Two weeks ago, you didn't want to have anything to do with me on a personal level, and now you're acting like you're controlling things."

"Oh, it's like that. Okay, I'm outta here. I'll see you at the party." Boom walked to the door, exited, and slammed it hard.

"These so-called hip-hop rivalries might help to sell records but they're also putting young black men in the ground too damn early."
　　—Tisha Ariel Nikkole, speaking at a college "Preserving Hip-Hop" panel

Chapter 21

The Playboy Mansion in Los Angeles was the hottest spot to be for *Life Music* magazine's and World Music Records' party for Shout. All of hip-hop's luminaries were there including rappers, R&B singers, and record label executives.

The pool, patio and dancing areas were full of people and photographers. Around 12:45 A.M., Shout got out of a platinum-colored stretch Hummer with his entourage of about twelve standing around him. Celebrity photographers took several pictures of Shout, who smiled and posed for the camera with one finger up.

"Number one, look over here!" a photographer said. Shout gave the peace sign and continued to pose for the photographers as he inched his way to the entrance. Shout and his entourage went straight to the red, chained-off VIP area. Shortly thereafter, a waiter came over.

"Let me get six bottles of Cristal," Shout said.

"Yes sir," the waiter replied and walked away.

Shout got up and Greasy stood also. Shout walked up three steps into a balcony area gallery where he could see the entire dance floor. Several platinum disco balls rotated with a rainbow of lights glowing from them. Green, red, and yellow laser lights shot through the air. Shout stepped down from the balcony and punched Greasy playfully in the shoulder.

"Who should I be on the lookout for tonight, Shawn?" Greasy asked.

With a sheepish grin, Shout said, "There you go."

"Nah, man, you got sumptin' on your chest, get it off."

"You got me. You got me. You remember the girl in D.C.?"

"Yeah, the smooth skin and tight-body chick with the Timbs?"

"Yeah, yeah, yeah. I'm catching feelings right there."

"Word? You ain't never talk about no chickens like that before."

"She ain't like them groupie broads. She's smart. She's learning this music game. I want her on the team."

"What you really know about her though?"

"Nothing, but a lot at the same time."

"Your instincts haven't let us down yet. Do ya thing, man. Do ya thing."

"Thanks, Greasy. You my man."

Shout shook Greasy's hand before running his index finger and thumb over his moustache. "Be on the lookout for her tonight. If you see her, have one of the crew bring her to me."

****

Around 1:30 A.M., Tisha walked into the dance area of the Playboy Mansion. Most of the photographers were no longer taking pictures. She flashed her platinum shiny all-access pass to security and was allowed in. The moment she stepped inside, she saw Boom, who grabbed Sydney's hand and walked over to Tisha.

Boom hugged Tisha. "You look fabulous," he said, checking her out from head to toe. "And you're in Gucci." Boom looked at her bag, then down at her feet, "You haven't missed a detail."

Tisha blushed. "Stop putting the spotlight on me, please." She nudged Boom.

Boom touched Sydney's back. "You remember Sydney, right?"

"Definitely. Hi, Sydney. How are you tonight?" Tisha asked.

"It's a madhouse. But I'd rather us be on the top with this artist than on the bottom with another one."

"No doubt."

Sydney stepped closer to Tisha and lowered her voice. "You really outdid yourself with that piece you did on Shout. I hear that he adores you."

Tisha stepped back. "Oh, really? That's news to me. I'll see y'all later." Tisha stepped off and walked toward the bar. A young, bald, light-skinned man in navy-blue velour sweat suit stepped toward Tisha.

"So what do you do?" a man asked.

"Excuse me?"

"You have an all-access pass. You must be a VIP, so what do you do?"

Tisha looked down at the pass and touched it. "Oh this. I'm a journalist, a writer."

"That's dope. I'm Jay-Z's cousin. I've helped make all of his records platinum."

"Can I get you anything to drink?" the bartender asked.

"Yeah, a cranberry juice with some ginger ale," Tisha said.

The man continued, "I know P-Diddy, 50 Cent, Eminem, all of them. I've written some songs on some hot albums."

"Oh, really," Tisha said, rolling her eyes. "Well, why aren't you in the VIP area?"

Before the young man could answer, Shout and Greasy surrounded Tisha. Greasy stepped in front of the young man who had been speaking to Tisha. Shout put his hand on her waist. "What's up, beautiful?"

"You betta get ya hands offa me," Tisha said. She turned around quickly, grabbing the hand before realizing it was Shout. "Oh, Shawn, I thought you were—"

"I was who?" Shout took a step forward. "Oh, it's like that?"

"I was talking to the guy sitting next to me. I thought he had lost his mind by touching me, I mean."

"Oh."

Three women approached Shout. One lady in a one-piece leopard suit asked, "Shout, can I get a dance?"

Shout shook his head. "Maybe later, honey."

Another woman in a pair of low-rise leather pants and a white halter top stepped up to him, but Greasy raised his hand to her. "Step back."

She leaned her head forward. "Shout, can I go home with you tonight?"

Tisha felt herself shrinking as she stood next to Shout. He leaned back toward her and pulled her closer. He grabbed her hand and squeezed it. She squeezed his hand in return.

"Greasy, it's coast-to-coast time."

Greasy stood to the side of Shout and Tisha. He moved with them through the crowd until they stepped up into the roped off VIP section. Passing the main area, they went into a private room in the back of the mansion.

"I see you got the outfit. It fits well," Shout said. He twirled Tisha around, checking out her figure. Shout stared at Tisha as she walked to a leather stool in the room. He smiled and began to walk slowly behind her.

"Yeah, thanks. How many outfits like this have you bought?"

"None."

"Yeah, right."

"I haven't. You can believe me. I don't buy shit for nobody but my moms. I don't want nooooobody to get no relations twisted."

"Oh, I understand."

Tisha wrapped the all-access pass around her finger.

"What's wrong with you tonight? You seem stressed." Shout stood with his legs spread and leaned against the wall.

Tisha got off the stool and walked away from Shout. "You know our lives are so different. My life is about reality, living with real things. Your life is this fantasy—glitter, money, and cars. Fantasy doesn't mesh well with reality." Tisha fidgeted with her legs.

"What does that mean?"

Tisha looked at the wall.

"What does that mean?" Shout asked again.

Tisha looked at the floor.

"I know you hear me," Shout said loudly.

"It means I'm pissed off that some chickenhead answered your cell phone today. I'm mad that you bought me this outfit because you're trying to make up for something. And mad that I have to guess, but I already know what that is. I don't like playing games. I'm pissed off that you want me to play them."

Tisha kicked one of her Gucci slides at the wall. Shout walked over to her and picked her up. The other shoe hit the floor as he put her in his lap.

"This is new for me. I've been all over the world. There are women everywhere throwing their panties at me, but I don't feel anything. It's just people. The first night that we were at my house, I knew you were the one. But now I gotta figure out how to do this."

Tisha got down from his lap and turned toward him. "You need to know if you're serious with me, I'll be serious with you. But, I'm not settling for you having sex with groupies, chickenheads and anybody who wants to suck your dick. I'm not her."

"I gotta change my lifestyle. I haven't done that in a while. But I'm willing to change it for you." Shout pulled Tisha closer.

Tisha leaned her head on Shout's chest. "If I have to share you with ten million fans for your music, I don't want to share you with even one groupie. I don't want to and I..."

Shout kissed Tisha on the mouth. She put her arms around his neck and hugged him.

Greasy knocked on the door. "Ey yo, Ey yo. Greasy, Greasy, Greasy."

Shout screamed back, "Yo, it's cool."

Tisha jumped off Shout's lap and adjusted her dress. She noticed her slides on the other side of the room so walked over and bent down to get them.

"Jordan from the record label is here. She wants to see you now. She's mad, having a fit and whatnot," Greasy said.

"Word? I'll be right out. Tell her I was in the can."

"Cool." Greasy exited the room and closed the door.

Shout intertwined his fingers with Tisha's. "I ain't no angel, but I believe that you were sent to me. I want to spend time with you like crazy. Don't give up on me." He kissed her sweetly on the neck.

Tisha and Shout left. Tisha sat alone at VIP table. A group of Shout's relatives and friends occupied three tables next to Tisha. A couple of them were speaking to scantily clad women. The cigar, cigarette, and marijuana smoke was burning Tisha's eyes and the smell of the eclectic mix of colognes and perfumes was putting her nose in a frenzy. Just above Tisha's booth was a mirrored ceiling. She looked up and felt like she was in a carnival.

****

On a stairwell, near the back of the mansion, Shout saw Jordan. Her hair was gelled down and slicked back. She was wearing a black pleated skirt, floral blouse and black Jimmy Choo heels.

"What's up, Jordan?"

"What in the hell took you so long? I've been waiting like fifteen minutes."

"I'm here now. What's up?"

"Everything with your mom is straight. I still have security at the safe house but I feel real good about the women."

"Thanks. I appreciate it."

"You know I went out of my way for you."

"I know. That's love right there."

Jordan ran her hand over the top of Shout's shoulder and said, "You know I want a payback."

Shout moved slowly away from Jordan's hand. "I'ma take care of you."

"I see your friend from the bus is here."

Shout looked toward the booth where Tisha was sitting. He lifted his chin and smiled.

"I don't think it's good for your image to be seen with one woman so often," Jordan said.

"What is this, new record company strategy? I don't think it matters who I'm with in the VIP lounge. Let me step off. We can talk some more tomorrow." Shout turned and headed toward Tisha's table.

Jordan grabbed his arm and pulled him hard. "I wasn't done yet."

"Jordan, you need to chill." Shout looked at her hand and snatched his arm away.

"We need to have a meeting at the hotel in my suite at 10:00 A.M."

"Alright." Shout stepped away from Jordan. "I'll see you later."

Shout sat down with Tisha at the table. Jordan walked by. She looked at Shout and Tisha and smiled sheepishly. Shout put his arm around Tisha's shoulder.

"What's her name again?" Tisha asked.

"Who?"

"You know who, the record company lady."

"Oh. Her name is Jordan."

"What does she do?"

"She promotes my records."

"She seems like she wants to do more than promote your records." Tisha rolled her eyes and stirred her drink.

"You buggin'."

"Oh, I'm blind now?" Tisha took a sip of her cherry cola. "Remember what we just got finished talking about with reality versus fantasy."

Mario Marks, a new record producer of mixed African and Chinese heritage, walked toward Shout's booth. Greasy turned to Shout and gave Mario the go-ahead.

"What's up? I love you, man. You da illest." Mario reached into his leather jacket pocket. "Here's a CD of my five hottest tracks. They are blazin'. Pick one. My number is on the CD."

"Alright, man. Good lookin' out. Peace." Shout nodded and shook Mario's hand.

Underneath the table Shout pinched Tisha's thigh. Tisha slapped his hand.

A young lady approached Greasy who turned to Shout then looked at Tisha. "Go ahead. Let's find out who she is," Tisha said.

Shout motioned to Greasy to let the young woman come back. Wearing a purple beaded tank top, skin-tight blue sequined jeans, and matching sandals, the woman said, "It's nice to see you again. You may not remember me.

My hair was platinum last time you saw me. I'm Jamaica Jones, the celebrity stylist."

"I remember you at The Source Awards," Shout said.

"Right." Jamaica extended her hand to Tisha and said, "Hi. It's a pleasure to meet you. Love the dress." She gave Tisha a card and sat down next to her. "Shout, when are you gonna let me do some work for you? I know you have a video shoot coming up."

"Give your info to my peeps," Shout replied.

"Who?"

Shout pointed. "That man sitting over there in the Pittsburgh Steelers jersey. Give him your digits."

"I'll do that. You shouldn't sleep on me. My stuff is legitimately hot." Jamaica got up and shook Shout's hand. She then walked across to the man Shout had pointed out.

"Hello all," Jordan said curtly when she returned a few minutes later. "Shout, I need to speak with you."

Tisha looked up at Jordan and exhaled.

"Tisha, I'll be right back," Shout said. Tisha reached into her bag and grabbed her two-way. She sent a message to Boom. WHAT DO YOU KNOW ABOUT JORDAN FROM WORLD MUSIC? SHE SEEMS TRICKY.

After a few minutes, a message came back: SHE'S BEEN COOL EVERYTIME THAT I'VE WORKED WITH HER.

Tisha responded, THANKS. I'M GETTING READY TO LEAVE. WE'LL TALK SOON.

****

"Follow me," Jordan said sternly to Shout. Both he and Greasy followed her out of the VIP area. As Shout walked through the crowd. Jordan took Shout to the far right side of the club and three men approached them.

"Shout, this is Chris Markowitz, Jeff Leiberman, and Ron Smith," Jordan said with a big smile. The three gentlemen shook Shout's hand. "These are our key allies in the independent record stores in California. Through them, you're able to secure the whole state."

While shaking Smith's hand, Shout said, "That's peace."

Leiberman said, "We're really pulling for the record. You have the best placement in all the stores."

"Great," Jordan said proudly. "We'll be doing an in-store signing tomorrow. For all their support, Markowitz has a favor to ask of you."

Tisha walked out the VIP area of the mansion. Shout noticed. He and Greasy both looked at each other as Jordan tapped Shout's arm.

"A favor. What do you need, Chris?" Shout asked.

"I'm having a bar mitzvah for my son, Andrew, in two days. He would love it if you could come and do a song."

Without responding, Shout looked over at the exit. He heard his phone ringing and picked it up. He was relieved that Greasy had gotten his cue and placed a fake call to him. "Hello. What's up? Is it an emergency?" Shout asked, stepping away from the group. "I'm on my way." Shout looked at Jordan. "Family emergency. I gotta roll. Let's connect and talk about the bar mitzvah tomorrow."

Shout and Greasy left the mansion and hurried to catch Tisha who had gotten into a black limousine.

I blue streak like Martin
I changed the game
You saw the size of that diamond
Well mine's the same
They ask who is movin' units
Shout's the name
They thought hip-hop was over
But now they're glad I came...
—Shout, from his song, "Shout's the Name"

Chapter 22

As her limousine pulled in front of her hotel, Shout and Greasy saw Tisha get out.

"Man, I'm going to go up and try to hook up with Tisha," Shout said and pulled his baseball cap low. He hid his two platinum chains in his shirt and took his platinum Rolex off and dropped it into his pocket. "Call me in the A.M. on my cell."

Shout gave Greasy a pound and stepped out of the truck. He passed by the bellhop and took the side door upstairs until he got to the tenth floor. After several minutes, he stuck his head out of the door. He looked up and down the hallway before quickly jogging to Suite 1023, where he slid the hotel key in the lock.

Shout looked at the bedroom clock and realized it was 4:00 A.M. He hopped into the shower and began singing, Usher's "Burn." After the shower, he put on some gray sweats and a blue tank top with sweat socks and athletic slides. He called Room 1112 and let the phone ring six times but no one answered. He called again a few minutes and still there was no answer. He looked over at the dresser and saw the other hotel key for Tisha's room. He quickly got off the bed, brushed his hair, and put on his blue du-rag before slowly walking to Room 1112 where he lightly tapped on the door.

"Tisha, Tisha." No answer.

"Tisha, it's Shawn." No response. Shout took out the hotel key and opened the door. He walked over to the bed. Tisha was asleep. Her blue-and-cream satin scarf was neatly secured around her head. The blanket covered her up to her neck. Shout walked to the other side of the bed to see her face. Even without makeup, her skin was flawless. Shout sat on the bed and looked toward her.

"Tisha, wake up. Tisha, wake up."

Tisha turned over. Shout walked around to the other side of the bed and kneeled in front of her. "Tisha, I want to talk to you."

With her eyes closed Tisha said, "Shawn, I want to talk to you too. You don't understand how much we belong together. You were meant for me."

Shout looked at Tisha, and shook his head. "Tisha, wake up. Tisha, this isn't a dream."

Tisha sat up in bed, opened her eyes, looked at Shout, and rubbed her eyes. He stood and sat on the bed near her.

"How did you get in here?"

"I had a key. Remember, I dropped your gifts in here earlier."

"Oh."

"Why'd you leave the party without saying anything?"

"You were busy." Tisha leaned on her side.

"You could have still stepped to me."

"If you look busy, I'm not stepping to you."

"You understand my business. Why are you saying that?"

"It just seems like it's more than business. Jordan wants more from you than that."

"There's always gonna be people who want something from me, but that don't have nothin' to do with us."

"I feel like anybody could try to take you from me. So maybe I shouldn't try to be with you like that."

"You act like you talking to the brotha who has the nine-to-five gig who can be at home every day at 5:30. You're in the biz, you know how this shit is."

Tisha got up and went into the bathroom. She closed the door for a moment, and Shout heard the toilet flush.

"Do you believe in fate?" Tisha asked, coming out of the bathroom with her hands on her hips.

"Do you?" he asked.

"Yes, I do."

"What does fate have to do with us?"

"Everything. A part of me would love to be with you, but the other part hears the groupie on the phone. Another part sees Jordan trying to have sex with you, and don't even mention all of the groupies who just want a piece. All of those things come to my mind."

"I can't promise you anything. It's one day at a time. I don't know what tomorrow will bring." She climbed on the bed. Shout grabbed the back of her leg and kissed her. She playfully squirmed beneath him, and they began to wrestle.

"I feel an energy when I'm with you. It's almost magical, but I don't want to go too fast and make a mistake," Tisha admitted.

"You must be one of those old-fashioned girls. You ain't the type to be givin' some on the first night, huh?" Shout smiled, but looked deeply in Tisha's eyes.

"Ha-ha. Very funny. *Romeo Must Die* is on HBO. Feel like watching it?"

"Aaliyah was off the hook in that movie. You know the answer to that." Shout reached out to touch Tisha's arm and examined it. "Where are your tattoos?"

Tisha just looked at him.

"You really are old-fashioned."

"Don't worry about my tattoos. You have enough for the both of us." Tisha laughed. "When I get a tattoo, it's gonna mean something. It ain't just gonna be a butterfly on my back."

Tisha got under the covers. Shout lay on top across the foot of the bed. Shout's blood was boiling. His erection was practically puncturing a hole in his sweatpants. Being around Tisha, all he could think about was sex. But if it happened the same time that he'd had sex with all the groupies, how would it be any different?

Before DMX's character was killed in the movie, they had both fallen asleep.

****

Since Jordan knew that Shout left The Playboy Mansion, she estimated that ten pages to Shout's two-way were never returned. She thought her email system wasn't working. Seven calls to Shout's cell phone went straight to voicemail. Shout's manager called Jordan back, but never Shout himself. Whenever Jordan spoke to his manager, she lied about her purpose for calling Shout. The whole world didn't need to know that she had fallen for him. Back in the hotel Jordan thought about getting Juicy to help her get through to Shout, but she hadn't had a real friend to confide in since high school.

Shontae Hargrove was Jordan's best friend in high school. They went to the skating rink, movies and dances together. Shontae and Jordan shared the same philosophy about boyfriends, "Use them before they get the chance to use you." The duo went through high school like teen heartbreakers, dropping one boyfriend after the next. They selected boyfriends strictly on their ability to provide some money, jewelry and a ride to wherever they wanted to go. Toward the end of their senior year, Shontae started dating Jose "Baby Benz" Barrio. A handsome Puerto Rican, Jose wore nice clothes, jewelry and like his moniker, pushed a Mercedes Benz 190. When he stepped to Shontae, she couldn't resist him. She wanted to be able to use him, before he used her, but Shontae had a weakness for Jose. Jordan and Shontae graduated from high school on the fifteenth of June and on June twenty-third Shontae started a pre-college program at Temple University. By June twenty-sixth, Jordan had begun creeping over to Shawn's house after her father went to sleep. When Shontae visted Jose on July 2, she was shocked to see her man butt-naked, having sex with her best friend. Shontae hadn't spoken to Jordan since.

"Juicy, I need you to help me get to Shout," Jordan said to her speakerphone on the walnut colored nightstand.

"Are you still on that?"

"Yeah, it's my job."

"That's my area. I'll get back with you in a coupla days," Juicy hung up the phone.

Jordan stretched out in her bed and fell fast asleep. For yet another night, she dreamt of Shout holding her, caressing her and being with her.

****

At 9:00 the next morning, Boom heard a knock on his hotel door. Boom ignored the knock and put the pillow over his head.

"I know you're in there. You better open this door," Sydney yelled.

Boom turned over slowly and went to the door wearing black striped Calvin Klein fitted boxers.

"What?" he yelled through the closed door.

"We need to talk," Sydney responded. Boom opened the door and went back into his bed and laid down.

Sydney waltzed into the room wearing a cropped lime green linen pants set with off-white mules. "I don't appreciate that shit you said about me last night."

Boom didn't respond.

"How are you gonna call me a freak? I thought you knew me better than that."

Boom still didn't respond.

Sydney went into the bathroom and grabbed the ice bucket. She turned on the tub's cold water and filled the bucket. She walked over to Boom and poured the cold water over his head. Boom yelled.

"What the hell are you doing?" He got out of the bed and went into the bathroom, grabbed a towel and shut the door.

"You can't stay in there all day," Sydney screamed as she leaned on the door.

Boom walked out of the bathroom with a white towel draped around his shoulders.

"You got a problem?" Boom said.

"Yes, I do. I don't appreciate my partner and my friend calling me a freak just because an old friend stopped by my hotel room."

"Whatever."

"It's not whatever. You're calling me names and you don't even know what the situation is."

"It looked like it was a booty call about to happen. That's what it looked like," Boom responded.

"Oh okay. Well, from the booty call man himself, you would know wouldn't you?"

Boom rubbed the towel over his head again.

"But for your information, just because someone comes to see me doesn't mean I'm up for a booty call with him. It takes two to tango. And anyway, you're the master of the booty call. You so much as told me that you don't want a relationship with me. So, why are you acting like this?"

Boom went into the adjacent room and laid on the bed. Sydney followed.

"I'm not going to allow you to walk away from me or from the things that you say to me. If you want us to have a relationship then say so. If not, then say that too. But don't be wishy washy with me. It's not called for."

"I don't want you having sex with other men," Boom replied.

"Why not? I didn't think you were exclusively mine. So, how does it make a difference?"

"It makes a difference, Sydney. That's why I didn't want to go here with you. You don't know what kind of man I am and what I expect from my woman. Maybe you're not up to the task."

"Maybe I am, but you just don't want me to be. It's easier for you to simply look at me as sex instead of something real. Relationships are real. Our relationship would be."

"Sydney, listen. I'm tired. I'm going to sleep. I shouldn't have called you out ya name last night. My fault. Maybe we can talk about this later."

"I'm not leaving until we do talk about it."

"Well, you must be getting some sleep too then."

"I guess I am." Sydney took off her outfit, kicked off her shoes and got in the bed.

"Love is most elusive to the ones who chase after it. The more you want to be in love, the harder it is to find the real thing."
—Tisha Ariel Nikkole, excerpted from her magazine article, "Looking for Love"

Chapter 23

Washington, D.C.

When I'm with Shawn, he doesn't seem like the biggest rapper in the world. He doesn't seem like the person on BET and MTV every day or on all of the magazine covers. When I talk to him and when we spend time together, it almost seems like he's my man. A week had already passed and Tisha couldn't stop thinking about Shout. Tisha closed her journal and went over to begin working on her laptop.

A few minutes later, her telephone rang.

"Hello."

"How's my girl doing?" Shout asked.

"Who's ya girl?"

"You betta quit trippin'."

"Nah, I'm just playin'. I'm alright. Just trying to get another article done."

"Oh."

"What's up with you?" Tisha asked.

"I'm in the studio today. I'm doin' the title song for a Halle Berry movie."

"Where you at? New York?"

"Nah, Atlanta."

"Oh. I love Atlanta."

"Yeah. It's nice down here. I want you to come visit me."

"When?" Tisha asked.

"Tonight."

"Umm." Tisha exhaled and looked at her laptop, focusing on the lines of her unfinished story.

"Do you miss me?"

"Maybe."

"Maybe? That's all I can get is a maybe?"

"You know I miss you."

"Aiight then. D.C. to Atlanta is direct. I'll have a ticket for you at the Delta counter and we'll have the record label's private jet for the trip back."

"I don't know, Shawn. I'm on a crazy deadline."

"I really want to see you. I thought the feelin' was mutual."

"Don't go there. You know how it is."

"I know how it is. But you can be here by six."

"If I come to Atlanta, I'm still going to be writing."

"No problem. I'll be in the studio, so it's all good."

"Who's picking me up from the airport?"

"Me and my boys."

"Ya boys?"

"Tisha, I gotta go. I'll see you around 8:30."

"Bye."

Tisha hung up the phone and began packing the Louis Vuitton duffle bag that Shout had given her. She picked up her purple polka-dotted journal, her laptop, packed a bathing suit, pajamas, underwear, a couple of pairs of jeans, some short-sleeve shirts, and her toiletries as well as a baseball cap and a head wrap. As she bounced down the stairs, a taxi cab was driving down the block. She waved it down, hopped in, and headed to Reagan National.

****

It was at least ninety-five degrees when Tisha reached Atlanta. She unbuttoned her shirt and her red tank top peeked through. She looked up and down the pick-up lane, but Shout wasn't anywhere. Tisha looked at her watch. It was 8:45. Ten minutes had already passed since she had gotten off the plane. Tisha sat on a bench by the door.

Shout pulled up riding shotgun in a white Escalade. Greasy was driving. Two guys were in the third row and two guys were in the middle. Everyone in the truck was wearing World Music Records T-shirts with Shout's name on them.

Greasy spotted Tisha and hopped out of the truck. He opened one of the passenger doors and an unfamiliar face popped out. Tisha looked at all of the people in the truck and was puzzled by the crowd. She reluctantly got in and plucked Shout in the back of the neck with her middle finger. "What's up with the welcoming committee?"

Shout looked at her in the sideview mirror.

"We was all in the studio and wanted to make a food run."

"Oh. This is a food run? I didn't know that."

Tisha sat back as Greasy drove with the music blasting. They stopped a few minutes later in front of the Marriott Marquis, a towering hotel with a curved driveway in the heart of downtown Atlanta.

Greasy got out of the truck and took Tisha's bag out of the trunk. Tisha got out and looked to the left and right. She looked over at Shout in the passenger side, and he blankly stared back. Shout powered down the driver side window and yelled, "Tisha, I'll catch up with you after the studio."

Greasy gave Tisha a room key and her bag. He jumped in the truck and drove off. Tisha looked at the truck turning the corner and dropped the bag.

****

The heavy gold draperies perfectly matched the light blue wallpaper in the hotel room. The bed looked big enough to sleep ten people. Tisha flopped on the end of it, took the remote control off the nightstand, turned on the television and proceeded to channel-surf.

Besides the sound of the television, it was really quiet. Tisha went out to the balcony and looked down at the pool's fluorescent glow under the night sky. Tisha decided to call Charmaine.

"Hey, Charmaine."

"Hey."

Tisha took the portable phone and sat on the balcony, reclining in one of the patio chairs. "Charmaine, something is wrong."

"What do you mean?"

"Shout called me today and asked me to come to Atlanta. He flew me down here but didn't say anything to me on the way from the airport."

"Really?"

"Yeah. It was so strange. It was like he was purposely not being himself."

"Did you try to talk to him?"

"I couldn't. He brought four of his friends and his bodyguard. He sat in the front. I sat in the back. All the times we've been together, I've never seen him this distant. Something is wrong."

"Do you have any idea of what it could be?"

"No, not a clue. Everything is going well. We talk all the time, and every available moment we both have, we get together. I don't know."

"Maybe he has some chickenhead business going on in Atlanta. You never know."

"Come on, Charmaine, let's think deep on this one."

"Well, we can talk about it all night, but what can you do about it?"

"I don't know. I'll think about this some more. I'll talk to you later."

Tisha hung up the phone and pulled some bubble bath and bath beads out of her bag.

The telephone rang.

"Hello?"

Static sounded on the other end.

"Hello!"

Tisha hung up. She went to turn the faucet on and dumped some bubble bath and bath beads in the tub. She was taking off her tank top and jeans as the phone rang again.

"Hello?"

"Tisha, why'd you hang up on me?"

"I didn't know it was you. What's going on? You're acting funny."

"What do you mean?"

"You fly me to Atlanta and then you pick me up with your whole crew and don't say two words to me the whole ride. And now you're calling on the phone? For all of that I could have stayed where I was."

There was a knock on the door.

"Hold on." Tisha grabbed a towel from the bathroom and wrapped it around her chest, and threw the phone on the bed.

"Who is it?"

"Room service," a male voice responded.

Tisha opened the door. Shout was standing in front of her with his cell phone to his ear, smiling.

"You're full of yourself today, I see," Tisha said. She turned her back to Shout and put the phone on the cradle. "I'm packing my stuff. I'm outta here. You're wasting my time and your money."

Shout walked over to her and grabbed one of her wrists. "Hold on, Tisha. I want you to come with me."

Tisha held the towel tightly around her chest.

"For what?" She turned around and ran to the bathroom and cut off the water.

"I want to talk to you."

"I'm busy. I'm getting ready to take a bath."

"I'll wait, or better, I'll join you."

"Nah, that's alright."

"Can you just get your jeans on? It's important."

Tisha grabbed her jeans and tank top from the chair in the corner and stood behind the closet door and put on her clothes. She slipped on her flip-flops and got her hotel cardkey. She folded her arms across her chest and followed Shout.

At the hotel pool, they sat at a patio table as the moonlight illuminated the water. Tisha sat at the table pouting as she leaned backward in her chair.

"I want us to make it official. I want you to be my girl."

"What?" She temporarily lost her balance.

"I have strong feelings for you, and I want you to be by my side. I'm tired of doing this alone."

Tisha got up and began to walk away as tears streamed down her face. After several steps, Shout jogged toward her and touched her arm. Tisha was trembling.

"I need you to come to my room for a minute."

"Okay. If I can get a ride."

Tisha jumped on Shout's back, and they got on the elevator headed to the twenty-sixth floor.

Upon entering Suite 2686, Tisha got off Shout's back when she saw two young men sitting in the living room.

"It took you long enough," one of the guys said.

Tisha looked at Shout puzzled, and stopped, short of the living room.

"I need to ask you a favor," Shout said to Tisha.

Tisha looked at the Cristal champagne bottles and the buckets of ice throughout the suite. She went into the master bedroom where Shout was sitting on the edge of the bed and noticed two more bottles of Cristal champagne on the dresser.

He grabbed her hands and looked up at her. "In my business, it's about favors and it's about family. You see those two guys out there?"

Tisha nodded.

"They're my family, and I need you to do something for me."

"What?"

Shout paused and spoke slowly, "I want you to have sex with them to show your loyalty to me."

Tisha stepped back and turned away from Shout. She went into the bathroom and shut the door, grabbing her stomach as she fell on her knees and leaned over the toilet. She thought that she'd vomit. She sat on the floor for a few moments, then got up splashing cold water on her face. She just stared at her reflection in the mirror. "Do I want him so much that I'll show that kind of loyalty to him?" Tisha asked to herself.

****

Tisha yelled through the bathroom door, "Shout, cut off all of the lights and send them in one at a time."

Shout got off the bed, walked toward the bathroom door then hesitated. He turned around and cut off all the lights in the master suite.

"Go ahead, Trevor."

"What?"

"You know the deal."

"Word? Good lookin'."

Shout left the suite with his head down, grabbing a bottle of Cristal on his way out.

****

Tisha heard someone sit on the bed. She grabbed one of the bottles of Cristal off the bathroom counter. She opened the door, but it was so dark she couldn't see where the edges of the bed were.

"Turn around, girl. Let me see ya ass," a voice said.

"You turn around first."

"Oh, you must be kinky. Good lookin' out, cousin," the voice yelled.

Trevor turned around and Tisha smashed the champagne bottle on the side of his head. "Tell your cousin good looking out for that, dummy."

Tisha ran out of the suite and down the hall to find her room. Tisha threw all of her stuff in her bag and left the hotel. She walked down the street outside and as a car approached, she ducked into the bushes, crying uncontrollably. She got her cell phone out of her bag and called Boom. "Boom, I need your help."

"Tisha? What's wrong? Are you crying?"

"Shout flew me to Atlanta, was acting strange then set me up to have sex with his friends. I hit somebody in the head with a bottle. I want to go home. I need a ticket home."

"Okay, I'll do it now. Go to the airport, and I'll call you back with the airline info."

"Thanks, Boom. Thanks."

Tisha saw a cab coming up the street and waved both hands. The cab stopped and she hopped in. "Take me to Hartsfield International Airport."

He said the bridge was over
But what KRS never told ya
Was about the dawning of this soldier
In the way that my rhymes spit
Make you grab your stomach and vomit
I'm the toilet, the paper, the whole shit
Them other rappers be clowning
In my sweat they be drowning
You might as well call me the black sea
There'll never be another just like me...
—Shout, from his song, "Rhymin' and Bullshit"

Chapter 24

The next day Tisha was back home in Washington, DC. She woke up at 3:00 P.M. She slowly massaged her face with her left hand and felt puffiness on her eyelid and the area below her eyes. She also noticed her lip was split. It must have happened in her tussling with Shout's family in the hotel. She looked down at her outfit and realized she hadn't changed clothes. She turned on the shower and stepped in with her clothes on and leaned her back against the shower's wall and cried.

****

New York, NY

Shout was at the Sydney Warren Public Relations office, sitting across from Boom.

"How was Atlanta?" Boom asked.

"I got in some studio time for the soundtrack I'm working on. But I blew it with Tisha."

"Blew it? What are you talking about?" Boom asked.

"You know I like the girl but I'm a superstar, I gotta test her. I gotta know when she's not with me that nobody will be able to get over on her or take advantage of her. I got to know that," Shout explained.

"I understand that, but what did you do?"

"I asked her to do a couple of my family members. It was a loyalty test."

"Shout, how could you have been so stupid? Tisha would never have sex with anybody to show loyalty to you. She's not the kind of girl. You treated her just like those groupies that you have sex with after the shows."

"I know, I know. But you know about the suite in Atlanta. Everybody in hip-hop takes their girls to this suite to see if they'll turn into a freak. I had to do it."

"You were right when you said you blew it," Boom stated.

"They say that suite has its own lucky charm. As the tale goes, this room has the power to bring the freak out of a church girl. Rappers and groupies alike know about this room. Rappers brag about what they got the women to do and groupies brag about how many times they've been to the suite and with whom. I didn't want Tisha to be there, but if she's going to my girl, I had to know what would happen."

"No disrespect, but you can't believe everything that people talk about. If you like Tisha, great. If you don't, just leave her alone. She's too good to be cheapened by this industry," Boom said.

"Jordan paged me a little while ago, I gotta get ready to meet her," Shout said.

"For what?"

"I think she wants to talk about additional promotional tour dates."

"Oh. If you need me, call me or hit me on my two-way."

"Thanks, Boom."

Shout left the office and hopped into a waiting limousine where Greasy and Shout's manager, Pockets, were sitting.

****

Jordan and Juicy were in Jordan's office.

"When the guys come in, stand over in my closet. I'll need you to take some pictures of me getting busy," Jordan said, adjusting the lens on the camera. "It's automatic focus, so all you have to do is point and shoot."

"What are you going to do with these pictures of you and Shout having sex?"

"I got a couple of ideas. Maybe I'll send them to *Playgirl*," Jordan said, then laughed.

"Shout and Pockets are here," Jordan's secretary said a few minutes later.

Jordan walked over to her desk, motioned to Juicy to get into the closet, and said, "Send them in."

"What's up, Jordan?" Pockets said as he and Shout sat on the couch.

"I wanted to talk about extending Shout's promotional tour. As you know, we've had strong sales spurts along the east coast and in the Midwest but we need to do more to spark sales on the west coast."

"I just looked at our stats, we're doing well. We moved 215,000 units last week," Pockets said.

"Yeah, but how many of those sales are from the west coast region?"

Pockets just looked at Jordan.

"That's my point, I think we could be doing better," Jordan stated. "I'm thinking about ten cities—a real short tour—L.A., Oakland, Sacramento, Las Vegas, and a few more."

Just then, Jordan's phone rang.

"Dan Bellows is on the line," her secretary said.

"What's up, Dan?"

"Are you still meeting with Pockets and Shout?"

"Yeah, right now."

"Well, could you send Pockets up to see me now?"

"No problem."

Jordan hung up. "Pockets, Dan wants you to go up to his office. Alone."

Pockets looked at Shout. "I'll be back."

After Pockets left her office, Jordan walked over to her door and locked it. Shout had stretched out on the couch, and Jordan sat on the end next to him.

"You've been quiet today. What's going on with you?"

"Nothin', man. I've just been chillin'."

"I've been thinking about that favor I did for your mom. I've figured out a way that I want you to pay me back."

"Is that right?" Shout said.

Jordan stroked Shout's calf.

"What's the deal, Jordan?"

"Now, on a personal level, I did help you out with your mom, right?"

"Correct."

"What if I asked you for a personal favor?"

"I'd have to see what it was."

"Well, I haven't been with anybody in a long time, and I really feel like I'm losing it. I want you to have sex with me."

"You're kidding, right? You're pretty enough to find a man."

"It's a favor—that's all I'm asking from you. You don't have to go 'cross state, you don't have to spend no money. It's just a favor in return for a favor."

"If I do you this favor, I don't want to hear from you no more. Don't call my cell phone, don't page me. I don't want to have nothing else to do with you. Understand?"

"Yeah."

"Alright, when?"

Jordan got some Courvousier from the bar and poured herself and Shout a drink. She raised her glass and they clinked glasses.

"Now." Jordan looked at the floor. "Here is fine with me."

He got another drink.

Jordan pushed her skirt up to her hips. Shout finished off his drink as Jordan was pulling down his pants. Jordan leaned over to kiss Shout, but he turned his face away. Jordan handed Shout a condom and watched as he slid it on. Jordan climbed on top of him and straddled his dick. Shout was lifting Jordan up with the palms of his hands. Fifteen minutes later, Jordan turned toward the closet and smiled at Juicy, who had been taking pictures the whole time.

****

Washington, D.C.

I haven't spoken to Shout since he asked me to have sex with his cousins for "loyalty's sake." I've been crying every night. It's already been seven days. No matter what I do, I can't stop thinking about him. I can't believe that I actually thought that there was a real relationship forming between us.

Tisha finished writing in her journal and began typing on her laptop:

"Love, Rap, and Roll" by Somebody's Fool

You don't know me but you probably pass by me every day. I wear long skirts on the subway and short skirts at the club. I wear tank tops, sweaters, and bra tops. My hair is long, short, straight, and curly. Sometimes I'm smart. Sometimes I'm not. I thought I could make the hottest, most popular rapper on the planet fall in love with me. It almost worked until I realized that he did not see me any differently from all the other girls who threw their panties onstage.

By all standards, I'm a groupie. I never called myself one. I never wanted to admit it, but I'm no different from the young girl who sprays her chest with a water bottle at the concert so her breasts will show. I guess I owe the out-of-the closet groupies an apology. I'm not any better than you— we're one in the same. Some days, I know for a fact that you are better than me. The groupie knows not to expect love from a one-night stand, she knows that having sex with the star is all she's ever gonna get. Getting his heart is absolutely out of the question. But a fool doesn't know that. I didn't know.

When I began my relationship with the hottest rapper in the country, I thought that it was possible for him to fall in love with me for who I was—inside and out. I didn't realize that was simply a figment of my imagination.

Tisha wrote for another two hours then called Wanda, an editor at *Aura* magazine.

"I want to submit a personal story to you but I don't want my identity revealed."

"What's the story about?"

"My relationship with the biggest rapper in the country."

"Is the story done?"

"Yeah. I'll email it to you and you can give me your feedback."

"Great, I'll look for it."

Tisha sent the story and went over to the couch and turned on the television. Shout was on television being interviewed on a video show.

"The song 'Nicole' is off the chain. We gotta ask, was that inspired by anybody special?" the host asked.

"Yeah, it was."

"Can you go a little deeper."

"It was just a friend of mine."

"Oh, here we go. Guys always be downplaying their relationships. That's how you're going to play us today?"

The audience began to whistle and clap.

"We'll be right back with Shout to learn more about his friend."

The video show cut to commercial.

Tisha hit the off button, turned over on the couch, and fell asleep.

****

For seven days, Shout had been having dreams about Tisha, mostly of them having sex. But sometimes they'd been in a swimming pool. A force would pull Shout to the bottom of the pool. Tisha would try to save him, but his two cousins snatched him away.

Shout left the television studio and called his mom.

"Mom, I've been having some crazy dreams lately."

"What about?"

"Tisha."

"The girl you brought up here who hit Trent?"

"Yeah."

"Well, you need to leave her alone. She practically made him a vegetable and Damani an only child. She sounds loony."

"But Mom, that was my fault. I set her up. And now I keep dreaming about her."

"Mmph. Do you believe that the dream is trying to tell you something?"

"Sometimes. Or, it's telling me that I need to resolve something. Yeah. I need to talk to her, Mom."

"Well, if you do, be careful. She seemed sweet at first, but my goodness, violence is a no-no."

"Right. Right. Mom, I love you. I'll talk to you later."

Shout hung up and dialed Tisha's number. It continued to ring so he hung up.

****

As Tisha stepped off the porch, a car sped by blasting "Nicole." As she jogged, thoughts of Shout crowded her mind. *Did he ever really care about me? What would have happened if I had sex with his cousin? Would we still be together? How can you ask somebody to be your girlfriend in one breath then ask them to be a hooker the next?*

Tisha stopped running and bent over by a tree where she saw a family of ants entering a small anthill carrying little white crumbs. She walked over to an old park bench and sat watching a young couple laughing as they walked passed her. They smiled at her. She tried to smile, but couldn't. She got off the bench and ran as fast as she could.

An hour later, Tisha was breathing heavily as she sat on a step outside Charmaine's Georgetown townhouse. Her best friend's red Accord coupe wasn't outside. Tisha walked back down the street and saw a tall clock. It was 5:10 P.M. She stopped in a coffee shop and got a bottle of water. Walking back up the street, she got a chill as she looked at a poster of Shout. She quickly looked down at the ground and kept walking. Approaching the townhouse, she saw Charmaine's car. She walked up the steps, each thigh feeling like a college trunk being lifted up a flight of stairs. As she prepared to ring the doorbell, Charmaine opened the door.

"Well, surprise, surprise."

"Hey."

"You look tired. Where you been?" Charmaine looked at Tisha. "Don't tell me you ran all the way over here."

Tisha looked at Charmaine and fell down on the brown leather couch.

"Yeah, I ran."

"Still trying to run through your heartache."

"Something like that."

Charmaine gave Tisha a towel and held her nose.

"You smell. Go upstairs and take a shower."

Tisha turned her lips down.

"I'll pull out some clothes for you and put them in your room."

"Chey-e-n-n-e. I don't feel like moving," she whined.

"Come on now. You're stinking up the living room. I got clean clothes and new panties for you, so don't worry."

Tisha crawled up the steps with the bottle of water in hand.

****

Shout's cell phone rang.

"Speak."

"It's Jordan. Where are you?" she asked.

"Taking care of personal business."

"Well, I want to spend some time with you."

"Listen, I don't want to hurt your feelings but I'm not feeling you like that," Shout replied.

"You wasn't saying that last week," Jordan stated.

"Yeah and last week, I told you not to call me or page me. Listen Jordan, the truth is, having sex with you let me know how much I miss my girl. There's nothing between us, but business." Shout hung up the phone before Jordan could respond.

"Rap star Crusha C has broken the rap sales record for a female artist, selling 300,000 units in one week. She's recently been nicknamed the female Shout."

—Tisha Ariel Nikkole, excerpted from her magazine article, "Crusha C on the Rise"

Chapter 25

Jordan had The New York Daily News spread across her desk. She had cut several letters from various pages of the paper and placed them on her credenza. Once she finished cutting, she placed her pearl handled scissors back in her desk drawer. Standing in front of the credenza, Jordan positioned the letters on two pieces of paper. The first page read: BITCH STAY AWAY FROM SHOUT. The second page read: OR YOU'LL DIE!!

Jordan glued the letters down and pulled her list of addresses from her file cabinet. She walked out to her assistant's desk and printed a label from her computer with Tisha Ariel Nikkole's address on it. A few moments later, Jordan exited the World Music office building, walked five blocks and dropped the stamped envelope in a blue mailbox.

****

Driving on I-95 South, Shout adjusted the rearview mirror of his Aston Martin. He turned on the radio and his song "Nicole" was playing on a hip-hop station. He turned

the dial to a strictly R&B station and listened to "Old
Friend" by Phyllis Hyman, "If You Don't Know Me By Now"
by Patti Labelle and "Through the Fire" by Chaka Khan,
until his cell phone rang.

"Speak."

"Where you at, man?"

"I had to break. I gotta handle some personal
business."

"Shout, you're too big for this shit, man. You can't
just step off whenever you feel like it."

"Man to man, Greasy. I got personal issues I gotta
handle. I'll be in D.C. for the next day or so."

"Is this about that girl?"

"I told you already."

"Personal or not, you can't be in the city by yourself
no more. You're bigger than that."

"Greasy, I'm out, man. Thanks for lookin' out for a
brotha."

Shout turned off his phone and opened up his two-
way to read the address on his pager display. Boom had
sent Tisha's address to him an hour ago.

****

Around ten, Tisha and Charmaine were sitting in the
living room watching Law & Order: Special Victims Unit.
Charmaine was braiding Tisha's hair into big cornrows with
added hair.

"Thanks for supporting me over this past week. I
know you never really thought much of my 'relationship'
with Shout, but it was so real to me," Tisha said during a
commercial.

"I'll always be here for you. It doesn't matter if you're
in a relationship with Shout or Tremont or Big Joe, I want
you to be with someone who is gonna treat you right."
Charmaine hugged her.

Tisha smiled. "I'm gonna get over Shout. No matter
what happens in my life, I'm gonna get over him."

Charmaine threw up her hand for a high-five.

"Grab the phone for me," Charmaine said as it
started to ring.

"Hello." The line went dead. "Nobody's on the line. I want to check my answering machine. I'm expecting some feedback on one of my stories."

Tisha dialed her voice mail. "You have six new messages."

"My life is picking up," Tisha said.

"This is Wanda from *Aura* magazine. I love the story. We're going to run it with some minor editing. Call me when you get a chance—or send me an email."

Laying the phone on her thigh a few seconds later, Tisha said, "That's so strange."

"What?"

"I had six messages, but five times whoever called let the tape record them breathing, but no messages."

"You mean you heard someone breathing on your answering machine?"

"Yeah, I think so."

"Is the breathing anybody you know?" Charmaine laughed and continued to braid.

"Haha. The fifth person was from *Aura* magazine. I gotta go home and look at my story. Will you give me a ride?"

"What? You mean you don't feel like running across town?" Charmaine laughed.

"Not tonight."

****

Shout turned the corner in Northwest DC, looking for Tisha's apartment. He rode down the block and found a space in front of her apartment. He pulled his hoodie over his head and looked at his duffle bag in the backseat.

Shout walked up the steps and rang the buzzer for her apartment. A few minutes passed and no one answered. Shout looked up and down the street and walked away dejectedly. He got back in his car, reclined in the driver's seat, and turned on the radio.

A few minutes later, a car pulled up behind Shout's. He saw the headlights in his rearview mirror. He sat up and noticed a young woman with a baseball cap and sweatpants getting out of a car. She ran up the stairs to Tisha's apartment.

It was too dark to see if the girl was Tisha. Quickly getting out of the car, keeping his hoodie pulled over his eyes, Shout jogged to the house and rang the buzzer.

"I'll be right down."

Tisha trotted down the steps with Charmaine's sweatpants and shirt in her hand. She opened the door and saw Shout standing in front of her and her face tensed.

"What the hell are you doing here? Where's Charmaine?"

"Charmaine?" Shout questioned.

Tisha stuck her head out the door. Charmaine's car was nowhere to be found.

"Who's Charmaine? The person who just dropped you off?"

"Yeah."

"She's gone. She ain't out here."

"Well, I gotta go. I don't have time for no fake ass." Tisha tried to pulled the outside door close.

Shout held the other side of the door. "Wait. I want to talk you."

"What you want ain't my problem."

"Why won't you let me talk to you?"

"Shout—or whatever you want people to call you—I don't have anything to say to you, and you have nothing to say that I want to hear."

"If you let me talk to you now, I can explain everything. I promise you."

Tisha looked at the floor then walked up the steps. Shout followed. Once they entered her apartment, Shout stood in the living room.

Tisha stood behind the bar in the kitchen. "Why are you here?" Tisha asked, grabbing an apple off the counter and taking a bite.

"I wanted to talk to you."

"Well, talk."

"Can you come over here?," Shout stated as he sat on the couch.

"I can hear you from right here."

"I know you're mad because of last week. But I didn't want you to have sex with them."

Tisha looked at Shout with disgust, rolling her eyes and snaking her neck.

"I had to test you. I had to know that you would say no."

Tisha got a glass of water. "Did you just make that up? Or do you really think I'm that stupid?"

Shout got off the couch and walked toward Tisha.

"Stop where you are!"

"I have feelings for you. I had to know that you had feelings for me, but that your respect comes first. I can't be with a girl on any real level who doesn't have respect for herself."

Tisha walked past Shout, making sure to be out of arm's reach and sat on the couch.

"These hoes out here would do anything to be with a rapper—my girlfriend can't be like that. Remember you're supposed to be my girlfriend." Shout smiled at Tisha.

"How many times have you pulled that stunt? How many times have you set up a girl who you claimed you wanted to be your girlfriend?"

"Since I've become famous I haven't wanted a girlfriend." Shout hesitated.   "Until now." He sat next to Tisha. "I apologize if I hurt you. I didn't want to. I know you're a special girl. My special girl." Shout ran his hand over the top of Tisha's head, her neck, and her chin. He enjoyed looking at Tisha's small nose, almond-shaped eyes, and small, pouty mouth.

Tisha smacked his hand away. "Whatever Shout. I can't trust your words. As far as you're concerned, I'm just lyrics in a song. Nothing you say means anything to me. Your actions matter. Period."

Tisha walked to the front door and opened it.

Shout stood up.

"I want you to leave."

"You're going to give up that quickly? You're going to give up on fate that quickly?"

"I didn't give up on fate. You threw it out the window."

Shout stepped toward the door.

"Out of respect for you, I'll leave. But I also know that we were meant to be together."

Shout walked out of the door and shut it. For a few moments, he stood in front of Tisha's door. He heard footsteps come to the door and then he heard locks being turned.

****

Thirty minutes had passed since Shout left Tisha's apartment. He sat at the steps of the apartment with his hood over his head. It was hot and humid that night, but he'd rather be hot than to be seen by his fans. He stepped of the stoop and looked up at the light coming from Tisha's window.

"Tisha," Shout yelled.

Tisha didn't come to the window.

"Tisha," Shout yelled again.

Tisha came to the window and lifted it up.

"Why are you being loud?"

"That's how I got my name."

"Well be loud in somebody else's neighborhood."

"Ima yell until you take me back."

"You gonna be yelling all night."

Tisha slammed her window.

She heard Shout yelling her name for another 15 minutes. She looked out her window and saw some of her neighbors came outside.

Tisha went downstairs.

"Shawn, stop yelling. We can talk upstairs if you agree to stop yelling."

"Are you gonna take me back?"

"No"

"Tisha, everybody makes mistakes," Shout yelled to the top of his voice.

Tisha felt nervous and the crowd outside was getting larger.

"Okay, let's just go inside."

Shout followed Tisha inside her apartment.

"You lucky nobody recognized you. I suggest you don't do that again."

"I don't care about nobody recognizing me. I care about gettin' you back. So what's up?" Shout took off his hoodie, revealing his white tank top.

"Can you be for real for a minute?" Tisha paused. "I don't know if I can forgive you or accept your apology. You made me feel like a piece of meat. You made me think that our friendship meant nothing to you. I know about the groupies and what you deal with but come on. There has to be a better way."

Shout stepped over toward Tisha who was sitting on a barstool.

"If you were me, how would you handle it?" Shout asked.

"I know I wouldn't ask my boyfriend to have sex with my relatives. If I had feelings for somebody, I would be real with it. And see what happens. I wouldn't set up a sting operation. "

"I was wrong for putting you through this. I was wrong because you're the right person for me. But it you were the wrong person, we wouldn't be having this conversation."

Shout stepped within inches of Tisha's face and stared directly into her eyes. "I want to be with you. No bullshit." Shout extended his arms and put hands on Tisha's petite waist.

Tisha looked down and exhaled. Shout lifted her chin up with his hand and kissed her.

"No more tests. We're done."

Tisha wrapped her arms around Shout's neck.

A solitary tear rolled down her right cheek.

"I missed you."

Shout kissed her on the mouth and tasted her strawberry lipgloss. He carried her to the bedroom and laid her on the bed. He took off his tank top and stood over Tisha with a bare chest. He laid next to her and pushed up her shirt. He ran his hand over her taut stomach and firm breasts. He kissed her all over. He suckled her nipples like a child with a pacifier.

"You taste like honey," Shout said.

"Umm." Tisha let out a low groan and rested her head against the pillow. As Shout pulled her shorts down Tisha's legs were trembling. Shout stood up and took off his pants and boxer shorts. Shortly after putting on a condom, he grabbed Tisha's thighs and pulled her to the edge of the bed. Tisha pulled her legs close to her and lifted her bottom off the bed. Shout kissed her on the mouth and allowed his tongue to move around for a moment. Then he leaned forward and stuck his hardness inside of Tisha. Tisha exhaled and smiled.

****

Sydney and Boom were sitting in his office.

"What's the status on Denim being a presenter at the Soul Train Music Awards?" Sydney asked.

"It looks good. They want Shout, so I told them they came as a pair."

"You're always working your magic."

"What's up with Mike Lopez?" Boom asked.

"We already talked about that in L.A. That's a dead issue."

"Does he know that? He called three times today for you. The last message was to let you know that he's in town."

"Nothing is going on there."

"Well, tell him to stop calling you."

"He's an important radio executive. He's connected. I can't just tell him to stop calling."

"Do you want me to tell him to stop calling?" Boom asked.

"You are the most jealous man I have ever met."

"Jealous? I don't know what that is. I know about protecting my assets. You're one of my assets."

"Oh, now I'm your property?"

"Sydney, don't go girl power on me. You know what I mean."

"Yeah, I know. But, if I tell you nothing is happening, nothing is happening. I'm not going to lie to you. That's not my style."

The phone rang again, Boom answered. He looked at Sydney. "It's Mike Lopez for you again."

Sydney looked at the phone and exhaled, "I'll take it in my office."

"I'm not attached, and I don't discuss my private life. It's better seeing what the magazines make up."

—Shout, interviewed in for the magazine, "Behind the Man"

Chapter 26

Tisha's phone rang and the answering machine came on. Fifteen minutes passed, and there were three quick knocks on her front door. A few minutes later, there were three knocks again. Charmaine opened the door with her key, turned on the light in the kitchen, and began to walk to the bedroom. Charmaine wore a pair of cropped pants with African symbols on them and a black t-shirt. "Tisha, I just came by to..." she said as she noticed a man in the bed.

"Tisha, who's that?" Charmaine demanded. "Tisha. Tisha, wake up."

Tisha opened her eyes and rubbed them. "Girl, get off me. Get off me."

Shout got out of bed and walked to the bathroom, wearing only his fitted black boxers. His back muscles were well defined. The tattoo on his back of a black panther and the African warrior Shaka Zula shone on his skin.

Perplexed, Charmaine said, "What is going on?"

Tisha smiled and said, "He really wants me to be his girlfriend."

"Obviously, I missed something. Weren't you the girl crying all last week? What happened?"

Tisha got out of the bed and took Charmaine to the living room. She began whispering and laughing. Charmaine hugged her.

Shout exited the bathroom, went back into the bedroom, and put his jeans on before going into the living room and sitting in the recliner.

Charmaine and Tisha looked at him and both smiled before looking at each other.

"What, you ain't gon' introduce me to family? Come here, girl."

Tisha smiled and walked over to Shout and sat with him in the chair. "Shout, this is my best friend, Charmaine Johnson."

Tisha motioned toward Charmaine, who got up and walked over to their chair to shake Shout's hand.

"It's a pleasure to finally meet you, but don't be messing over my friend. She's a good girl. Don't blow it again," Charmaine stated very matter-of-factly.

"I won't." Shout looked at Tisha. "She's as feisty as you, huh?"

"That's right, feistier," Charmaine said as she walked back over to the couch.

"I need to ask you a favor," Shout said, looking at Charmaine.

Charmaine stopped, narrowed her eyes and angrily stared at Shout.

Shout put up his hands and said, "Yo, chiiiilll. I need you to get my bag from the car."

"Would you, Charmaine?" Tisha asked.

"No problem. Where's the car and your keys?"

Shout pointed to the keys on the counter. "My car is parked out front. It's a gray Aston Martin."

Impressed, Charmaine grabbed the keys and went outside. Tisha put her arms around Shout's neck and hugged him tight. "I'm so glad you're here. What do you want for breakfast? I can make you pancakes, bacon, and eggs. Is that cool?"

"Yeah. Can you cook for real?"

"Of course."

"That's rare. I'll mess around and move in wit' you."

Charmaine opened the door and carried in the designer duffle bag. She dropped it on the floor and put the keys on the counter. "I'm on my way to work. Call me later. Have fun." Charmaine looked cautiously at Tisha, then shot a steely glance at Shout.

"Peace," Shout said, realizing that Charmaine was giving him a warning.

He got up and began digging in his bag. "Tisha, come here for a minute and close your eyes."

"What you doin'? I ain't into nothin' freaky."

"Girl, stop buggin'. Keep your eyes closed." After he seated her he said, "You can open your eyes now."

Tisha looked down and saw a platinum-link chain with "Nikkole" written in diamonds hanging around her neck. "It's beautiful. It's really pretty."

"Just like you," Shout said.

Tisha hugged him, then looked at the necklace again. The brilliance of the diamonds filled her eyes. Underneath "Nikkole" were the letters "KG."

"Shawn, there are other letters on my chain."

"What letters?"

She pointed to the KG.

"Oh, that. That means Keyshawn's girl." He looked at her and winked.

Tisha went into the kitchen and began to cook breakfast.

****

"All you can expect from him is sex and you got that. Move on," Juicy said as she drove her Escalade through Brooklyn.

"You're right. I didn't even feel anything anyway. It was all in my head."

As Juicy drove through the Marcy projects, she pointed to some young girls who had been turnin' tricks for her on the down low. There were three girls who were seventeen and eighteen. They had dropped out of high school and were looking to make some serious paper.

"Those girls are pretty. But these projects don't have nothin' for them. I'm helpin' them and you should be helpin' me."

Jordan looked out the window.

"When Lizia turns 18 this month, I'm getting them a crib outta the projects."

Jordan thought about all the conversations that she had with Dan about Shout – the times that Dan told her to use her body to get next to him. Dan asked Jordan to be a prostitute for the sake of World Music Records and yet she wasn't benefiting from World Music's profits. Her paycheck was the same whether she had sex with Shout or not. But even a prostitute can see an increase in pay when she uses her body.

****

A few hours later, Shout and Tisha were in the living room of her apartment, watching TV.

"I know you want to get out of the house," she said.

"No, I'm cool. I'm here with you."

"Your pager and phone haven't been going off."

"I cut them off when I decided to come down here and get my girl back."

Tisha kissed him on the lips.

"I would love to see the new Morgan Freeman movie," Tisha stated.

"We need a theater that ain't in the city. We gotta go to the latest show. And we have to enter after it's dark in the theater."

"That's a lot of precautions."

"I don't have to go to the movies at all. I just want to be with you. But if that's what you want, I'll do it for you."

"Nah, you're right. We shouldn't go to the movies right now. But I want to go to the video store and get us some movies for tonight. Will you be able to stay?"

Shout looked down at the front of his pants and said, "What you think?"

"Oh, maybe we can do something else before we go to the video store."

Tisha ran into the bedroom and Shout chased her. Tisha jumped on the bed.

"You ain't getting' none. Get a way from me." Tisha said as she giggled.

"You know you dying to give it to me."

Shout took off his sweatpants and t-shirt and just looked at Tisha.

"You got a bangin' body," Shout said as he moved closer to the bed.

Tisha anxiously jumped around from one side of the bed to the other.

"Flattery gets you no where." Tisha smiled.

Shout slowly crawled on the bed. Tisha stood perfectly still. When Shout reached her, he pulled down her pajama bottoms and licked her clitoris until she came. Tisha fell down on the bed. Shout laid on top of her and pumped his thickness inside of her. Tisha reached up and felt his hard nipple. She grabbed his index finger and put it in her mouth.

"Awww," Shout yelled as his semen filled the condom.

****

Boom and Sydney were in a coffee shop on Lexington Avenue where they picked up a copy of *The Village Voice*. A review appeared on Shout's recent performance at Madison Square Garden, and there was a bunch of pictures of Shout with various people.

"Sydney, did you notice that there are lots of pictures of Shout with Jordan in the background?"

Sydney looked at the picture. "Yeah, she's everywhere."

Sydney sipped her latte and Boom sent Tisha a two-way. HOW ARE YOU DOING? I HOPE ALL IS WELL.

"You've been kinda quiet lately," Sydney said.

"You know our workload. It's been impossible working with Denim and Shout. Denim is a diva beyond compare and Shout, well, he's his own man. Sometimes that's a challenge all unto itself."

Sydney ran two fingers over Boom's hand. "You know I'm really happy when I'm with you."

"Yeah, I'm happy with you too."

"I just want you to know that."

"I do know that."

"Hip-hop, the most testosterone filled industry outside of professional sports, a forum where the worse diss is when one rapper calls another rapper gay, still won't acknowledge homosexuality within its ranks. But hip-hop is reflective of society. And just like homosexuals exist in schools, churches, and doctor's offices, they most certainly exist in hip-hop."
—Tisha Ariel Nikkole, excerpted from her newspaper article, "The Gay Rapper: Man or Myth"

Chapter 27

Tisha laid on top of Shout on the couch watching *Matlock* reruns. "I love you being here with me." Tisha rubbed her hand over Shout's bicep.

"I know."

"I don't want you to leave."

"I gotta work. I gotta turn my stuff back on."

"I know. I know."

Tisha sucked her teeth and put her hair behind her ear.

Shout turned his cell phone and pager back on. Within minutes, both were chirping and buzzing.

"Whaddup?" Shout said, seeing Jordan's number on his Caller ID.

"Where you been? I've been setting stuff up for you."

"You should call Pockets. You know he's my manager. He handles my schedule. You don't have to call me direct."

"Oh, it's like that now? You wasn't saying that when your mom needed security."

"Don't go there. Man, I'm just letting you know if it's business, call him, that's all. No disrespect."

"I have a photo op for you to go to in New York."

"What is it?"

"It's a hip hop roast. I want you to go with Denim, the R&B singer. It'll be huge."

"What you mean go with? I roll with my boys."

"It'll keep your name in the paper if you showed up with her. She's the biggest R&B star right now and you're the biggest rap artist. It's the perfect match."

"That sounds wack."

"I thought you were cool with her camp."

"We are cool, but I ain't trying to roll with Denim like that."

"Why you gotta be so triflin'?"

"Call Pockets. I'll speak with you later."

Shout hung up before Jordan could say good-bye.

****

Tisha jogged for two miles. On her walk back, she stopped at a small grocery store. She picked up a new copy of *Aura* magazine. Her article, "Love, Rap, and Roll" was inside. She screamed and ran all the way home. Opening the door, she yelled, "Shawn, Shawn."

Shout was in the shower singing "U Saved Me" by R. Kelly . Tisha opened the bathroom door.

"Guess what? My article 'Love, Rap and Roll' got a cover mention in the latest issue of *Aura*."

"What article?"

Shout cut off the water and snatched a towel from the top of the stall.

"When we were apart, I wrote an article about rappers and relationships. I thought it would help me feel better about the situation so I wrote it."

Shout blew air through his lips and walked into the bedroom. "I can't believe you did that, Tisha."

"What?"

"You took our relationship and you put it on blast."

Shout dropped the towel, turned around, and put on his boxers.

"I didn't put us on blast. I simply wrote about the challenges that rappers and people who may date rappers might face."

"Is that all I am to you, a rapper? I should be your man first."

"Why are you so mad?"

"Our relationship is private—the other parts of my life aren't. I want to keep our shit private—no articles, no media, no flashbulbs—just me and you. The other shit is a distraction." Shout pulled his T-shirt over his head and grabbed his matching baseball cap out of his duffle bag. "People violate my private space every day. I didn't think you'd be stupid enough to do the same thing."

"Now you're calling me stupid?"

Shout walked out of the bedroom and grabbed his duffle bag. He went into the living room and sat on the edge of the couch to put on his Timberlands.

Tisha followed. "Shawn, I apologize if you're offended or feel that I violated you or our relationship but I am a journalist. I share my experiences with the world. That's my job."

"You can talk about your experiences, just don't talk about mine."

Shout stood and headed for the door.

"You leaving?"

Shout did not look back. "Yeah."

"Can I get a kiss good-bye?"

Shout put two fingers over his lips, kissed them, and pointed them at Tisha before closing the door.

****

Later that day, Tisha sat at her desk opening her mail and jotting down ideas for upcoming stories to pitch to magazine editors. She opened a plain white envelope with the two pages inside that read: BITCH STAY AWAY FROM SHOUT OR YOU'LL DIE!!

Tisha threw the papers on the floor and stepped away. "What the hell is going on?," she fumed. Tisha picked up the envelope and examined it. Outside of the New York city postmark, nothing else stood out on the envelope. Tisha's telephone rang and she jumped three feet in the air.

"Hello," Tisha stated with her heart beating fast.

"Can I speak to Tisha?"

"This is she."

"Oh, I didn't catch your voice today. It's Wanda from *Aura*."

"Hey, thanks for all of the emails."

"Well, I got some even better news. *Aura* wants to offer you a contributing editor position."

"Oh my God, really?"

"Yeah."

"Would I have to move?"

"No, not yet. But we would want you to come to some editorial meetings in New York. We'll send an offer sheet for you to consider."

"Great. This seems like a wonderful opportunity."

Tisha hung up the phone, then she ran her fingers across the chain that Shout had given her and remembered that he was mad at her. She sat back down solemnly and thought about the threatening letter.

Tisha slowly typed a message to Shout in her two-way. DON'T BE MAD. EVERYONE MAKES MISTAKES, EVEN YOU. I NEED TO SPEAK TO YOU. I JUST GOT SOME HATE MAIL.

She pressed the send button. Exhausted, Tisha showered and climbed into bed for a quick nap before Shout's Washington, DC platinum party. Her phone rang. She looked at the Caller ID, but the number was unavailable. "Maybe it's Shout calling from a hotel or something," she mumbled.

"Hello."

"Is this Tisha Ariel Nikkole?" a female voice asked.

"Yes, who's this?" Tisha asked.

"It's the bitch who's gonna make your life miserable. I better not ever see you with Shout or it's over."

The line went dead in Tisha's ear.

****

Tisha checked her watch. It was midnight and Shout had not arrived at his own platinum party at Washington, DC's Dream nightclub. Boom wasn't there yet either.

"Perhaps they're together," Tisha thought to herself. As Tisha looked around the room, her eyes connected with

Jordan's. Jordan had been staring at Tisha for the past ten minutes. She'd hid her gaze behind a Shout look-a-like ice sculpture. Tisha looked away and walked toward some barstools next to a Cristal champagne waterfall. A few moments later two bodyguards approached Tisha.

"Miss, you gotta go," a beefy white bodyguard said to her.

"What are you talking about," Tisha asked.

"We're taking you out of here."

"No you're not. I was invited."

One of the other bodyguards grabbed Tisha's arm.

"Get off of me," Tisha screamed to no avail.

"World Music Records said you gotta go," the beefy bodyguard yelled.

Tisha looked over at Jordan who smiled at her while the two bodyguards man-handled her. Jordan turned her back as the bodyguards carried Tisha out of the building.

"Just because we don't all hang out and act like Rodney King, that doesn't mean there's an east coast / west coast rivalry or any real beefs beyond what's on wax."

—Shout interviewed in the magazine article, "Shout: Hip-Hop's Reigning King"

Chapter 28

On the train ride to New York City, Tisha thought about being thrown out of Shout's party, the hate mail and her late-night phone call. *Who is behind all of this nonsense? Is Shout that mad at me?* Tisha thought. "Maybe he didn't want me at the party to prove a point. But, that still doesn't explain the hate mail or the evil phone calls from the chick with the weird voice," Tisha mumbled to herself.

Tisha thought of ways to make up her privacy breach to Shout. *What can I do to not violate that trust? Can I be a journalist and Shout's girlfriend at the same time?*

Boom met Tisha at the train station in his black Mercedes G500 SUV. She spotted him and waved. Boom got out of the truck and hugged her. He opened one of his back doors and threw in her bag. They jumped in and he pulled off.

"Ah, the city and the people. I love New York," Tisha said.

"You should stop playin' and move up here."

Tisha continued to look in the distance.

"What the hell happened with you and Shout in Atlanta?"

Tisha paused and responded coolly, "He was just testing me."

"It seems as if the storm has blown over. Have you all made up?"

"Sort of."

"Girl, you can't downplay it to me. He already called me, got your address, and told me everything. I know you two are doing a whole lot more than what you're letting on."

Boom pulled up in front of The 40/40 Club and walked straight to the bar and ordered two Long Island Ice Teas. Tisha sat in a bar stool and stared at the gray Italian marble.

"What's been going on?" Boom asked.

"Just trying to do my writing and what-not."

"What's up with you and Shout?"

"Nothing."

"That's not what he told me."

"Are you kidding me? He told you he's mad about that article. I can't believe that."

"No, he didn't tell me, but you just did."

"Boom, please don't say anything. I'm already in hot water."

"You play a dangerous game, Ms. Nikkole."

"What do you mean? You're taking his side?" Tisha turned away and looked toward the back of the restaurant.

"It's already extremely difficult to be in a relationship with a high-profile individual—the media is gonna be all over you as soon as they get a whiff. So, what reason could you have to put the media on your scent?" Boom took a drink from his glass.

"It wasn't like that. We were apart. I was in pain. I didn't think we'd be together so I wrote the article. I didn't want to hurt him."

"What's the status of your relationship now?"

"We're in a potentially serious relationship. We both have intense feelings for each other."

"Well, I want to tell you about something that I wasn't really sure about, but it kinda happened and I still don't know if it's the right thing."

"What?" Tisha asked as her eyes widened.

"I've been having sex with Sydney for the past couple of weeks. Our relationship is getting kinda serious."

"Sydney? Your partner Sydney?"

"Yeah, that's the one."

"How did that happen?"

"She kept coming on to me. I didn't stop her."

"But I thought you didn't believe in relationships."

"I don't."

Just then a crowd appeared at the door of The 40/40 Club. Boom and Tisha looked to the door where three photographers began snapping shots every two seconds. The flashbulbs looked like exploding lights on a Christmas tree.

The crowd began to part. Shout walked arm in arm with R&B star Denim. They were led upstairs to a VIP room by Greasy and the maître d'.

Tisha's face turned the color of 1,000 beets. She adjusted herself on the stool and used a finger to wipe her eyebrow.

"I hate to do this to you, but he's my artist. And there aren't supposed to be any photo opportunities of him without my knowledge. This was obviously staged. I'll be right back," Boom said.

****

Boom walked to the VIP area and was stopped by Greasy. Shout saw Boom and signaled him to come back.

"What's up, man? How you feel?"

They shook hands.

"I feel good." Boom looked at Denim, grabbed her hand, and kissed it. "Hi, Denim. You look fabulous tonight." He paused, then looked at Shout. "I need to speak to you for a minute." Boom nodded at Shout, who got up and stood to the side of the table.

"Who set this up—you coming here with Denim?"

"Jordan."

"When?"

"She called Pockets this morning, and she said the label wanted me to do it."

"Is that right? Is she here?"

"No."

"Well, I'll have to talk to her. Enjoy your dinner."

Shout tapped Boom's shoulder. "Hold up. What are you doing here?"

"I'm having drinks with one of my best friends from college, Tisha Ariel Nikkole." Boom walked away.

"Oh man," Shout mumbled and exhaled. He looked at Denim and managed a half-hearted smile.

Within moments, Tisha appeared in front of Shout and Denim's table.

"What's up Denim? It's so nice to see you again," Tisha said, rolling her eyes at Shout.

"Girl, sit down. Thanks for the story. Everybody loved it."

"No problem, you're worth it. Your fans deserve to see you in a positive light." Tisha smiled.

"You know Shout, right?" Denim asked.

"Barely," Tisha replied sarcastically. "I heard his career was over."

"Very funny, Tisha," Shout said and sipped his drink.

"Well, Denim, enjoy your dinner," Tisha said, looking at Shout before leaving the table.

Tisha looked down at her two-way pager and read the screen: BITCH YOU BETTA STAY AWAY FROM SHOUT. Tisha studied the message and could see that it was sent from an Anonymous source. She shut the case of her pager.

****

Jordan and Juicy sat in the back of a chauffeured limousine that turned and twisted along a quiet road in Las Vegas, Nevada. Jordan didn't know where they were headed. The destination was Juicy's surprise. As the limo stopped, Jordan and Juicy stepped out of the car. They stood in front of a modest building with a bright red neon sign that read BUNNY'S BROTHEL.

"From strip clubs to whore houses... You think I need to be inspired?"

Juicy chuckled and motioned Jordan to follow her into the establishment.

Inside there were women strippers, waitresses who wore bunny ears and fluffy tails and men who drooled.

Juicy walked back to a large office with zebra carpet and a matching couch. There was an executive desk that faced the couch. Juicy sat on the desktop and looked at Jordan.

"Why are we here?" Jordan asked while she looked around the office. "And by the way, you look awfully comfortable on somebody's desk."

"It's my desk Jordan. It's our desk," Juicy replied.

"What? What are you talking about?"

"This is our business. Prostitution is legal here. You said you needed a change and you said you'd help me if I needed you. I need you now."

Jordan sat there. Her eyes were wide. She got up and walked out of the office, looked at the bar and stared at the stage.

"This could be my chance to start over. I could leave World Music in the dust," Jordan mumbled. A feeling of optimism overcame Jordan. She went search for Juicy and found her in the hallway.

"I got ya back. I gotta go to Miami and tie up some loose ends. When I return change the name of this joint to J&J's kittens."

Jordan hopped in the limo.

"Driver, take me to the airport."

"Founding hip-hop entrepreneur Roland Simpson says, 'successful hip-hop businesses are redefining the way urban culture is looking at making money in America.' And it's about time. Finally, urban youth can look toward a way out of the ghetto that doesn't involve bouncing, carrying, or hitting a ball."

—Tisha Ariel Nikkole, excerpted from her magazine article, "Hip-Hop is Big Business"

Chapter 29

Shout's limousine dropped Denim and her entourage off at the Essex House. Before Denim could close the car door, Shout was dialing Tisha's cell phone.

"Yes," Tisha answered sleepily.

"Why'd you leave the bar?"

"I had no reason to stay."

"I was there."

"Yeah, with another woman. Watching my man enjoy dinner with another broad isn't exciting to me. Sorry."

"You know that was staged. Where you at now?"

"In the hotel."

"Which one?"

"Why do you want to know?"

"See, there you go!"

"Nah, Shawn, you were mad at me the other day, then this stuff tonight. I ain't feeling you right now."

"Which hotel?"

"How do you think I feel?"

"You gon' make me call Boom and ask him, huh? That's how you gon' be tonight, huh?"

"Where's your date at, Shawn? Where's she?"

"She's been dropped off. I'm trying to get with my baby, but she ain't feeling me."

Tisha smiled.

"I know you're smiling. Get your stuff. I'm coming to get you."

"I'm at the Sheraton on 7th Avenue."

"I'll call you back when I'm out front. I'm taking you to the Trump Plaza tonight."

"Yeah, you gotta do something to make up for that fiasco tonight."

Tisha got up and started getting her clothes together.

****

The marble floors, crystal chandelier, and overflowing water fountains brightened Tisha's eyes. She had never been to a place so beautiful. The plants in the foyer were all green, not a brown or yellow leaf in sight. The old doorman smiled, and the concierge appeared willing to help. As Tisha and Shout entered the luxurious Trump Plaza hotel, she grabbed his hand.

Shout and Tisha walked through the lobby to the elevator. Once inside Shout kissed her and whispered in her ear, "You turn me on."

She playfully moved away from him. "Yeah, that wasn't what you were saying at dinner tonight."

He placed his arm around her upper body. She tried to pull away but he grabbed her and affectionately pulled her in front of his pelvis.

"Are you trying to give me a hint?" Tisha asked, squirming.

"Yeah." Shout smiled at her. They got off the elevator.

Inside their palatial suite, complete with Jacuzzi, king-size bed, sofas, and a marble kitchen, Shout asked, "Why are you in New York anyway?"

"I have a meeting tomorrow."

"With who?"

Tisha just looked at him.

"I didn't give you permission to talk to nobody." He smiled and winked.

"Ha ha. I have a meeting with *Aura* magazine." Shout removed his pager and cell phone from his hip. "What now? You've already told them ev'rything."

"No, I haven't."

"Okay, whatever you say."

"They want to offer me a job."

"That's good. I'm proud of you. Handle your business, Tisha."

Tisha leaned over and kissed him. He pulled her down and hugged her, and they rolled over on the bed.

"Yeah, I'm excited. It's more money, not as much hustling. I would enjoy it."

Shout took off his boots.

"By the way, this is a huge bed," Tisha said.

"That's 'cause I got big things planned." Shout stood and grabbed his crotch.

"With all that humor, you need to be in the movies."

Tisha and Shout laughed.

Tisha walked over near the closet and saw a large flat cardboard box and a flat envelope.

"What's this?"

"Oh, that's stuff for my girlfriend but you don't know her."

"Stop playin'."

"I ain't playin'. If you're her, you can open that. If you ain't, she gon' get you for messin' with her stuff."

Tisha tore into the box and found a life-size poster of Shout.

"This is fine, just like you. Thanks for my poster." Tisha ran over and kissed him. Shout tapped her on the behind.

She lifted the flat envelope off the floor and pulled out a picture of the two of them on their first date at the restaurant.

"How did you get this done? You didn't even like me back then."

"I liked you the first time I ever saw you, I just didn't know where your head was at."

Tisha jumped on his lap, and Shout fell back on the bed. She kissed him on his forehead, his eye, his cheek, his chin, and finally his lips.

"I love—" She stopped herself mid-sentence and bit her lip, afraid of telling him that she loved him.

"You love what?"

"I love the poster of you. I'm gonna put it right over the bed, so even when you're traveling, you'll be there with me."

"I love it too." He just looked at Tisha, knowing that wasn't what she was gonna say.

"Can we just lay here tonight?"

"Girl, you know what's up with me."

Tisha smiled. "I want to always remember what it was like on my first night at Trump Plaza. I want you to hold me."

"I'll hold you afterward. Let's celebrate. Let's get buck wild," he said with a wide, cheesy grin.

"Shawn, be serious. I'm being serious."

Shout moved Tisha on top of him.

A few moments passed, and Tisha looked Shout in the eyes. "Okay, enough of the memories. You up for trying the hot tub?" she asked.

"Definitely."

Tisha ran into the bathroom and turned on the Jacuzzi.

"I got a surprise for you. Get in the tub and wait for me." Shout went into the bathroom and waited for the tub to fill. Tisha dressed herself in a red bustier with nipple openings, a red crotchless g-string, and red 5 inch heels. She played Beyoncé's song, "Naughty Girl" on her portable cd player and entered the bathroom. Shout was sitting in the tub.

"Oh shit."

Tisha went over to the tub and kissed Shout on the mouth and danced for him. As she shimmied, he nipples moved. Shout's erection was getting harder and harder by the moment. As the song came toward the end, Tisha stepped into the tub and began to strip. She turned her back toward Shout and bent over. He saw her pubic hairs peeking through the crotchless panties. He leaned forward to her, but Tisha quickly turned around. She took her panties off and saw the head of his penis sticking out of the water. Tisha leaned down and grabbed his shaft with one hand and then kissed the head. She sucked him deep as he moaned. Tisha spread her legs and sat on his erection. She tongue kissed him and then got out of the tub. She grabbed a towel and laid on the bed.

Shout looked at his erection, "We ain't done yet." Shout got out of the tub. All the lights were off in the bedroom. Shout couldn't see anything.

"I'm being naughty tonight. If you want me, you'll have to find me. And you can't turn on the lights." Tisha said and scurried over to the fireplace in the living room. Tisha was lying on a blanket and heard Shout's footsteps coming closer. Her nipples got hard. Shout got down on his hands and knees and felt the bottom of her foot. As he moved closer, he pushed her legs apart. He put both of his hands on her buttcheeks and then spanked her with one hand.

"Hurt me." Tisha said and giggled. "Hurt me." Shout began to massage her ass and moved his legs up by Tisha's head. He laid on the floor and pulled her wet center to his mouth. Tisha felt his penis on her cheek. She opened her mouth and slurped. As Tisha's juices flowed, Shout could feel her muscles vibrating on his chin. As she vibrated, her tongue made passionate circles around his shaft and pressure kisses at the tip. As he felt his ejaculation coming, he pulled away from Tisha and squirted the entire room.

****

Tisha and Shout were still sleeping when the phone rang at ten-thirty the next morning. The loud noise startled Tisha. Shout rolled over and took the phone. "What?"

"You missed your flight to Miami."

"What?"

"You missed your plane."

"What plane?"

"Pockets was supposed to tell you about a conference you have to go to in Miami."

"Oh."

"You gotta come."

"Book another flight for me."

"When?"

"In five hours."

"Okay. You'll be flying at three."

"Cool, and get a ticket for Tisha Nikkole. She's flying with me."

Jordan hung up the phone.

****

Tisha rushed to make her noon meeting at *Aura*. The conference room was all gray with royal blue chairs and a white writing board. The meeting was being run by Editor-in-Chief Lana Chez Van Buren.

"Everyone, let's welcome Tisha Ariel Nikkole to our editorial staff."

The staff clapped.

"Whenever we have a new person on board, I explain the person's role to the staff so that everyone has a grasp of how the new person should fit."

Tisha nodded.

"After the feedback of Tisha's article, we're developing a monthly feature that involves relationship analysis based on real life told in the first person. Tisha will continue to come up with stories similar to the one that was run in this issue. The goal is to peak the interest of our readers with real relationship stories."

Tisha heard Shout's voice in her head, "You violate my privacy. Keep my name outta your articles. You're supposed to be better than them." Tisha began to sink in the chair.

Three hours later, Tisha arrived back at Trump Plaza and entered the room. Shout was sitting on the couch talking on his cell phone. He quickly wrapped up the conversation.

"Who were you talking to? Your mom?"

"Yeah, that's my number one girl, but you're a strong number two."

Tisha barely cracked a smile. She went into the bathroom and splashed some water on her face, then sat in a chair across from Shout.

"What's wrong wit' you?" he asked.

"Nothing."

"What happened at the magazine?"

"Nothing really. I just gotta be able to produce what they want."

"You can do that. Don't sweat that because it's a new gig."

"You're right. I'll stay focused. Are you ready to go yet?"

****

Boom and Sydney were in Boom's Miami hotel room.

"It's funny to hear you say that it's time for another strategy meeting," Sydney said before drinking from her bottled water.

"Jordan from World Music Records has been calling the management of our artists and setting up publicity opportunities. Remember Shout being seen with Denim?"

"Yeah, I remember that."

"That's not her forte but for some reason she seems real interested in Shout. Tisha has been getting a real negative vibe from Jordan and now Jordan's meddling in our PR business. I think it's time you made a call."

"To who?"

"Dan Bellows."

"Is it that serious?"

"Yeah, I think so. Shout's been telling me that she's been calling him directly a lot and his manager. She's been telling them that the label wants him to do a lot of different things that should have been discussed with us first."

"That's a serious problem."

Boom sat on a barstool next to Sydney.

"It gets worse."

"You're kidding. What else?" Sydney asked.

"Tisha is getting threatening phone calls, hang-ups, threatening messages, she was pulled out of one of Shout's parties and she thinks it's Jordan."

"Why would Jordan dislike Tisha like that?"

"Tisha is really Shout's girlfriend."

"Seriously?" Sydney asked, raising her brows.

"Seriously," Boom replied.

Just then they both heard a knock on the door. Sydney walked back into the bedroom and shut the door as Boom answered the door.

"Hey Jordan," Boom said as he opened the door. "What are you doin' here?"

"I wanted you to be the first to know that I'm leaving World Music Records."

"Why?"

"I want more control over my future. I'm going into business for myself."

"Really? Good for you," Boom walked over to the desk and began separating VIP and photo passes. Boom moved a picture to the side of the desk and chucked. It was a photo of Tisha and him. But Tisha was on her hands and knees barking like a dog. Jordan glanced at the photo.

"Isn't this the writer who's been covering Shout a lot?" Jordan asked.

"Yeah, we're friends from college. I came across it the other day and I'ma clown her when I see her."

Just then, Sydney walked into the room.

"Excuse me Boom, I need to speak to you for a minute."

Boom and Sydney walked back into the bedroom. Jordan picked up the photo again. "This photo must be about 8 years old, but they look exactly like they look now," Jordan mumbled to herself. She put the photo in her totebag.

I was born in the streets
It's how I earned my name
Rappin' to a drumbeat
It's how I earned my fame
Rhymin', passin' time
And bullets whizzing by
Life in the 'hood
Gave no time to cry
So a boy became a man
In a matter of time
—Shout from his song, "Manchild"

Chapter 30

Miami, FL

Tisha and Shout were staying at The Fontainebleau Hilton, one of Miami's plushest hotels and resorts. Built in a curve with palm trees throughout the estate and a waterfall, the resort was a couple's romantic paradise.

They were in the penthouse suite playing the *NBA Ballers* Playstation 2 video game. Shout was beating her unmercifully. Tisha frowned and looked around the room, absolutely frustrated with the simplicity of the game.

"I don't want to play anymore," she pleaded.

"Take this beating like a woman," Shout said, laughing.

"I can't take no more beatings like this." Tisha threw her joystick on the bed and walked away. "Anyway, you should be getting ready for dinner."

Shout leaned back, and Tisha stared at his arm. She reached out and touched it.

"How many tattoos do you have now?"

"I never counted."

"They're nice."

"Thanks."

"Why do you have a microphone attached to a gun on your arm?"

"It's a choice I had to make. Either I was gon' be a gang banger or I was gon' do music. Every time I want to walk away from music, I know the other choice."

"But you have more choices than that."

"Yeah, but I didn't back then. It's a reminder of where I came from."

"Why do you have this tear over this picture with the name on it?"

"That's for Vonni. I wish he was still here."

Tisha and Shout lay on the bed, looking up at the circular designs on the ceiling.

"I might get a tattoo."

"Yeah, right." Shout laughed.

"I'm serious. I know what I want on it."

"Me too. *Keyshawn* on your chest." Shout smiled.

Shaking her head, Tisha said, "No. I don't think so. It's gonna be a surprise."

"I will be surprised if you get one. I'm getting ready to take a shower," Shout said.

"No. You gotta beat me to the bathroom." They both jumped up and ran to the bathroom at the same time.

"It was a tie, so what now?" Shout said.

"I ain't leaving," Tisha responded.

"I ain't either."

"Oh well." Tisha turned on the shower's faucet and jumped in. She heard the door closing behind her. "Sore loser," she said, mumbling under her breath.

The shower door slid open and Shout stepped in. Standing behind Tisha, Shout rubbed the soap all over her body. He started with her neck, then squeezed her nipples and then rubbed her ass. Tisha turned around and rubbed the soap over Shout's chest and formed a circle with her hand and played with his penis. Shout lifted Tisha up and leaned against the shower's wall. Tisha's legs were wrapped around his back. They made love as the water drenched them until they both climaxed in unison.

****

Jordan sat next to Clayton, a college-aged computer geek at a copy center in Miami. He printed out a copy of the freshly altered photo.

"This looks good," Jordan said. She studied the photograph, which now featured Tisha performing oral sex on Boom while wearing a dog collar and leash around her neck. Jordan had paid Clayton $200 to change the photograph. It looked like an original.

"You could have a big future with me. Keep my card, especially my cell number on the back." Jordan handed Clayton her card and left the copy center.

****

The next morning, Tisha ate eggs and toast at the VIP breakfast for about twenty-five music executives from across the country. Shout was sitting at a head table and Jordan sat next to him.

Jordan looked over in Tisha's direction and said to Shout, "I see you brought your little friend to the breakfast."

Shout put another forkful of pancakes in his mouth.

"When are you gonna realize that women only want you for your money? They don't care about you."

Shout drank his ice water.

"And that girl you got, she looks like a gold digger anyway. Mark my words, she's probably slept with ten other rappers just like you."

Shout put some bacon in his mouth and turned to his manager Pockets and whispered in his ear. Pockets then turned to Dan Bellows and whispered in his ear. Dan signaled to Jordan to get up from the table and follow him.

"Jordan, Shout is offended by you and repulsed by you." Dan paused and looked at Jordan sternly. "He and his manager don't want you working with him anymore."

Jordan folded her arms and leaned against the wall. "This was your idea, not mine. I told you all rappers aren't alike. Shout is difficult."

Once back in reception area, Dan Bellows thanked the attendees for coming to the breakfast in honor of Shout before Shout stepped to the podium.

"Thank you for all your help in making my music successful. I couldn't do what I do without y'all. One love," Shout said.

Shout and Greasy exited through the door. The attendees began to get up.

Barbie Waxman, a fellow journalist, came over to Tisha.

"Hey, Tisha. I haven't seen you in a while. How are you?"

"I'm doing great."

"Loved that article in *Aura*."

"Thanks."

Tisha was trying to walk to the door, but Barbie kept stepping in front of her.

"Word is you're close with the Shout camp. Is there any way that you can get me a one-on-one with him?"

Tisha smiled and gently shook her head. "His publicist, Boom Tillman, is here. I'm sure he'll hook it up."

"No, you don't understand. I want you to hook me up with him for a—you know, so I can get some."

Tisha stood back from Barbie with a perplexed look on her face.

"Sex?" Tisha asked.

"Now, you're getting the picture."

"I could never set him up like that. You're on your own."

"Are you sure you're not trying to do the same thing? That's all your article was about anyway." Barbie looked Tisha up and down and rolled her eyes.

****

Boom stood in the back of the room. In the front right of the room, Sydney was sitting down talking to a mixed group of male and female journalists. As she got up from her table, Mike Lopez stepped behind her and put his right hand on her butt and gave it a squeeze. Sydney turned around, looked at Mike and moved his hand. Tisha came walking toward Boom.

"The breakfast was great," Tisha said, smiling.

"Uh huh," Boom tightly replied.

"What's wrong with you? You act like somebody is sleeping with your wife. But, hey, you're not married." Tisha chuckled. Boom didn't. "I saw Sydney in here. I was wondering where you were."

"I was here, I was in the background today. Shout could handle it," Boom responded.

"Do you wanna talk about anything?" Tisha asked.

Boom continued to stare at Sydney as she stood next to Mike Lopez. "Nah, that's alright. Let's bounce." Tisha and Boom left the room.

****

Shout and his crew were in a ballroom rehearsing. Shout recited 4 songs and then sat on an oversized speaker watching a technician as he adjusted the lights for Shout's upcoming performance. Jordan entered. She waved to Pockets and pointed to Shout.

"I wanted both of you to know that I'm leaving World Music. It's been fun, made some money, but now I'm stepping out on my own."

Shout looked at Jordan whose face wore a sly smile.

"Where you goin'?" Pockets asked.

"I got a business in Vegas. When I get settled, I'll fill you in."

Jordan gave Shout an envelope containing the doctored photograph of Boom and Tisha.

"Have a great performance and good luck with everything," Jordan said, then she exited the ballroom.

Jordan stood in front of the doors because she wanted to hear Shout's reaction.

"That bitch," Shout yelled, "I'ma fuck him up."

Jordan laughed and went to the ladies room. Inside a stall she lit a marijuana joint and then she called Wanda from Aura magazine.

"Wanda, I don't know how to tell you this, so I'll just be direct. World Music Records has reason to believe that Tisha Ariel Nikkole is part of some illegal sex and prostitution scheme that involves some of the biggest artists at our label. I gotta keep this on the hush hush now, but if I were you, I wouldn't keep hiring her to write articles for Aura." Jordan inhaled the joint and kept it in as long as she could. Jordan listened to Wanda's grateful "Thank-Yous" over the phone.

"Your welcome. It was no problem. We go way back, so I didn't want you to lose your job over some bitch."

Jordan hung up the phone and laughed so loud that her voice echoed through the bathroom.

****

Tisha stepped up on the risen stage where Shout and other World Music executives had been sitting. There was a tote-bag with a visible PDA inside. Tisha reached into the tote-bag and walked into the lobby. She turned on the PDA.

"Jordan Ellis" appeared on the small silver screen. Tisha fidgeted with the various features until she reached the email function. She punched the email's history and saw numerous emails that were sent to her two-way.

"Oh my God. Jordan has been the one threatening me all along," Tisha said to herself.

Tisha put the PDA in her backpack and dialed Shout's cell phone. He did not answer. Tisha paced the floor.

"Jordan's been sending the hate letters, got me thrown out of the platinum party. What else is she gonna do?" Tisha asked herself. As she walked back and forth, her phone vibrated. She looked at her caller ID. It was Wanda from Aura magazine.

"Hey Wanda," Tisha said in a somber tone. Tisha listened intently as Wanda told her that Aura was rescinding its editor position. For some reason, an executive at a record label had accused Tisha of plagiarizing. Tisha hung up the phone and screamed.

"Why would Aura magazine believe that I've been plagiarizing my articles?" Tisha yelled. "And what music executive could possibly threaten to pull financial support if Aura continued to work with me?" Tisha fumed. Her eyes turned a crimson red and angry tears rolled down her face.

"Jordan. Jordan is doing this."

Tisha called Shout's cell phone again, but he did not answer.

"Don't criticize black artists for perpetuating wealth in their videos by wearing excessive jewelry. They're renting their jewelry from the same place the Hollywood types are renting theirs on Oscar night." – Tisha Ariel Nikkole being interviewed on a news talkshow

Chapter 31

Boom and Sydney were sitting in the bar area of the Fontaine Bleu hotel. Boom had thought many hours about not being able to trust Sydney.

"Sydney, as much as I like you and as much as I like us working together, I can't be with you in a personal relationship. It's affecting our business relationship."

"What are you talking about Boom?" Sydney asked, raising her voice.

"This thing you have with Mike Lopez, I just ain't feelin' it. Before you tell me ain't nothing happening. I saw him feel on your ass earlier today. I can't have my girl going out like that. That's just weak."

"But I told you," Sydney replied with tears welling up in her eyes.

"That—," Boom pointed to a white envelope on the table, "has my resignation in it. Within the month, I'll be starting my own PR business and I'll be taking Denim and Shout with me."

"I can't believe you would do this to me."

"Sorry Sydney, it's the way it has to be."

"You can't do this, you signed a non-compete agreement. I'll sue you for everything you have."

"Do what you have to do, Sydney."

Boom got up from the table and walked to the elevators.

****

Boom sat on the couch in the sitting area of Shout's hotel suite. As Shout walked from the bathroom, Boom approached him. Shout raised his right hand and connected with Boom's jaw with the power of an earthquake. Boom hit the floor. Shout jumped on top of him and kept punching him. Boom was dazed and bloodied on the floor. Greasy ran over and pulled Shout off of Boom.

"Man, get out before he kills you," Greasy yelled.

Boom got up and stumbled. He crashed into a coffee table. He got up again and walked to the door. One hand was holding his jaw and another was outstretched feeling along the walls to assist with his balance. As Boom leaned against the wall, a maid saw him bleeding and called an ambulance.

****

Shout stood in the shower for forty-five minutes. The water burned his skin. He hoped it would burn the love that he felt for Tisha out of him. He felt destructive and alone. Two of the closest people to him had betrayed him.

With a towel wrapped around his waist, Shout stepped into the master's bedroom of the suite. He approached the king-sized bed and noticed a familiar face sticking up from the sheet.

"How'd you get in here?" Shout demanded.

"I came to cheer you up," Barbie, the journalist, replied.

"Ha ha. That's funny. Now get out."

Barbie sat up on the bed and exposed her negligee. She wore a white see-through outfit where the nipple areas were open. Shout looked at her breasts. He needed a release from his frustration. He took off his towel and got in bed. He closed his eyes and could see Tisha's face. Barbie tried to kiss him, but he turned his head. He roughly moved his hand over her breasts and to the bottom of her panties. He felt the moistness revealed by her crotchless panties. He jabbed his finger through the opening. Shout climbed on top of her and forcefully penetrated her. With each thrust Barbie's body moved back until her head was hitting the headboard. Her discomforting wails were not heard by Shout. Every painful thrust was an attempt for Shout to fight the pain he was feeling. He climaxed and his whole body shook. Barbie smiled. Shout looked down at her. He didn't see Tisha's face. He withdrew from her. And at that moment he realized that he wasn't wearing a condom.

"Get the fuck out," Shout yelled.

Barbie smiled, pulled up her jeans, threw on her t-shirt and left the room.

"That was too easy," she said to herself.

In the sitting area of the hotel suite, Barbie slipped on her high-heels and noticed an envelope on the floor. She picked it up and left.

"Asking a rapper if he ever fears for his life is a stupid question. I won't even answer that." – Shout on the red carpet attending an awards show in Los Angeles

Chapter 32

Boom laid in a hospital bed having received 20 stitches all over his face. The swelling in his jaw had gone down. His cell phone rang, but a heavily sedated Boom didn't have the strength to answer it. He laid in the bed drifting in and out of consciousness. He wondered why his best client had attacked him. He drifted off to sleep.

****

Tisha was in the lobby of Shout's hotel. She had just tried to reach Boom and she'd been calling Shout for the past hour and a half. No one answered their cell phones. Tisha thought about going up to Shout's suite, but no one answered in his room either. Barbie saw Tisha and walked up to her laughing. Tisha turned around.

"What's so funny?"

"You are...," Barbie responded.

"I don't get the joke."

"All this time I thought you were with Shout. I gotta admit you're one undercover bitch."

Barbie handed the envelope to Tisha. "I just got this from Shout's bedroom. What's next, a video?"

Tisha stood with her mouth wide open. Words would not come. She breathed heavily and tears streamed down her face.

****

Jordan dialed Dan's cellphone.

"Dan, I quit. I'm not working for you and your bullshit anymore. Find another colored girl to be your whore," Jordan hung up and smiled.

She dialed J&J's Kitten Club in Vegas and spoke with Juicy.

"I've tied up my loose ends. I'm ready to start over. I'm flying to Vegas tonite."

****

Tisha went outside and got into her rented convertible. She rode around for a while then she stopped at a traffic light in front of Shout's hotel. She looked over to her left and noticed a lady who looked like Jordan. She was about to cross the street. Tisha stared and recalled the outfit that Jordan wore earlier. It was identical to this person's outfit. As the lady stepped off of the curb, Tisha knew it was Jordan. Tisha pulled her baseball cap closer to her head and lifted her foot off the brake as Jordan got midway of the car. Tisha floored the accelerator and hit Jordan's body, throwing it 50 feet. Tisha didn't take her foot off the accelerator until she was 65 miles north of Miami.

"The average hip hop executive is in their 20's or 30's. Their ambition, intelligence, and determination is the greatest underused and overlooked asset in the African American community." – Tisha Ariel Nikkole speaking at a "How To Get Into The Entertainment Business" college lecture

Chapter 33

In a plain hotel room Tisha sat and thought about her relationship with Shout, her job with Aura magazine and her life, period. She looked in the mirror. Her eyes were red and swollen from crying. She looked at her cell phone and picked it up from the bed. She dialed Shout's cell again. At the beep she left a message.

"Keyshawn, I know you're mad at me because of the picture with Boom. But that picture is fake. That was a prank photo from college. Please believe me."

Tisha disconnected the call and dialed Charmaine's number. Her phone rang three times and then voicemail came on.

"Charmaine please go to my apartment and get the photo of me and Boom from inside my nightstand. Fax the photo to this hotel as soon as possible. I'm in room 323. It's a matter of life or death."

****

Shout picked up his cell phone and listened to the messages from Tisha. Her last message shocked him the most.

"Key, I ran Jordan over with the convertible. I might have killed her. She's been the one threatening me, harassing me, sending the letters. When I saw that she altered the photo of me and Boom, and you wouldn't answer my calls, it was the last straw. I gotta talk to you. I don't know what else to do."

Shout sat with the phone in his hand.

"I don't believe that shit. These chicks got game."

Shout grabbed the Playstation game controller and sat on the bed. His cell phone rang again. He refused to answer it. The voice mail light blinked. He turned on the TV and picked up the phone and listened.

"Keyshawn if I ever meant anything to you, come to my hotel. I'm at the Fairfield Inn off of I-95, north of Miami."

As he hung up the phone he saw a newsflash on the TV. The police were looking for the driver of a blue convertible.

"Greasy. Greasy, come here!" Shout yelled.

"What's up?"

"Call the Miami detective that squashed those traffic tickets for us a couple of months ago.

"For what?" Greasy asked.

"We're gonna return a favor." Shout put on a red doo-rag and his red and white Phillies cap and headed for the door.

****

Boom looked at the TV when he saw the newsflash. He felt cooped up already in the hospital. He decided to walk around. As he got to the emergency corridor, he saw Jordan being pushed down the hallway on a stretcher. The color in her face was gone. Her body was practically lifeless. He approached one of the EMT's from the ambulance.

"What happened to the woman who was on rolled down the hall just now?"

"Do you know her?" the EMT asked Boom.

"Yeah, she works with me."

"She got hit by a car that was going really fast. She's goin' to be operated on and then goin' into intensive care."

Boom thought about Jordan. "Tisha was getting lots of threats. Tisha had a blue convertible here. Oh my God, my cell phone!" Boom yelled.

Boom hobbled quickly to his hospital room and shut the door. He listened to five frantic messages from Tisha. She had told him everything. Now Boom understood why Shout had hit him. He had to get to Tisha's hotel as soon as possible.

****

Tisha had been in a fitful sleep for about two hours. Then there was a knock on the door. She jumped up and looked through the peephole. Shout stood on the other side. She opened the door and wrapped her arms around Shout. He broke her embrace. Tisha stepped back, "What's wrong with you?"

"Nuttin'. What's with the calls?"

"Everything that's been happening to me. It's all been Jordan. I got her PDA. It has those emails that prove she was threatening me."

"You talkin' crazy. You was tryna play me." Shout stared at Tisha, emotionless.

"You don't believe me? That picture of me and Boom wasn't real."

Shout blankly looked at Tisha.

"If you don't believe me why are you here?" Tisha yelled while crying.

"I'm here to show you what happens to people who betray me," Shout said as he waved to the detective who was waiting outside. The detective came in and handcuffed Tisha.

"You're a Judas Keyshawn, a fuckin' Judas," Tisha screamed as she tried to free herself from the detective's tight grip on her shoulder.

"You betrayed me first. Remember that."

Shout slammed the door and wanted to feel better, but he did not. A feeling of nausea rose from the pit of his stomach.

He sat on the edge of the bed with his head between his legs. A scraping sound came from the bottom of the door. Shout walked over to the papers and picked them up. The fax cover page was attached to a fuzzy picture of Boom and Tisha. It was captioned: OMEGA & DELTA SPRING INITIATION 1998, NORTH CAROLINA CENTRAL UNIVERSITY.

Shout breathed heavily and punched his hand into the wall.

****

Forty-five minutes later, Boom walked up the steps to Tisha's hotel room. The door was ajar. He slowly walked in. Shout turned around and looked at him.

"Man, my fault. I thought you betrayed me."

Shout hugged Boom.

"I understand," Boom replied, "Where's Tisha?"

Shout sighed, "I turned her into the police." He slumped down in a rigid chair against the wall.

"What have I done? This was all about Jordan. Jordan wouldn't stop." Shout got up and punched another hole in the wall. Boom walked over to him and grabbed his shoulder.

"Shout, we gotta focus. We gotta help Tisha."

Shout put both hands over his face.

The End

Letter to My Readers

This book was originally titled, **Platinum Changes Things** and was originally previewed in the self-published edition of *The Blueprint for My Girls*. The idea for this book has been a part of me since 1998. Before I started writing books to help teen girls, I worked in the entertainment industry as a magazine publisher and journalist.

My time in the entertainment industry has been fascinating, shocking, uplifting, disappointing and encouraging all at once. There's a certain element that affects all who actually work within that particular field. Through this fictionalized story, I hope that I captured its essence.

People have asked how I write both motivational based non-fiction books as well as entertainment based fiction and I tell them that I lead a double life – a life that empowers young people to make the best decisions of their lives and a life that draws upon creating entertainment possibilities. As much as I love conducting workshops on self-esteem, I equally enjoy conducting my "How to Get Into The Entertainment" Business lecture series and writing novels that reflect my adoration of music, culture and people. I believe God would not have given me this duality if he had not intended for me to use it. So, I write, speak, create and conduct my life in a way that encompasses all of my passions.

As a former magazine publisher who truly enjoyed interviewing artists and chronicling hip hop culture, I absolutely had to write at least one book that reflected the entertainment industry. When I began to write **The Blueprint for My Girls**, **Exclusive** would still talk to me at night. **Exclusive** would not let me rest until I got this book out of my system. Now that it's out, watch out! Afterall, seeing **Exclusive** published was another step out on faith and of me continuing to follow my dreams.

Thanks for reading and I hope to meet you soon,

Yasmin Shiraz

Yasmin Shiraz
Email me: yshiraz@yasminshiraz.net

My Thank Yous

I pray all the time. I pray for ideas. I pray for ways to share my experiences with others. I pray for God to give me the tools that I need to survive and thrive. I thank God for this book.

The Blueprint for My Girls readers who sent me letters, emails, checks and money orders requesting this book. Your show of support encouraged me to publish this work.

Michael for quietly supporting me and helping me blossom. Macoia for encouraging me with all the love and sparkle a little girl can bring to your life. Yamir for being the happiest little kid on earth. Your personality helps keep my life in perspective.

Mary Anne Sykes for challenging me to be the best, working with my often hectic schedule, and being the greatest Gigi on earth. And, Reginald Sykes for being a great part of this support system.

Witchell and Ricky Ward for supporting all of my wild and crazy ideas and never telling me, "You can't do that."

Steve Wilson for listening to a dreamer dream and then helping a doer do. Tracy Grant and Dave Goodson for giving me superior advice and direction, and lending their talents to help my visions become successful. Where would I be without y'all?

The book distributors and the numerous bookstore owners, thanks for giving me a chance to show that my books would sell. Your feedback on my products has been a tremendous blessing. I appreciate you for allowing me into your world.

Much love to the journalists, radio stations, magazines, newspapers, television, and internet outlets that have shown me love on my projects.

Privacy:
The sequel to Exclusive

Tisha and Shout's story continues in the follow-up novel, *Privacy*. Will Jordan survive the hit and run? Will Tisha be charged with attempted murder or 2nd degree murder? Can Tisha and Shout's relationship withstand legal pressures, sinking record sales, and emotional dependency? Their *Privacy* will definitely be breached in this steamy follow-up novel.

Coming soon!

For more info visit:

www.yasminshiraz.net